D1713725

Not By Chance

Christian Fiction

A Series of Chances #2

Diane Lil Adams

♥

♥

All the glory to God
and all my thanks to Tank!

♥

Author's Note

Not By Chance begins one moment after Another Chance ends. It's best to read the books in A Series of Chances in order.

Another Chance: Dr. Michael Grant, administrator of Casey's Institute for Juvenile Offenders, breaks with protocol to offer Anna Brown a position in an experimental dog therapy program. After Michael's first wife committed suicide, he vowed to remain single, but Anna puts his resolve to the test. Anna's first marriage left emotional scars and her experiences as a widow haven't improved her opinion of men. When she is attacked by a disturbed Casey's employee, both Anna and Michael realize it is time to confess their true feelings and take another chance on love.

Trust in the Lord with all your heart
and lean not
on your own understanding …
- Proverbs 3:5

♥ Chapter 1 ♥

Michael Grant sat beside Anna Brown on the stairs just outside the back door of his house. Beyond the fence, he could see Casey's Institute, set amongst the hills of the Missouri Ozarks. He couldn't help smiling as the sun cleared the horizon and brilliant colors emerged with the dawn. Had there ever been another morning such as this? The blue sky was cloudless, the air had never smelled so fresh and clean. He was in love with Anna Brown, and miraculously, Anna was in love with him too.

"When will we have the wedding?" he asked. Michael teased himself that she might say they could arrange it that afternoon. When Anna didn't answer, he turned to check her expression and discovered that she had fallen asleep.

As administrator of Casey's, he should not entertain a woman in his home without a chaperone. Nonetheless, Michael lifted Anna in his arms and carried her into the house, gently placing her on the couch. Smoothing her long, dark hair away from her face, he inadvertently exposed a ring of dark bruises around her neck. He could feel his muscles tense as he imagined Bruce Carlisle twisting the collar of Anna's blouse into a noose. Thank God for Charlie, one of the pet therapy dogs who had somehow escaped his pen and come to the rescue. Michael wished he had followed his instincts and gone downstairs to check on Anna himself. After he received her text message – *made other plans* –

he had jumped to the wrong conclusion: Anna must have discovered the truth about his past and decided to sever all ties. Rather than face that possibility, he sent Russell to the basement in his place. Russell had served Casey's as a security guard for many years and Michael trusted him to be discreet.

Russell found Anna in the Dog House, in the midst of an altercation with Bruce Carlisle. Bruce was shielding one eye, and blamed Anna for his injury. He was carrying a copy of an old promotional book about the school – one that included a wedding photo of Jeanne Casey and Michael.

Michael felt certain that the picture had prompted Anna's curt text message. He had stressed the importance of absolute honesty in their relationship, then deliberately deceived her about his past. He feared that she would be repulsed by a man who had driven his wife to suicide, and apparently he had been right.

Anna wouldn't answer the door when he went to the dorm to check on her, but just before dawn, she had been forced to summon him to an emergency. Assuming it would be his only chance to set the record straight, he stammered out his story. Instead of labeling him a monster, Anna had confessed that her motive for marrying Paul Brown had been equally self-centered. Dismissing both of their pasts, she went on to say that she loved him, that she wanted to take care of him, that she wanted to marry him!

And now, she was sleeping on his couch.

He went to the linen closet and returned with a pillow and quilt. When he raised Anna's head, to slide the pillow beneath her cheek, her eyelashes didn't even flutter. He tucked the quilt around her shoulders and feet, then settled on the coffee table, content to watch her sleep.

If you go, you will regret it the rest of your life – Jeanne's words crept into his consciousness unbidden. He hadn't understood that she meant to kill herself, but he *should* have. How many times had she protested the future that Michael and her father had planned? To be asked to live on the grounds of the prison where she had been incarcerated …

Michael had ignored her threat and spent the day at Casey's, watching as the construction crew poured the concrete foundation

2

for this very house. When he returned to the apartment that night, Jeanne was asleep. Taking advantage of the unexpected peace, he ate a sandwich and showered before he went to wake her. The moment he touched her shoulder, he knew …

Anna said that he had done enough penance, but Michael believed his sins were unforgivable. He had sentenced himself to a lifetime of solitude – there would be no second marriage, no children. Did he dare release himself from that vow of loneliness? Was it possible that God's grace extended this far?

♥

Anna Brown thought she must be dreaming. She found herself curled up on a blue couch under a handmade quilt and didn't know how she got there. She yawned hard and the scenery didn't change … she must be awake. She sat up and looked around.

Not ten feet away, Michael was tipped back in a leather recliner. Gone were the jeans and T-shirt he wore when he hurried to the dorm before dawn. Now he was clad in his familiar uniform – dark slacks and a pale blue shirt with a striped tie threaded through the collar. Anna had once asked whether he wore a tie to watch TV … She looked around the room and didn't see one. Maybe it was hidden inside a large oak armoire? The cavernous space was sparsely furnished with quality furniture and only a few pictures on the walls. Anna wasn't surprised by the lack of clutter – Michael kept his office exceedingly tidy too.

She stretched, then winced with pain. Less than twenty-four hours ago, she had been attacked by a fellow employee and had the injuries to prove it. Her hands went to her neck, gingerly touching the bruises. She had been certain that she was going to die …

Don't think about it, she counseled herself.

The living room windows faced Casey's campus, with a gorgeous view of tree-covered hillsides. She wanted to tiptoe across the room and gaze into the backyard, where Michael had planted a virtual sea of pansies. She had been so moved by this display of affection …

Had she really been the one to propose marriage?

3

Anna covered her face as she blushed with shame. Thankfully, Michael had accepted her proposal, but what had happened in the interim? She must have fallen asleep and he had carried her into the house.

Rising quietly, Anna crept to the recliner and knelt beside it, catching a whiff of Michael's scent – something woodsy and clean. She took a moment to admire him, to begin to believe that she would soon *marry* him. A hint of silver hair feathered his temples, giving him a distinguished look. His skin was bronzed – had he acquired his tan while planting pansies? Though he was stretched out in the recliner, fast asleep, it did not diminish his size.

Michael Grant was a big man and she was a small woman. They were alone, a good distance from any of the other buildings. Given what had happened the day before, shouldn't she be wary of Michael?

No! she told herself. She would not allow Bruce Carlisle to destroy their future. She closed her eyes and prayed for God's presence and peace. Then she listened for the Holy Spirit and felt the warm glow of renewed faith. "The Lord is my helper; I will not be afraid," she recited silently, as she rose and perched on the arm of the chair.

"Good morning," she whispered, and touched her fingers to Michael's cheek.

♥

Michael opened his dark brown eyes and his surprise quickly turned to delight.

"Good morning," he said, scooting to one side to make room for her. "Was I dreaming, or are we engaged?"

"We are!" she chirped, slipping in beside him. "You proposed to me, right before I fell asleep."

"And did you say 'yes'?" he played along, cradling her against his chest.

She giggled. "I would think you no less a gentleman if you reneged. We were both very tired."

"If one of us backs out, it won't be me," Michael assured her.

4

"I've been contemplating this for a long time."

Anna laid her arm across his waist. "How long?"

He gazed at the ceiling. "I rehearsed a proposal on the way to St. Louis, when I brought your contract last summer. 'What would she say,' I wondered, 'if I offered her a different sort of contract instead?' "

"Yes," she said happily. "She would've said 'yes.' "

"If only I had known." He kissed her then, and she molded her body to his and kissed him back.

Michael broke away first, pulling the lever and snapping the chair to an upright position. Scooping Anna into his arms, he carried her to the counter that bordered the kitchen, placing her on one of the cushioned stools. "We're attracted to one another," he said with a smile. "We shouldn't put ourselves in the way of temptation, by being alone in a private setting." They were her words, nearly verbatim, and he waited for recognition to dawn.

"Helen said you have a photographic memory," Anna mused. "I'm going to have to be careful what I say, if you're going to quote my words back at me."

"I am blessed with an exceptional memory," Michael agreed, going to the kitchen. He held the coffee pot under the faucet, but watched her over his shoulder. "Sometimes it doesn't feel like a blessing though, when I'm forced to recall foolish things I've done." He poured the water into the reservoir, then slid the pot into place.

"I find it hard to believe you ever do anything foolish," Anna said, resting her elbows on the counter, framing her face with her hands.

"You'll quickly be dispelled of that notion," he promised. "Consider Bruce Carlisle, for example. I should've fired him long ago, with or without evidence of wrongdoing." He peeled a coffee filter from the stack and folded it into the basket.

"Let's don't talk about that right now," Anna said.

"Let's do," Michael insisted. He watched as her hands went to the neck of her sweatshirt, easing it away from the bruises. "So I won't have yet another foolish thing to regret," he added.

Anna exhaled noisily. "I know what you're going to say - that I should report him."

5

"You don't agree?"

"Eventually," she said in a small voice.

Michael leaned his forearms on the counter and gazed into her eyes. "Eventually meaning *after* the scrapes heal and the bruises disappear?"

"Eventually meaning … after breakfast?" she tried to bargain.

"All right," he said with satisfaction. He straightened and scooped coffee into the filter. "We don't want to give him time to get too far away."

She sighed with resignation. "What will they make me do?"

"The police? They'll want a detailed statement and pictures of your injuries."

Anna closed her eyes and her voice wavered. "What's a rape kit?"

Michael was unable to hide his shock as he spun around.

"He didn't rape me!" Anna said quickly. "But what if the police make me do it anyway?"

Michael rested his hands on his hips while he studied her body language. *Was there a chance she had been raped and didn't want him to know?* "The police will not *make* you do anything. You're coming to them in good faith, reporting a crime in the interest of protecting some other woman, or girl." He pressed the switch on the coffee brewer and came to the stool, rotating it so that they were face-to-face. "Did he rape you, Anna?" The thought that Bruce might have touched her in that way … Michael felt both sick and furious.

"Bad enough he tried to kill me, without raping me too," she said with a shudder.

"I would far rather you had been raped than murdered!" Michael protested.

Anna crossed her arms, as though she were cold.

Michael cupped her chin in his hand, forcing her to look into his eyes. "Did he *try* to rape you? Please tell me the truth. Don't keep secrets because you're afraid I'll get upset."

Anna pushed his hands away. "He didn't do anything like that."

"It won't help your case, if you change your story later," Michael warned.

She frowned at him. "Why would I lie about it?"

"You might be in denial. Sometimes, when we don't want to deal with something unpleasant, we try to pretend it didn't happen."

"Is this what the police will do?" Anna asked warily. "Try to intimidate me?"

"I'm sorry," Michael said, raising his hands and backing away. "That was not my intent." He perched on the stool beside her, and gave her a moment to calm down. "I watched the video, but Bruce had apparently studied the layout of the Dog House and knew where the blind spots were."

"I forgot about the cameras!" Anna said. "I could've signaled to the guards that I needed help. Can you see when he attacked me?"

Michael thought she sounded hopeful, and he took it as a positive sign. "It's not very incriminating. The two of you are conversing, then he moves out of range. You appear to be making a phone call, then he grabs your hand and you both disappear."

"He took my phone," Anna explained, growing upset. "I was trying to text you, but he yanked it out of my hand and held it just out of reach. Couldn't you hear what he was saying?"

Michael shook his head. "The videos are visual only."

Anna's face fell. "So it's my word against his. Both times."

"The cameras hadn't been installed the first time," Michael reminded her. He wanted to comfort her, but he could not play two roles at once. "I'm surprised he didn't try to take you off campus."

"He wanted to," Anna said. "He invited me to go somewhere for coffee."

"Before or after he showed you the picture?"

She pressed her fists to her temples. "After. He accused me of committing adultery."

"He knew how that accusation would upset you," Michael guessed.

"I didn't believe him, that you were married," Anna said, looking into Michael's eyes. "That's when he showed me the picture. But I didn't get as upset as he expected. You said you weren't married, that first night, and I knew you wouldn't lie

7

about it."

"Thank you," Michael said, though her trust added to his burden of guilt.

"I said maybe you had gotten divorced, but he said John Casey wouldn't let you be administrator if you divorced his daughter. I thought maybe she died, but I didn't know why you wouldn't have told me that, since I told you about Paul."

"I should have," Michael allowed. "I was afraid you would dislike me, once you heard the whole story."

"You don't have a very high opinion of me," she said sadly.

"On the contrary," Michael disagreed. "I saw you as someone with extremely high standards. That's not a bad thing, Anna. I admired you for it." He waited for her to look up, before he spoke again. "What did he say then?"

"I don't remember." She raised her shoulders. "I just know that's when he really got mad. I could see it in his eyes. I was terrified and I guess he could see *that* in my eyes. I tried to put the table between us. The grooming table. But he grabbed me and ..." She paused, blinking back tears.

Michael rested his hand on her shoulder, but resisted the urge to take her in his arms.

"He yanked me across the table," Anna went on. "That's how I hurt my back."

"That's how *he* hurt your back," Michael specified.

She drew a deep breath. "I remembered a trick my brothers taught me." She tucked her thumb between her fingers and held up her hand to show him. "I couldn't aim. I just ..." She thrust her fist into the air, to demonstrate. "I poked him in the eye. It was horrible! He practically screamed with pain."

"That doesn't mean he was seriously injured," Michael said calmly. "The eye is very sensitive. Even the slightest touch will make a person react dramatically."

"That's true," she said with a wan smile.

"I don't see Bruce as the sort of person who can withstand even a suggestion of discomfort," Michael added. "Do you?"

"I don't know anything about him," she said in a pleading tone. "That's what's so hard to understand! How could he hate me when he doesn't even know me?"

8

"It's not you he hates, it's me," Michael explained.

"Maybe so, but ..." Anna shook her head. "How could he do those things to someone who's never done anything to him?"

"That's an issue we deal with every day at Casey's," he reminded her.

"I know, but ... he's a counselor! He should be better than the rest of us, not worse!"

"It doesn't work that way," Michael said gently. The dark smudges under her smoky green eyes gave her a haunted look. "He obviously has unaddressed issues of his own. If he's arrested, he'll be forced into counseling. It might be the best thing that could happen to him."

"As if I care," Anna said angrily. She grasped her elbows and hunched forward. "I want him thrown into a dungeon."

"Chances are, he won't even serve time," Michael said with regret. "Not for a first offence. But it should prevent him from working in another school." He waited a moment, then pressed on. "Once you hit him, did he let you go?"

"No," she said stonily. "It just made him madder. He grabbed the back of my shirt and ... twisted it. I couldn't breathe!" She paused, obviously trying to gain control of her emotions.

Michael gave in and put his arms around her. "What happened then?" he asked quietly.

"I felt like I was going to pass out. I thought I was gonna die! But all of a sudden, he let go. Because of Charlie. He was growling and showing his teeth and the hair on his back was standing straight up. I've never seen him be mean before."

"He wasn't being mean," Michael corrected her. "He was being loyal. He was defending you."

"I want to keep him," Anna pleaded. "I'll never stop wondering what would've happened if he hadn't gotten out of his pen."

"We *are* going to keep him," Michael said. "We'll go and get him as soon as we return from the police station."

She pressed her face into his tie. "Will you stay with me?"

"Of course I will."

"You said they'll want to take pictures of my back and my arm?"

"And your neck."

"Will they make me …"

Michael wasn't sure what was frightening her. "They won't force you to do anything," he promised, concerned that she might back out.

"They won't make me undress?"

"No," he said. "You can just pull your clothing far enough away to expose your injuries, as you did with me."

"Will you stay with me while they're taking the pictures?"

"I won't leave you for a minute." He smoothed her hair away from her face. "I'm going to ask you one more time – did he rape you, Anna? Please, do not allow him to get away with it if he did."

"He did *not* rape me," she said, pushing him away.

"If you allow him to go unpunished, he's likely to find a job at another school. Without evidence, I can't legally reveal what you're telling me, even if they were to call and ask for a reference. His next victim could be a student. A child."

"I thought you already fired him," Anna said. "That's what he said."

"That I fired him?"

"I think so. I know he said it was his last day."

Michael crossed his arms and tapped his fingers against his biceps. "Did he call you and ask you to meet him downstairs?"

"I was afraid you'd think that," Anna said with depression. "Especially if you found out I saw that book."

"You would naturally be curious, once you learned of its existence. How did you come to be downstairs alone?"

"Can I have a tissue?" she asked, wiping her eyes with her fingers.

Michael moved to the end of the counter and brought back a box of Kleenex. "I know this is unpleasant for you, but you need to recall as many details as you can, before you speak to the police."

She exhaled with drama. "Dawn was feeling sick, so I walked her to the clinic. Then I realized I didn't have my phone."

"Why didn't you come and get me, before you went back down?" he scolded gently.

"I tried to! I came to the office, but the waiting room was packed. Someone said Tina had gone home sick and you'd been called away on an emergency. I was afraid *I* was the emergency. I thought you had tried to call me and when I didn't answer, you got worried and went downstairs to look for me."

It was easy to follow the progression of her thoughts, and it gave him some solace.

"I looked for a security guard, but I couldn't find one," she sniffed.

"Nearly half of them are out sick."

"I decided it was an exception to the rule." She blew her nose and looked up at him. "I was just going to grab my phone and run back upstairs, but you said never to leave the area until I set the alarm. While I was doing that, I noticed that a couple of the dogs had spilled their water. Those bowls need to fasten to the wall, instead of the gate," she said sternly. "They're too easy to knock down." She paused, as though offering Michael a chance to comment. "I'm sorry," she sighed. "It was a totally stupid thing to do."

"I'm not going to disagree," Michael said. He returned to the coffee pot and removed two mugs from the cabinet above. "After we get married, we'll rearrange the cabinets, so that you can reach things more easily."

"I would never have gone downstairs if I had stopped to think that he might be there," she said, ignoring the opportunity to change topic. "What are the chances that he would catch me alone, both times when I broke the rule?"

Michael thought the chances were astronomically high. He couldn't help wondering whether she had broken the rule on other occasions, without being caught. He carried the mugs of hot coffee with care, and set one in front of Anna. "He didn't give notice, so he must have believed I would fire him over something he had done," he said thoughtfully. "Something he assumed I knew about, or would find out about. Or maybe he was certain I would fire him once I found out what he had done to you."

She scrubbed her face with both hands. "Why does he hate you so much?"

Michael wasn't sure of the answer. "I confronted him with the rumors that were going around campus. I let him know I was aware of the way he treats women. And I asked the security guards to keep a close eye on him. I'm sure he felt boxed in, and blamed me."

Anna sighed. "Just promise to stay with me, all right?"

"I can't imagine why you're so frightened of the police," Michael said with concern. "Have you gone through this before?"

Anna shook her head. "I used to watch a lot of detective shows with Andy. I know that's fiction, but ..."

"I promise I'll be no more than an arm's length away, the entire time." He glanced at his watch and made a face. "Unfortunately, I do need to desert you now though. There are so many people out with that virus, I've got to make sure all the bases are covered."

"Are you going to leave me here alone?" Anna asked, eyes widening.

"I don't want you alone until after Bruce has been arrested," Michael said firmly. "I thought I'd ask Russell to stay with you."

Anna shivered. Though Russell was a security guard, she didn't want to be alone with any man other than Michael. "Will I have to go to court and testify?"

"Unless he confesses."

She gnawed on her lip. "I *have* to do it," she said.

"Yes, you do," Michael agreed. "When I get back, we'll go to Briarton. And then we'll get Charlie and make him a steak dinner."

Anna fidgeted with the neck of her sweatshirt. "I should've bent his little finger back instead. Or stomped on his instep. Wait'll I tell my brothers about *this*."

♥ Chapter 2 ♥

When Russell arrived at the stone house, he and Michael spoke quietly for a few moments, beyond the range of Anna's hearing. She tried to believe they were talking about a Casey's matter that had nothing to do with her, but suspected it was wishful thinking.

"I'll be back in an hour or less," Michael called, just before he went out the door.

Russell remained in the dining room, his thumbs tucked into his belt, regarding her with a curious stare. He obviously wasn't comfortable with the situation.

"Would you like a cup of coffee?" Anna offered.

"No thank you," Russell said politely.

Anna knew he wasn't normally so austere. "You must be a healthy guy," she said, hoping to induce him to talk. "Seems like you're one of a few who hasn't come down with that virus."

"I'm just old," Russell said with a straight face. "I've probably had it a time or two and I'm already immune."

She smiled, uncertain whether he meant to be funny.

He smiled too, then came to the counter, where Anna sat nursing her coffee. "I need to make you an apology, Mrs. Brown. If I had realized you were hurt, I would've gone after Mr. Carlisle and hauled him upstairs to Dr. Grant. He would've been arrested

13

and we wouldn't be in this mess."

"I'm the one needs to apologize," Anna said, lowering her eyes. "It was my fault for going downstairs alone."

"Doesn't matter," Russell said. "You ought not to need protection from a fellow employee."

It was a good point, and one that gave Anna comfort. "Are you sure you wouldn't like a cup of coffee?"

Russell considered it. "I don't feel right helping myself to Dr. Grant's stuff."

"I'm sure he wouldn't mind," Anna said, folding her hands on the counter top.

"I'm sure he wouldn't either," Russell said, "but I'm not takin' it for granted."

Anna rubbed her eyes and wished Michael had taken her with him. She could've sat in Tina's chair while he did whatever he needed to do in his office. "Actually, I was thinking of looking for something to eat," she said bravely. "I skipped dinner last night and didn't have any breakfast. The coffee is making me sick to my stomach."

Russell pursed his lips. "Would you like me to call Dr. Grant and ask whether he'd be okay with that?"

Anna was sure Michael wouldn't mind, but she didn't want to argue with the security guard. She wondered if this was the first time he had been summoned to Michael's house early in the morning, and found a woman in residence. She hadn't fixed her hair before she left the dorm, or applied makeup. She hoped Russell wasn't jumping to the wrong conclusions.

"Sorry to bother you, Doc," Russell said into his cell phone. "Mrs. Brown's feeling sick to her stomach and we wondered if I could find her some crackers." He eyed Anna as he listened to Michael's response, then reached up and rubbed his eyebrow with two fingers. "All righty," he said, and pressed the button to end the call. He replaced the phone into a holster on his belt, then laced his fingers across his flat belly. "So, that's how it is," he said knowingly.

"Pardon?" Anna said, feeling her face begin to flush.

Russell laughed. "I had an inkling."

Anna tried to maintain a neutral expression. "Did he say I can

14

fix something to eat?"

"He said I should encourage you to make yourself at home. Kind of a telling remark, wouldn't you say? I'll guarantee you this – I haven't ever heard those words come out of his mouth regarding any other woman."

Anna slid off the stool and went to the kitchen. Opening the drawers one by one, she hunted for a rubber band, then settled for a shoe lace.

"Rumors have been going around," Russell said, watching as she tied her hair back. "I didn't know what to make of it, since he generally avoids even the hint of impropriety."

"Even though this situation might look improper, I hope you'll believe it's entirely innocent," Anna said.

"I'm sure it is," Russell agreed. "I don't know you very well, but I *do* know Michael Grant."

Anna opened the refrigerator and perused the shelves with interest. *What sort of things did Michael like to eat? Did he cook from scratch, or eat frozen dinners?* There was a head of lettuce, a few Roma tomatoes in a dish, a carton of eggs and a bottle of milk. There were a number of storage dishes, but she suspected Russell would object if she inspected the contents. She found the expiration date on the milk – it was fresh.

"Can I get you something?" she asked Russell, as she began opening cabinets, in search of cereal.

"No need to feed me," Russell said. "Just fix somethin' for yourself."

There was a full pantry and it contained a box of Bisquick. Anna decided to make pancakes, recalling how Michael had once made pancakes for her and her children. "I'm going to fix enough for Michael anyway," she tried to cajole the security guard.

Russell chuckled. "I'm not gonna ask whether he gave you permission to call him by his Christian name."

Anna wished she knew what Michael *had* said to Russell. "Dr. Grant mentioned that you've been at Casey's longer than he has. Were you hired when the school began?"

"Shortly thereafter, by John Casey himself."

"He's not very involved with the school anymore, is he?" She found a mixing bowl and measuring cups, removed eggs and milk from the refrigerator, then hunted for a griddle. She was impressed by how orderly Michael kept his kitchen.

"He doesn't need to be, since he's got Dr. Grant. 'Course, there wasn't much to the school in those days anyway. One building with a wing for the kids, and one for the staff. This was way out in the sticks back then. Briarton wasn't much more than four houses and a grocery. It's all built up on account of the school."

Coming from the D.C. area, and then St. Louis, it was still "out in the sticks" to Anna. "It's a beautiful part of the country," she said, pausing to gaze across the room, where she could see the view through the French doors.

"It is," Russell agreed. "Didja check whether he's got maple syrup?"

Anna had started to whisk the batter, but she stopped and went to the pantry. "Are you going to have a pancake with us after all?" she invited, holding up a bottle of Log Cabin.

"Maybe," he said. "Not that I need the carbs."

Anna put the griddle over two burners on the stove and turned the heat to medium. She imagined working in this kitchen over the years, until she and Michael retired. It would be a great place for the family to gather, after Paula and Andy married and produced grandchildren.

It would be even more fun if she and Michael were to have a child together. Or even two.

"Mrs. Brown?" Russell said.

"Sorry," Anna said. "Did you ask me a question?"

"Dr. Grant sent me a text. He wants you to write down as much as you can recall about the incident with Mr. Carlisle."

"As soon as I'm done here," she said reluctantly. "Did he say how much longer he'd be?"

Russell shook his head. "You've seen how his office fills up."

Anna knew there were often twenty people waiting to see Michael by seven o'clock in the morning, but maybe it wouldn't be as busy on a weekend. She turned the burners off and pushed the pancake batter to the rear of the counter. Eating probably wouldn't settle her stomach anyway. Not until *after* she'd been to the police station.

"I already wrote down what I witnessed," Russell told her.

16

"That dog was something else, the way he held Mr. Carlisle at bay."

Anna washed her hands, then refilled her coffee cup and fixed a cup for Russell. "Do you take cream or sugar?"

"Black," he said. "You need some paper?"

"I guess so." She boosted herself onto the stool and watched Russell text Michael, then eye the screen for a reply.

"He says there's paper beside the landline." Russell went to the other end of the counter and returned with a white legal pad and a BIC.

"Thanks," Anna said politely, though she had no enthusiasm for the task.

"How about if we work backwards," Russell suggested. "We'll start with what I saw, then you can add to it. I didn't actually see the man's eye, since he was covering it with his hand. He said you poked him?"

"Because he was choking me!" Anna said defensively. "Wait, no ... he started choking me *after* I hit him in the eye."

"Write that down," Russell said, gesturing at the paper.

"I was stupid!" Anna said, as she printed the words across the page. "I should've run, the minute I saw him."

"Were you in the hallway when you first saw him, or in the Dog House?"

Anna understood that Russell was trying to prod her memory. She forced herself to concentrate and soon had two pages filled with notes.

"You can always add to your statement, but don't write anything down if you're not sure of it," Russell advised. "If you remove it later, it'll look like you were lying."

"I'll leave a space, if I can't recall."

"Good," Russell said with satisfaction. His phone vibrated on the countertop and he quickly pressed in his code and read the message. "He's on his way," he said. "You wanna turn the griddle back on?"

♥

The women who resided on the third floor of Anna's

17

dormitory were gathered outside the front door when Michael emerged from the building.

"Dr. Grant!" Marianne Faraday called, scampering after him. "Could I ask you a quick question? I've been trying to call all morning."

Michael was letting his calls go to voicemail, only returning those that seemed urgent. "What can I do for you?" he asked.

"We're all kinda worried about Anna and Susie," she said, waving her hand at her friends. "In case they have the virus. We've been knocking on their doors and calling their cell phones, but neither of them answers."

"They're both fine," Michael assured her. "There's no need to be concerned."

"Okay, great," Marianne said, backing away. "Would you know where they are?"

"I do, and they're both well and safe," Michael said.

Marianne glanced at her friends. "Thanks!" she said.

Michael grimaced. Marianne was prone to gossip and he didn't want to guess what she would make of this situation.

He quickened his steps, anxious to take Anna to the police station before she changed her mind about going. Afterward, he hoped they could choose a tentative date for the wedding. He had pulled up his calendar for the entire year, and there were only a few events he couldn't reschedule.

He could smell the pancakes as soon as he opened the door. Russell was setting the table and there was a grin on his face. Anna looked exactly right, standing at the stove in his kitchen, flipping flapjacks. He barely resisted the urge to slide his arms around her waist and kiss the back of her neck.

Her neck … where red and purple bruises served as evidence of Bruce Carlisle's violence. Over the years, Michael had read many articles about women who had been attacked. It didn't seem likely that Anna would feel like making pancakes less than twenty-four hours later, while chatting amicably with the security guard. *Was she in a state of denial? Was it possible that she was repressing memories? Memories of a rape?*

♥

18

"Was it as bad as you anticipated?" Michael asked. He shifted into second gear and eased the Corvette over a speed bump, then pulled away from the Briarton Police Department.

"It wasn't bad at all," Anna admitted. "But only because you were with me. If I had been on my own, I'm sure I would've started crying. Or throwing up."

"And they would understand that. It's a natural reaction after you've been attacked."

"I did enough crying last night," she said, biting her lip.

"What did you mean when you said, 'There are worse things'?" The remark had alarmed him. "Were you referring to something specific? Something that happened to you?"

"There *are* worse things," she insisted. "Rape, murder …" She slid down in the seat. "This is probably a stupid question, but … have you ever been attacked?"

Michael debated whether to press for more information. "Of course," he said, deciding to drop the subject for now. "I have an older brother."

Anna giggled, relieving some of the tension. "Jasmine's husband. What's his name?"

"Jerome, after my father."

"Do they have children?"

"No," Michael said. "They're both very career oriented."

"So your parents don't have any grandchildren?" Anna said with sympathy.

"That's a blessing. I can't imagine either of them allowing a baby to wrinkle their clothes."

"Are they really *that* bad?"

"Not bad," Michael said guiltily. "We're just different. We have almost nothing in common."

"Do they still want you to quit your job at Casey's and become a defense attorney?"

"Sweeter words my father could not hear." He stopped at a stop sign and turned to look at her. "Do not start plotting how to fix my relationship with my family," he warned.

"I wasn't!" she assured him.

"Tell me more about *your* family," he suggested. "Your sweet sister, Nan, and the brothers who taught you how to defend

19

yourself. And your parents."

"I can't wait for them to meet you," Anna said. "Nan will fall madly in love with you. My mom will love you too, but she's too shy to talk to you very much. My dad will want your opinion on politics and the rest of them … They'll just tell stories on me."

"I'll look forward to that," Michael said. "I want to know everything about you. What subjects did you like in school? What did you play with – dolls or trucks?"

"Both, because it irritated my brothers when I messed with their things. Are you still in touch with your friends from childhood?"

"We exchange Christmas cards. What about you?"

"I lost touch with all of them, and I haven't ever attended a reunion. I have some pretty good friends in St. Louis though. I'll miss some of them."

"Having second thoughts?" He reached for her hand.

"Not at all," she said, squeezing his fingers. "It's amazing," she said in a dreamy voice. "How can one of the worst days of my life turn into one of the best days of my life?"

The statement brought an unexpected lump to Michael's throat.

"Are you going to drop me at the dorm?" she asked, when he started up the hill to Casey's. "I'd like to shower and change clothes."

"We need to bag the blouse you were wearing," Michael remembered. "In case it has a trace of Bruce's DNA."

"I threw it in the trash," Anna told him. "It was one of my favorite blouses, but I know I'll never wear it again."

"The trash in your room, or in the restroom?" Michael asked with concern.

"In my room. I hope nobody's around. I don't feel like making small talk. Should I come to your office afterwards?"

"I'm not going to leave you on your own," Michael said with authority. "Not until Bruce is in custody." He glanced at his watch. "Could you gather your things and take a shower at my house, after I figure out who can serve as our chaperone?"

"Scared to be alone with me?" Anna tried to tease.

Michael gave her a sidelong glance. "Casey's board hasn't ever drawn up a set of rules pertaining to my personal life, but I'm certain they wouldn't approve if I invited a woman to spend the night with me."

"Spend the night!" she gasped. "Couldn't you ask one of the female security guards to stay at the dorm? She could have my bed and I'll sleep on the couch."

"I wouldn't be satisfied with that," Michael said. "I had a hard enough time trusting your safety to Russell this morning, though I know he'd put his life on the line for you."

"I'd really rather you didn't say it like that," Anna said with a shudder.

"You need to take it seriously, Anna. Bruce has had plenty of time to consider the consequences of his behavior. It's likely he'll try to frighten you enough to prevent you from testifying."

Anna seemed to shrink to half her size.

"If they don't arrest Bruce before evening, I'll ask Russell to spend the night at the house with us," Michael thought aloud. "But two men and one woman isn't the ideal answer either."

"You could ask Marianne too," Anna suggested.

Michael barely restrained a groan. He parked at the front door of the dorm and Anna immediately jumped out.

"Anna, wait!" he called, hurrying after her. "So much for taking the threat seriously," he chastised, as they climbed the stairs together. He unlocked the door to her room with his master key, and went in ahead of her. "Get whatever you think you'll need for an overnight," he ordered. Then he stationed himself in the doorway.

♥

Anna fetched a tote bag from the closet and went around the divider, into her bedroom. She dumped in underwear, socks and a clean pair of jeans, as well as a sweater with a soft neckline. She tried to think what else she might need, but her weary brain wouldn't cooperate.

"How's Anna?" came Marianne's voice from the hallway.

"She's fine," Michael said. "Would you step in for a moment, please?"

Anna heard the door close and she heard Marianne clear her throat – a nervous habit her friend was trying to break.

"Have you already made plans for tonight?" Michael asked.

Anna came around the end of the wall in time to see Marianne's shocked expression.

"Anna was attacked yesterday," Michael explained. "Until the perpetrator has been arrested, she needs to be in protective custody. Would you be willing to serve as a chaperone?"

"Who attacked you?" Marianne asked, turning to gape at Anna. "Bruce again?"

Before Anna could answer, Michael held up his hand. "There's no need to discuss the details," he said firmly. "Are you available?"

"Well, yeah," Marianne blustered.

"Pack for an overnight then, and I'll have security come for you at 5:30."

"Overnight?" Marianne gasped. "Are we gonna stay at a motel?"

"I haven't decided," Michael said. "I'm trusting you to keep this to yourself, at least until after the man has been arrested."

Marianne met Anna's eyes. "No problem," she said, lifting her chin. "Anything special I should bring?"

"Whatever you need when you spend a night away from home," Michael advised. "Anna?" He motioned that he was ready to leave.

Anna knew she needed more than the few items she had thrown into her satchel, but she didn't want to make Michael wait.

♥ Chapter 3 ♥

"I forgot a lot of stuff," Anna said, peering into her bag once they were seated in the car. "Like soap and shampoo."

"I have soap and shampoo," he assured her. He pulled out his phone and began texting.

"What a moocher I am!" she said with disgust. "Please don't think I always take advantage of people this way."

He laughed, watching the screen for a reply. "On the contrary. I think you generally allow people to take advantage of you." He dropped the phone into his pocket and started the engine.

"Aren't we going to your house?" Anna asked, when he drove to the administration building instead.

"After we get Charlie," he reminded her. "And there are a few things we need to discuss before we link up with Russell and Marianne."

Anna wanted a shower, but she wanted to rescue Charlie even more. This was one time when she wouldn't mind if he planted his front paws on her shoulders.

Michael cast an anxious glance around as they got out of the car near a wooded area. He made Anna walk in front of him, reaching around her to unlock the gate, then the door into the building.

"Hey, Randy!" Anna said, when she spied one of the AHTs, cleaning out the kennels. "Is it your day to get stuck with the 'funnest' job in the Dog House?"

"It wasn't supposed to be, but Dawn and Anita are sick." He slouched against the wall with his broom. "I tried to talk the security guard into helping clean kennels, but for some reason, he preferred to wait in the hall." Randy suddenly spied Michael and his spine stiffened.

"I'm going to keep Charlie overnight," Michael told him. "Could you make a note so that the next AHT doesn't think he escaped?"

"Sure," Randy said, hurrying to the chalk board near the grooming table.

Michael went to Charlie's pen and opened the gate. "Sit," he said firmly, as Charlie bounded toward Anna.

Anna watched with amazement as Charlie sat, though his tail continued to wag with enthusiasm. "I can't believe it!" she said. "Even the dog behaves when you're around!"

"I've been working with him," Michael confessed.

Anna dropped to her knees and wrapped her arms around Charlie, burying her face in his wiry fur. "You're my hero," she whispered, hiding her tear-filled eyes from Michael. She leaned back on her heels and wiped her face with her sleeve.

"Did he wash your face?" Michael asked with amusement. "I doubt I'll ever be able to break him of that." He praised Charlie and gave him a treat from a jar on the counter. "Have you got a container for dry food? Too much 'people food' might not agree with him."

Anna went to a cabinet for a Ziploc and filled it with brown nuggets."

"You're one of the few who hasn't gotten sick," Michael told Randy. "What's the secret to your good health? Plenty of spinach?"

"My mom sprinkles it with sugar," Randy said with embarrassment.

Michael laughed and grabbed a lead from a hook near the door. "Thanks for picking up the slack. I'll be sure to make a note in your file." He headed into the basement hallway. "C'mon, Charlie," he called.

A young security guard was seated on the floor, texting on his cell phone. The minute he saw Michael, he leaped up, shoving the phone into his pocket. "Sorry, sir," he said nervously.

Anna noted the stern look on Michael's face, but it faded when he turned toward her and the dog. "So much for all the dog treats Charlie conned me out of, promising to be my best friend," he complained. "Looks like he isn't going anywhere without you."

As soon as Anna started walking, Charlie did too.

"Tell him to heel," Michael suggested. "Let's see if he'll obey you."

"Heel," Anna said. Much to her surprise, Charlie fell in beside her and trotted at a reasonable pace. "Does this mean we have to adopt him out?"

"Yes," Michael said. "We're adopting him out *to us*."

Anna glanced over her shoulder at the security guard, wondering what he would make of *that* remark. "Will you make a note in his file too?" she asked in a whisper.

"Yes," Michael said. "He knows better than to sit and play with his phone when he's supposed to be working." He glanced at her with a curious look. "That didn't seem too unpleasant for you. I was afraid it might be traumatic when you returned to the scene of the crime."

"Going in the back door, it almost seemed like a different place. Is that why you did it that way?"

Michael just smiled. "Have you thought of anything you could add to your statement?"

Anna made a face. "Could I please try *not* to think about it for a little while?"

"That's fine," he said, resting his hand on her shoulder.

"How long have you been working with Charlie?" she asked.

"All summer. I take him home for a few hours almost every evening."

"Why didn't I notice any changes?"

"Probably because you didn't give him the commands," Michael guessed.

"I had accepted that he was incorrigible," Anna said. "A terrible thing to admit when I work where I work."

"Incorrigible is not in the Casey's dictionary," Michael lectured with a smile.

Anna wondered if he would apply that to Bruce. "I forgot to

25

get the blouse out of the trash can."

"We'll get it tomorrow. Watch," he said, gesturing at Charlie as he unlocked the door to his office.

Charlie went straight to the front of Michael's desk, turned in a circle and laid down. He gazed up at Anna and wagged his tail, as though seeking approval.

Anna knelt down to pet him. "Good boy! Good dog, Charlie!"

"Make yourself comfortable," Michael invited, sitting down at his desk. "There are a few things I need to do, but it won't take long. You can nap on the couch, if you want."

"I'd better not go to sleep," Anna said, flopping down, much as Charlie had. "I'm so tired, you might not be able to wake me up until sometime tomorrow."

Michael chuckled. "Like that first night, when you fell asleep in the car?"

"That was embarrassing," Anna said, covering her face. "Paula said you had to get in my purse and look for ID, so you could call for directions."

"I was afraid you'd be angry about that," Michael said. He unlocked his desk and pulled a laptop from one of the drawers.

"How many keys do you have on that key ring?" Anna asked. She was amazed every time he pulled it from the pocket of his coat.

"Several dozen," Michael said, holding it up.

"How do you keep straight which one is for what? I'd have to paint them with nail polish."

"Not a bad idea," Michael mused. "I memorized the order. If someone wanted to seriously harass me, they could rearrange them."

"I'll keep that in mind," Anna teased, "in case I have trouble talking you into something."

"I don't imagine that will ever be an issue," Michael said. "Did I not just invite Marianne to spend the night?"

Anna giggled as she recalled the look on her friend's face.

He began typing, so Anna grew quiet, until her eyelids started to droop. Then she slid to the floor and crawled across the carpet. Propping her back against Michael's desk, she scratched Charlie behind the ears, unaware that she was gradually slumping onto

26

her side.

"Anna?" Michael called, leaning over the desk to peer down at her. "You said you didn't want to fall asleep."

She sat up and rubbed her eyes. "May I go and splash cold water on my face?"

"You may do almost anything you'd like," Michael assured her. "I'll be done with this in a minute, and then I'll try to be fascinating enough to keep you awake."

Anna wandered through the attached conference room to a small bathroom. Standing on tiptoe, to see in the mirror, she studied the bruises that circled her neck. She wondered how long it would take before they faded away.

What did Michael want to discuss? Was he going to back out of the marriage? He might suggest they spend more time together and see how they felt in a year. If only she could take back the proposal! She felt like such a fool!

"Anna?" Michael called. "Are you sleeping on the conference table?"

"Under it!" she called back. She washed her face and hung the towel neatly on the rack. When she returned to his desk, the laptop had disappeared and he was rolling up his sleeves.

"Where would you like me to sit?" she asked, as he tipped his chair back.

"Wherever you like. I'm going to be speaking as your future husband, not as the administrator of Casey's."

Her future husband ... Anna took a deep breath, then boosted herself onto his desk. "I always like to sit in the front row," she explained with a grin. "What did you want to talk about?"

Michael folded his hands on his chest. "Would you like to choose a date for the wedding? Other than a few events, my calendar is wide open for the next year."

Anna wasn't surprised that he wanted to push it off for a year.

"I guess it would be hard to put a wedding together in less than a year," he said placidly, when she didn't respond.

The remark confused her. "How big of a wedding do you want?"

He shrugged. "The details are up to you."

"I don't like big weddings. Paula and I argue about that all the

27

time. Even if she doesn't have a steady beau, she probably spends an hour a day planning her big wedding."

"Define big," Michael said, raising one eyebrow.

Anna considered for a moment. "More than four people?"

"Four?" he repeated, sitting forward in his chair.

She made a face. "I guess you'd want your family and friends and people from Casey's."

"No, no, and no," Michael assured her. "I'll tell my family after it's a fait accompli, and I have no intention of inviting friends or co-workers." He brought his fingertips together. "What about your parents? Won't they be hurt if they aren't invited?"

Anna pursed her lips. "Long car trips are difficult for them. And if they did come all this way, they'd want to stay a couple of weeks. It's kind of hard to start a marriage with house guests." She tucked her hands beneath her thighs and crossed her legs at the ankle.

"I'll gladly pay their airfare," Michael offered.

She shook her head. "Thank you, but … I think I'll do what you said – tell everyone afterward. Except Andy and Paula, of course."

"Of course," he agreed. "Would the two of them make up our quota of four?"

"Is that okay with you?"

"More than okay," Michael said agreeably. "They could serve as our witnesses. Do you think they'll approve?"

"Paula will probably offer to pay for the license. Wouldn't she have to be twenty-one? To be a witness?"

"I don't think so. Probably eighteen is good enough. What about Andy?"

"Andy is twenty-two."

"I meant, do you think he'll approve?"

"He'll be elated," Anna said with confidence. "He'll figure, now it's your problem to keep my old Volkswagen running."

Michael smiled, but he seemed to be waiting for her to say something more.

"Will your friends and family approve?" she asked.

"I don't care whether they do or not," Michael shrugged. "Did you have a date in mind?"

Anna turned her head and gazed out the window. She thought they probably *should* spend more time together, to make sure they were compatible. But if he had too much time to think about it, he might change his mind. *Either he wants to marry me or he doesn't,* she decided. "How about next weekend?" she said flippantly.

Michael laughed. "*Next* weekend?"

Anna felt her face grow warm. *If only she would learn to think before she spoke!*

Michael sat forward and looked into her eyes. "I'm afraid you're speaking impulsively, because you're tired. Maybe we should wait a few days to discuss this."

It was a good suggestion, given the events of the past twenty-four hours and her lack of sleep. "The longer we wait, the more complicated it will get," she predicted, ignoring the warning.

Michael's expression didn't change. "In the past, a blood test was required before the license could be issued." He laced his fingers together. "Do you want me to go online and see if that's still the case?"

Anna's heartbeat quickened. "Okay," she agreed.

"Do you want me to do it now?" he pressed. "I wouldn't want you to look back and say I rushed you into this."

Anna couldn't suppress a giggle. "Seems to me *I'm* the one rushing you!"

He pulled his laptop from the drawer and set it on top of his desk, a few inches from her hip. He brought up the Internet, then typed something into the search engine. While he was waiting, he looked up at her.

Anna thought he looked shell-shocked. "We're acting like teenagers," she said guiltily.

"Yes we are," he agreed. "But we've both been on our own long enough to know what we want. I want to marry you, Anna. I'm not going to change my mind if I think about it around the clock for the next six months." He checked the screen, then began to read. "We need to apply for the license in person," he said after a moment. "And they require a valid ID and social security card. I think we ought to take copies of the death certificates too, for both Jeanne and your husband."

"No blood test?"

"No blood test."

Anna studied his profile. Was she sure about this? She knew that she loved him, but … *did she know him well enough to marry him?*

"Do you want to have the ceremony here or in St. Louis?" he asked.

"I don't care, so long as it's in a church." *Should she admit that she was uncertain?*

"We might have a difficult time finding a pastor who will marry us on the spur of the moment," Michael said, tapping his fingers on the desk top.

"What about the pastor who did the commencement exercises?" Anna remembered that she and Marianne had been impressed by his graduation sermon.

"I don't know him, but I can certainly call and ask."

"You don't attend his church?"

"Sporadically, but I only shake his hand on my way out the door."

"My pastor in St. Louis would do it," Anna said. "Do you want me to call and ask if he's busy next weekend?" She caught her breath and held it. *Was she really pushing him to get married in one week?*

"Are you sure?" Michael rested his hand on her knee and stared steadily into her eyes.

"I'm sure," Anna said, though she wasn't sure at all. "Are *you* sure?"

In answer, Michael took his phone from his pocket. "Want me to look up his number?" he dared her.

"I know it by heart," Anna said. "He's been my pastor for over twenty years. Are you sure you're sure? I wouldn't like to call him back later and tell him the groom chickened out."

"That is not a concern," Michael said. "I've never been more certain of anything."

Anna dialed the first few numbers, then hesitated. "What about Casey's? Can you be away for the weekend?"

"I'm going to take a week," Michael told her. "At *least* a week."

"Won't the board members mind? It's short notice."

"We're getting married!" Michael said. "That qualifies as a good excuse, even for them."

"Even so ... shouldn't you ask first?"

Michael took his phone from her hand. He canceled the call, then closed his laptop and returned it to the drawer. He took a firm hold on Anna's waist and slid her to the left, so that she was seated directly in front of him. Resting his hands on her hips, he looked solemnly into her eyes. "Let's slow down," he suggested. "We need to consider both columns before we take action we might later regret."

"Both columns?" she repeated quizzically.

"The positive and the negative."

"Are you having second thoughts?"

"No, but I do have questions," he admitted. "And I'm sure there are questions you'd like to ask me."

"What kind of questions?"

"I didn't tell you about Jeanne," he said softly. "Aren't you curious whether there's anything else I failed to mention?"

Anna moistened her lips with the tip of her tongue. "Is there?"

"No," he said. "What about you? Is there anything you'd like to tell me?"

She lifted both shoulders. "I can't think of anything. I don't really have any secrets."

Michael caught her hands in his. "You once called a halt to our relationship because you saw me with Jasmine in the cafeteria. If you saw something similar in the future, would you jump to the same conclusion?"

"Anytime I see you kiss another woman, I'm going to be jealous," she said honestly.

"And how would you handle that jealousy? Would you give me a chance to explain before you gave me the cold shoulder?"

Anna tilted her head to one side as she contemplated this. "I don't know until it happens but I hope I'd confront you first."

"In tears or in a fit of temper?"

She pulled her hands free. "A fit of temper?"

"What did you call it ... getting your Irish up? Are you likely to do so in public?"

31

Anna was shocked by the accusation. "I have *never* raised my voice in public! Not even when the kids were misbehaving."

"Good," he said with approval. "Now it's your turn. What are you concerned about?"

Anna frowned. She couldn't think of anything to ask or say. "I noticed how neat you keep your kitchen. And your office." She swung her hand in an arc. "Nothing out of place."

"Is that a bad thing?"

"I don't know. Will you throw a fit if I leave a dirty dish setting on the counter?"

"I don't throw fits," he said evenly. "Your house is equally neat, Anna. As is your room at the dorm."

"Yes, but I'm not obsessive."

"I didn't think I was either. Was Paul obsessive?"

She nodded. "I didn't dare toss a sweater on the bed, or leave a pair of shoes outside the closet."

"I'm not like that," Michael said.

"How do you know? You've lived alone all this time …" She saw the hurt in his eyes and wished she had worded it differently.

"You might ask Charlie," he said. "He leaves his toys all over the living room."

Charlie's tail began to slap against the front of the desk and they both smiled.

"Suppose we agree to wait three months," Michael proposed. "How would we spend that interval?"

Anna wasn't sure what he meant. "Going on dates?"

"You'd be studying me, to try to determine what sort of husband I'd make. What would you be looking for?"

"Well," she said, touching her fingertip to her cheek in a thoughtful pose. "I already know you're a good kisser."

"Am I?" He looked pleased.

"Excellent," she said, bobbing her head. "Though we ought to practice a few more times before I give you a final grade."

"I think that would be a bad idea, under the circumstances. We are, once again, alone in a private setting."

Anna averted her eyes. First she proposed, then she recommended a speedy wedding. Now she was begging for kisses. "I'd want to know whether you leave the seat up on the toilet, especially in the middle of the night."

"I'm trying to be serious," he said, moving his hands to her waist.

"Okay," she said, feeling rebuked. She was quiet for a moment, as she remembered the issues that had caused trouble between her and Paul. "I'd want to know how you are about money. Will you get upset if I go over my budget at the grocery store?"

"You won't have a budget." Without warning, he captured her face between his hands and kissed her. "I told you," he said hoarsely. "Being alone is a very bad idea right now." He kissed her again, then leaned back and gazed at her with hooded eyes.

"Uh oh," she said nervously. "Charlie is not being a good chaperone."

Charlie's tail immediately began to thump against the desk. Anna giggled, breaking the mood.

"Is there anything else?" Michael asked.

"I don't know. You got me side-tracked so I wouldn't be able to think of what I want to say."

Michael scooted his chair back, so that she was out of reach.

"What would *you* do, if we waited three months?" she asked. "Rearrange the kitchen cabinets so I can reach the coffee mugs?"

"I'd help *you* rearrange the kitchen." He rolled his chair forward again and locked his hands behind her waist. "Sorry!" he said, pulling away when she winced. "Did I hurt your back?"

"It's okay," she said, draping her arms around his neck, ready to be kissed again.

"That's why I sat here, rather than on the couch," he said. "Because I knew how difficult it would be to keep my hands to myself." He got up and went to the window, staring out over the campus. "I didn't agree to a quick wedding because there's any reason to hurry," he finally said. "It's more that there's no particular reason to wait."

"Maybe we should pray about it," Anna said. "I promise myself I'll pray *before* I make decisions, then I always forget."

Michael returned to his chair and sat down, clasping her hands within his. He bowed his head, and Anna was quick to do the same.

33

She wondered if he would pray aloud, or if he was waiting for her to pray aloud. While he was accustomed to public speaking, she was not. She wasn't even sure what she was supposed to be praying about! Was he asking God whether they should get married, or skipping straight to when?

Anna! she chastised herself. *Stop worrying about his prayers and start figuring out your own!*

The silence suddenly seemed deafening.

Help! she said silently. *Am I getting myself into another big mess, or am I following Your will?*

She opened her eyes and peeked at Michael. She saw that his brow was furrowed and imagined he was praying that she wouldn't throw temper tantrums in front of the school board. In spite of her faults, he was willing to take the risk and marry her. He hadn't hesitated before he handed her his phone, so she could call her pastor – she was the one who had chickened out. There was no guarantee that their marriage would be happy, but no relationship came with a guarantee, no matter how long the parties had known one another. Michael was a Christian, he was kind, he loved kids and animals ... and he loved her.

Anyway, she reminded herself, *it's not about me.* She was meant to rescue Michael. It was the reason she had come to Casey's. She must take care of Michael so that he could take care of the children. She remembered how right this had seemed the night before. Once she acknowledged this fact, she had gone to bed and slept peacefully ... at least for a few hours. She heard Michael sigh. "Amen," she said. Though her prayer hadn't sounded much like a proper prayer, she knew God had been listening. "May I use your phone?" she asked politely.

Michael fished his phone from his shirt pocket and handed it over.

She dialed the number before she could talk herself out of it again. "Pastor Franklin?" she said in a cheerful voice. "This is Anna Brown. Guess what! I owe you an apple pie."

♥

Michael could hear a man speaking on the other end of the

phone, but he couldn't make out the words. He wondered why Anna owed him an apple pie. It must be a private joke between them.

"I was wondering if you're going to be busy next Saturday," Anna said. "I know it's short notice, but ... you would? That's great! Thank you so much!"

Michael's heartbeat accelerated. Were they really going to behave so impulsively? It went against his nature, but somehow, he couldn't force himself to call a halt.

"What time?" Anna asked. "2:30?" She waited until Michael nodded. "That works for us. Do you want to meet Michael ahead of time?"

She listened, nodding her head, as if the minister could see her. "Thank you again!" she finally said. "I'll call you as soon as I'm back in St. Louis." She pressed the red square and handed Michael his phone.

"What was that about apple pie?" Michael wondered.

Anna rolled her eyes at the ceiling. "I might have mentioned you last summer, when I filled in for the church secretary."

"And?" Michael pressed.

She giggled. "Pastor Franklin bet me an apple pie we'd be married before Christmas."

Michael merely smiled. "Saturday, at 2:30? Is that the plan?"

Anna bobbed her head. "Is that okay?"

He nodded serenely, though he was anything but calm. "What about a honeymoon?"

"We could go to Branson. There's a lot to do there, if you've never been."

"Do you have your heart set on that?"

"No," she said. "It's just close. And I know how to get discounts, after taking the kids every summer."

Michael didn't want to go where she had been before. "May I make the plans and surprise you?"

"Sure," she said. "Just let me know what kind of clothes to pack."

He handed her his phone again. "Do you want to call the kids?"

"There's no one you need to call?"

"I'll use the landline."

"Will we keep it a secret here at Casey's?" Anna asked.

"For the most part, yes." Michael wouldn't mind if Marianne *guessed* the truth and spread rumors while they were away. It would make the official announcement nothing more than a formality. He would tell Tina, his secretary, on Monday, but he should tell John Casey and the board members as soon as possible.

He lifted the receiver and dialed Loretta Boswick, the head of Casey's board, while his mind began to compile a list. They should apply for the license and purchase wedding rings on Thursday, allowing plenty of time to resolve any complications. Hopefully, either Paula or Andy could come home to act as chaperone. If not, he would stay at a motel. He wanted to do everything right and that meant avoiding too much time spent alone.

Anna slid off his desk and went to the couch, dialing his phone on the way. He heard the happy tone of her voice and it finally began to sink in – they were getting married! In a week! He tried to remember whether he'd ever been so excited about anything, but he knew he hadn't.

♥ Chapter 4 ♥

When Marianne and Russell arrived, Michael immediately led the security guard into his home office.

"How come your hair is wet?" Marianne asked Anna, once they were alone.

Anna frowned at her. "Because I washed it? *Before* Russell left to come get you," she added pointedly.

Marianne made a face. "Dr. Grant's not wearing a suit and you weren't there this morning. *Early* this morning. I'm not the only person who noticed."

Anna decided to ignore the insinuation. "C'mon. I'll show you where you're supposed to sleep." She led the way up the stairs and went into one of the guest rooms. Charlie followed, but halted just outside the door. "Dr. Grant said he couldn't give me permission to tell you what happened, but he couldn't forbid me to tell you either."

"So tell me," Marianne said in a cross voice. She leaned against the dresser, glowering over crossed arms.

"Susie's been real depressed and … she had a bad night last night. So I called him."

"You called Dr. Grant about Susie?" Marianne said doubtfully. "I thought this is about you getting attacked."

Anna fell back on the bed and stared at the ceiling. She wished she hadn't suggested that Marianne play chaperone.

"So? What happened with Susie?" Marianne asked.

"Her sister came and got her," Anna said, without sitting up. "I hope you won't spread that around." She knew the words would hurt Marianne.

"I won't," Marianne huffed. She dropped her backpack on the floor and sat down on the bed. "Are you allowed to tell me what happened to *you*?" she asked sarcastically.

Anna closed her eyes. "Bruce Carlisle caught me alone in the Dog House."

"The Dog House?"

"That's what we call the pet therapy area."

"How come you were down there alone? You said you learned your lesson last time."

Anna decided not to answer. It wasn't as if she owed Marianne an explanation.

"How come the dog is here?" Marianne wondered. She went to the hallway and stooped down to pet Charlie. "Isn't this the one you couldn't train? How come he didn't jump on me?"

"Michael's been working with him. He saved my life."

"The dog did, or Dr. Grant did?"

"The dog did." Anna sat up and felt light-headed. "Charlie did."

They were both quiet while Marianne petted the dog and Anna studied the pictures on the walls. She wished Marianne would get over her bad mood so they could go downstairs and fix dinner.

"You guys are like …" Marianne glanced at her, then looked away.

"If you mean we're a couple now, yes we are. If you think we're sleeping together, then no, we're not."

Marianne rolled her eyes as she stood up. "Are you gonna get married?"

Anna wondered what Michael would want her to say, in answer to a direct question. "I'm sure we will."

"At least you're bein' honest now." Marianne linked her hands behind her back and spread her feet apart, like a soldier at parade rest. "Are you gonna tell me what happened with Bruce?"

Anna pulled her sweater away from her neck, so Marianne could see the bruises. "He choked me." She pushed up her sleeve, so Marianne could see the fresh scab on her arm. "My back is all

38

scraped up too."

"Did the dog bite him?"

"No, he just growled and snarled, but Bruce was scared of him."

"He's done that kinda stuff to other women. Not chokin' them but … tryin' to get them to mess around."

"I wish they would go to the police," Anna said wistfully.

"You want me to sorta tell people about it?" Marianne offered. "Kinda suggest they should report him?"

Anna wasn't sure what Michael would say to that. "Maybe once he's been arrested?"

"I won't say a word unless you tell me too," Marianne promised. "I'm doin' a lot better with keepin' my mouth shut."

"It's not easy," Anna sympathized. "I know, because I have a hard time 'keeping a tight rein on my tongue' too."

"Well, you'd better learn in a hurry, if you two are gonna get married. I'm sure he'll tell you stuff he won't want you to tell anybody else."

"And you'll understand, if I can't repeat what he tells me?"

"Well, duh," Marianne said, rolling her eyes again.

♥

Michael pretended he wasn't watching as Anna and Marianne came down the stairs. Anna was wearing blue jeans and a pink sweater. Her hair was still damp, but neatly combed and tucked behind her ears. It was a good thing he had invited chaperones …

"All righty," Russell said, with obvious amusement. He was seated on the couch, facing Michael. "I'll order hot fudge sundaes for anybody who can climb the fence around the students' dormitory without getting electrocuted."

"I think that would work," Michael said, squashing his hands between his knees.

Russell laughed, and Michael wondered what was so funny.

"I think we oughta join the women in the kitchen," Russell said. "Make sure they don't use too much pepper. I can take it, but I imagine an old guy like you would get indigestion."

Michael got up and walked past him, without acknowledging

39

his remarks. He sat down on one of the stools at the counter, where he could watch Anna.

"Uh oh," she said. "We've got an audience, Marianne. I hope he didn't see you adding wine to the sauce."

Marianne looked at Michael, then at Anna.

Michael frowned.

"Just kidding!" Anna sang. "But she did bring hot sauce."

"Russell said he can't handle anything too hot," Michael cautioned.

"Russell did *not* say that," Russell disagreed, perching on a stool.

Michael shrugged, without even glancing at him. "What are you making?" he asked.

"We were going to fix oysters, but I couldn't find any in the pantry," Anna teased.

"Oysters?" Marianne said with a shudder. "No way."

"You don't like oysters?" Anna said with mock surprise. "Imagine that!"

"You sure sound cheery for somebody who almost got murdered," Marianne said with suspicion.

"I only had about two hours sleep," Anna said defensively. "Then I had to go to the sheriff's office and they took pictures of my injuries and made me go over my statement a thousand times."

Michael agreed with Marianne – Anna was not acting like a woman who had been attacked. "I think you're in shock," he said. "When it sinks in, I'm afraid you're going to fall apart."

"You don't know me very well then," Anna said sharply. "I do *not* fall apart. It's not in my nature." She turned to the counter, where she had assembled a variety of ingredients.

Michael didn't understand why he was in trouble, when he had only been trying to defend her from Marianne.

"What else do we need?" Anna asked Marianne.

"Tomatoes? Black olives? Corn. Umm … cheese. Oh yeah – chicken! Lemme think a minute. Can I scrounge around in your fridge?" she asked Michael.

"Help yourself," he said. "Let me know if there's anything I can do."

"Just don't give him a job of any real importance," Russell advised.

Michael frowned at him. He couldn't imagine why Russell was behaving so out of character.

"What's this?" Marianne asked, holding out a glass bowl covered with plastic wrap.

"Eww," Anna said, backing away. "Whatever it is, I don't want it in my Mexican Lasagna."

Michael got off the stool and came around the counter. He stood behind Anna and gazed over her shoulder. "Chop suey," he said, touching his hand to the small of her back. He inhaled the scent of his own shampoo in her hair. "It's only a few days old. There's nothing wrong with it."

"I still don't want it in my lasagna," Anna said.

"Have you ever had Bachelor's Buffet?" Russell asked both women.

"What's that?" Marianne asked doubtfully.

"When you get down to one spoonful of a bunch of different stuff, you throw it all on a plate and heat it in the microwave and call it Bachelor's Buffet."

"Eww," Anna said.

Michael slid his hand to her shoulder, then reluctantly let it drop.

"I'll cut up the chicken and start browning it," Anna decided. "You can make the sauce. Okay?" The question was aimed at Marianne. She seemed to have forgotten Michael was there.

"Sure," Marianne said. "Who's gonna grate the cheese?"

"Sounds like something I could handle," Russell said.

They all three turned to look at Michael.

"I'll just watch," he said, and returned to his stool. Twenty-four hours ago, he had sat on the same stool, listening to a message from Anna on the landline. He had wondered whether she would ever forgive him for allowing her to believe he had never been married. Now here she was, in his kitchen, cooking and laughing while secretly planning their wedding. Could this really be *his* life?

♥

Anna woke up and looked for a clock. It was after ten but the house was utterly quiet. Where were the others?

She jumped out of Michael's bed and straightened the covers. He had insisted that she sleep in his bedroom, while he slept in his recliner and Russell bunked on the couch. She had slept in his T-shirt too, and used his toothpaste and his shampoo.

She hurried to the bathroom to get dressed, wishing she had remembered makeup and hair pins. Hopefully, Russell would escort her to the dorm and wait while she did her face and hair.

When Anna opened the door, she almost tripped over Charlie. Dropping to her knees, she gave him a hug, then kissed the top of his head. As quick as she was to pull away, his long tongue slurped across her cheek. She emerged into the living room scrubbing the slobber away with her sleeve.

"Good morning!" Michael said, causing her to jump. He slapped down the lid of his laptop and hurried to capture her in his arms. "Do you have any idea how difficult it was to keep my hands off of you last night?" he asked in a husky voice.

"Where's Russell and Marianne?" Anna wondered nervously.

"Marianne's gone back to the dorm, and Russell was overdue to go home."

"How come they left us unchaperoned?"

In answer, he drew her up on her toes and kissed her with passion.

"Maybe they shouldn't have," Anna said, placing her hands flat against his chest.

"Not to worry," Michael assured her. "Russell knew I have a meeting in …" He checked his watch and made a face. "Twelve minutes."

"Were you going to leave me here alone?" Anna asked, thinking of Bruce.

"Bruce was arrested this morning," Michael said, as if he had read her mind. "When he returned to his apartment, there were two police officers waiting to escort him to Briarton."

Anna pressed both hands over her heart. "Will he get out on bail?"

"They're going to hold him at least 24 hours. I have the sheriff's word." He gathered her hair into a ponytail, smiling

42

down at her. "I should've gotten you up long before this, but I was busy working on the itinerary for our honeymoon."

"Do I get a hint?" she asked with excitement.

"Nope. And you only get breakfast if you hurry."

"I'll get something in the cafeteria," she decided. "Hopefully, I'll run into Marianne, so she doesn't think we're over here getting up to no good."

"She's going to think whatever she wants," Michael said with resignation. "Try not to worry about it."

Anna made a face. "I can't turn my worrier off. It doesn't work that way. I need to stop at the dorm, to get some hair pins … and makeup and deodorant. I forgot almost everything!"

"Will we ask someone else to pack your bags for the honeymoon?" Michael teased.

"Very funny," she said, poking him in the belly. "I'll be as quick as I can."

"I'm going to escort you," he said firmly.

"Do you have time?"

"I'll *take* time." He snapped the lead onto Charlie's collar and grabbed his tweed coat from the back of a dining room chair. He draped it over Anna's shoulders, ignoring her protests. "It cooled off last night and I don't want you getting sick before the honeymoon."

Anna turned her head and sniffed the collar. "It smells like you," she said happily.

"I should hope it wouldn't smell like some other man," he chuckled. "Charlie, are you going to behave or should I tie you up outside?"

Charlie barked and wagged his tail.

"He said he'll behave," Anna translated, as they reached the women's dorm.

Michael brought Charlie into the building, shortening the lead as they climbed the stairs. "Could you hand me my key ring? It's in my left coat pocket."

Anna handed it over. She thought they were already starting to act like an old married couple.

"I should have a new phone for you today," Michael said. "That will give us both some peace of mind." He opened the door

43

and went in ahead of her. "We need the blouse you were wearing on Friday. Let's do that first."

She pulled the trash can from underneath her desk. "Won't it have my DNA all over it too?"

"I'm sure it will. We just have to hope it has an incriminating amount of his." Michael lifted his coat from her shoulders and took a plastic bag from an inside pocket. He held it while she inserted the blouse, then he sealed it and wrote on the label with a Sharpie.

Anna remembered his meeting and hurried to brush her hair and fasten it into a bun. She would've liked to put on makeup too, but didn't want to make him late.

"Is that sort of like wearing a hat?" Michael wondered, bouncing his palm on her hair as they left the dorm.

"Would you rather I cut it and wore it in a different style?"

"No," he said without hesitation. "I love your hair."

"Who are you meeting with on a Sunday?" she wondered. "Students or parents or teachers?"

"John Casey is going to stop by. I wanted to tell him our news face-to-face."

Anna stopped walking and looked at him with anguish. "Will he be upset?"

"I don't think so," Michael said, nudging her forward. "I think he'll congratulate me and tell me he's looking forward to meeting you."

"I hadn't even thought of them," Anna said. "I don't think my brain is functioning very well."

"Mine either," Michael said. "You can claim bridal jitters, but what is there for me to blame it on?"

♥ Chapter 5 ♥

They parted company inside the front door, when Michael headed upstairs to his office. Anna knew he was worried about her, in spite of the fact that Bruce was behind bars.

There was a young guard at the podium, and he stooped to pet Charlie when Anna approached. "I need an escort to the Dog House," she told him. "I guess they'll need to stay with me while I clean the kennels."

"Maria felt well enough to come in," he said. "Another guard took her downstairs about half an hour ago." He led the way, being careful not to get tangled in Charlie's leash. "Maria was telling me about the pet therapy program. It sounds really cool."

"It is," Anna said with enthusiasm. "It's good for the kids, *and* for the dogs. Are you new to Casey's?"

"Just started last week. I'd like to teach here, once I get my degree. I'm going to school at night."

"That's admirable," Anna said. "I know how hard it is to work full time, go to school, and do homework."

"It'll pay off," he said with confidence. He stuck his head into the grooming area and waved at Maria. "Estoy bien!" he called.

Maria started laughing. "Buenos dias!" she called back.

He looked embarrassed. "I'm trying to learn Spanish, to impress her," he confided. "I'm listening to tapes."

"She's impressed," Anna told him, hiding her words behind her hand, "but don't tell her I told you."

"Thanks," he said gratefully. "Have a good day ... um ... what was your name?"

"Anna Brown," she said. *Soon to be Anna Grant*, she thought with elation.

"Have a good day, Ms. Brown!"

"Thanks, you too ... um ... what was your name?"

He laughed. "Scott. Scott Lively."

"Thanks," Maria told Anna, as soon as both guards were out of sight.

"What am I being thanked for?" Anna averted her eyes from the grooming table, trying not to think about Bruce.

"I've been trying to find out his first name," Maria admitted sheepishly. "I wondered where Charlie was!" she said, when his front paws landed on her shoulders. "Did you come in early and take him for a walk?"

"Dr. Grant kept him all night," Anna explained.

"So he finally told you! We all know you're sweet on him."

Anna knew her shock must be obvious.

"On Charlie!" Maria said, giggling and covering her mouth. "He's really cute, isn't he?"

It took Anna a moment to decide she meant Scott, not Michael or Charlie. "He is," she agreed.

"What happened to your neck?" Maria asked, leaning closer, to peer at it. "It looks like a rope burn. Did you learn anything else about him?"

Anna tried to raise her collar, and wished she had worn something else. "He's trying to learn Spanish, to impress you," she said, hoping Maria was talking about Scott.

"I know about ten words in Spanish," Maria laughed.

"You ought to tell the poor guy," Anna advised her. "He's got enough on his plate without trying to learn a language. Did you know he goes to school at night?"

"What's his major?"

"Ask him," Anna suggested. "It would be a good conversation starter."

"I'll do that ... if I can go to lunch at noon?" she hinted. "That's when he goes."

"That's fine," Anna said, though it meant she would have to go at noon too.

They cleaned the kennels together, then Anna retreated to her office. With no students around, it was a good opportunity to catch up on paperwork.

"Mrs. Brown?" Maria called from the grooming area.   "Dr. Grant wants to see you in the hallway."

Oh good, Anna thought, assuming he had come to deliver her phone. She hurried to meet him, and saw that he was with John Casey. She immediately remembered that she wasn't wearing makeup.

"Anna Brown?" John said. "I insisted that Michael bring me down to meet you."

"How do you do," Anna said politely, shaking his hand. "It's an honor to meet the person who started Casey's. I was hoping to have a chance to tell you that someday."

"Thank you," John said seriously, though his eyes were twinkling. "And I'm honored to meet the woman who managed to drag Michael out of that cave he's been hiding in. Please accept my congratulations and best wishes for your happiness. I hope we'll get to know one another, as time goes by."

"I hope so too," Anna said, certain her cheeks were flushed with red.

"So tell me about this thing you're doing with the dogs," John said, dropping a hand on her shoulder. "How's it work?"

Anna had to fight the urge to pull away. Though John Casey seemed harmless, she didn't want to be touched by anyone other than Michael. "The dogs are strays," she explained, leading him into the Dog House. "We get them from the shelter in Briarton, then the students train them to be assistance dogs. With the help of the AHTs," she added, gesturing at Maria. "Maria, this is Mr. Casey, the school's founder."

Maria wiped her palm down her pant leg before she shook his hand. "It's nice to meet you."

"Likewise," he said. "You enjoy working with dogs?"

"I love it! And I love helping people who are disabled."

"How's that?" he asked. "Pretend like you need to sell me on the program, Maria."

She looked nervous. "Well, first we teach them basic

47

commands. If they do well, we try and teach them the special stuff."

"What kind of special stuff?" John turned back to Anna. "Gimme an example so I can talk about it to the folks who help fund Casey's."

"They learn how to walk beside someone on crutches," Anna said, trying to decide what would sound impressive. "And how to walk beside a wheelchair, without getting their paws crushed. They can open doors ... some doors."

"And some gates," Michael said, winking at her.

"We teach them to pick up items that are dropped," Maria said. "Without chewing it up before they return it," she added, making a face. "They can turn on lights and open drawers. They can even help people get dressed and undressed. Socks and shoes and jackets – that kind of stuff."

"We try to teach them how to recognize danger, so they can protect their owner," Anna told him. "For example, if there's a car coming, they'll keep the person from stepping into the street. In an advanced training program, some dogs can predict when a person is about to have a seizure, and summon help."

"I think I heard about that," John said with a nod.

"Dogs are really good for people who are having emotional problems," Maria said. "We placed one dog with a veteran who is suffering from post traumatic stress syndrome. He says she gave him a new lease on life."

"You think you could get the dogs to perform on camera?" John asked. "I could send out a crew to make a video with the kids and the dogs?"

"I'm sure we could," Anna said with confidence.

"Give me a call when you get back," John told Michael. He turned to Anna. "Thank you again. You know what I'm talking about." He waved at the AHT. "It was nice meeting you, hon. I hope to see your smiling face in that video."

"I hope so too," Maria said, darting a glance at Anna.

Michael pulled a cell phone from his pocket and handed it to Anna. Then he followed John Casey out the door.

"Is Dr. Grant having surgery?" Maria asked with concern.

"What makes you think that?" Anna said with surprise.

48

"Mr. Casey said, 'When you get back.' Get back from where?"
Anna just shrugged, uncertain how else to respond.

♥

Anna sat across from Michael in his private dining area,
pushing food around her plate.

"What's the matter?" he asked. "You don't act like a happy
bride."

"Normally a bride wouldn't have to keep her wedding plans a
secret," she said dismally.

"You can tell people if you want, but not everyone will wish
you well."

"Like Helen? And Gayle? It's just that … I don't like being
dishonest. Maria thinks you're going to have surgery."

"Where did she come up with that?"

"I don't know. As soon as you and Mr. Casey left, she asked
whether you were going to have surgery. And she said people are
always bugging them – the AHTs, to find out whether we're an
item."

"An item?" Michael repeated with amusement. "I guess I've
never heard it put quite like that."

Anna giggled. "You will tell people we're married after we get
back, won't you?"

"Of course," he said, reaching across the table to stroke her
cheek. "I can't wait to announce it to the world. I'm only trying to
protect *you*. I can handle it when people get nosy or judgmental,
but you're so sensitive …"

"I am *not* sensitive," Anna objected.

"Really?" he said, with the hint of a smile. "I recall an
occasion when you burst into tears, because you said everyone
was attacking you."

"Attacking me? I don't think I said *that*."

He tipped his head to one side.

"Did I really?" she asked, covering her eyes. "I just couldn't
think what to say, after seeing you kissing someone in the
cafeteria."

"I wish you wouldn't put it that way," Michael grumbled. "I

only kissed her cheek and I'm sure Jasmine wonders why I've been holding her at arm's length ever since."

"I'm sorry," Anna said. "Do you see her very often?"

"She's coming this afternoon, with some paperwork I need to sign."

"Will you tell her about us?"

"No," he said firmly. "We agreed to tell our families *after* the honeymoon, right?"

"Doesn't it feel like you're lying though?"

Michael folded his hands on the table and grew quiet. "There are times when a couple has to keep secrets – not from each other, but from everyone else. We aren't responsible for the conclusions people draw, so long as we didn't deliberately mislead them."

"Which is sort of like lying," Anna insisted.

Michael nodded. "Secrets are very much like lies."

Anna crossed her arms. "Is this leading to a discussion about oysters?"

Michael hesitated. He was wary of starting an argument, but he didn't want to miss an opportunity to stress the importance of honesty in their relationship. "A moment ago, you said you fabricated a story, after you saw me with Jasmine in the cafeteria."

"I didn't make it up!" Anna protested. "It was true that everyone was giving me a hard time!"

"We'll leave it at that, then," he said, though he wasn't truly satisfied.

"Paula wants to have a shower for me," Anna changed the subject. "I told her I would ground her for a year."

Michael laughed. "How can you ground her when she lives in another city?"

"You think she wouldn't obey, if I said she wasn't allowed to go out?" She rolled her eyes. "Paula didn't do what I said when she lived at home."

"You did a good job raising those kids, Anna. Don't sell yourself short."

"Thanks," she said, beginning to pile trash on her tray. "If we're not supposed to keep secrets from one another, how come you don't tell me where we're going on our honeymoon?"

He frowned. "Do you want me to tell you?"

"No," Anna giggled. "I love surprises. Good ones," she specified.

♥

Anna walked a few feet behind Maria and Scott, trying not to eavesdrop on their conversation. She thought they looked especially cute together, since they were the same height. She felt extra short when she walked beside Michael, because he was extra tall.

She couldn't change her size, but she needed to change her attitude, and quickly. "Stupid oysters," she grumbled. If only she had spit the first one into her napkin! But they were dining at Michael's ritzy private club and she was trying to impress her potential new boss … anybody would've washed the oyster down with a gulp of water and lied that it was delicious.

"See you later!" Maria called to Scott, as he turned to head back upstairs.

Anna followed Maria into the Dog House, but her mind was stuck on the lunchroom conversation. Maria and Scott were just getting acquainted – were they totally honest with each other? She felt certain Maria would say they avoided certain topics, and didn't ask questions if they might not like the answers. Everyone skirted the truth when they were first getting acquainted … didn't they? She would like to ask the AHTs' opinion, but she didn't dare discuss Michael with anyone at Casey's.

Should she have confronted Michael after she saw him with Jasmine in the cafeteria? It wasn't as if he had pledged to be faithful. In fact, they had hardly known one another at the time. They hardly knew one another *now*, she thought with a twinge of concern.

"Anna?" Maria said warily. "Are you okay?"

"Sorry," Anna said with embarrassment. "I was daydreaming."

"Looked more like a nightmare to me," Maria said.

♥

51

Michael hung up his phone and debated what to do. Marianne had come down with the virus and couldn't play chaperone. Russell felt it was sufficient if he was on the premises, but Michael wasn't sure the members of Casey's board would agree. So long as Bruce was in custody, there was no real excuse to sequester Anna in his home.

He dialed the sheriff's cell phone, wanting some assurance that Bruce would not make bail before morning. He was pleasantly surprised to learn that two other women had come forward to back up Anna's claims. It meant Bruce would only walk free if he made a bargain with the district attorney. Even so, Michael decided to post two female security guards at the women's dorm, every night until he and Anna departed the campus on Thursday.

He opened his laptop and signed onto the Internet, verifying that all their reservations had been confirmed. According to Paula and Andy, Hawaii had always been Anna's dream destination, so that's where he would take her. He didn't want to spend their wedding night on an airplane, so he had reserved a honeymoon suite in Los Angeles. They would fly to Honolulu on Sunday morning.

Unlike Jeanne, Anna hadn't led a life of privilege. He felt certain she had never flown first class before, or stayed in a five star hotel. He wanted to lavish her with the best of everything. He wanted to spoil her so that she wouldn't even try to imagine life without him. He wanted to give her the perfect honeymoon, down to the last detail.

He checked his watch, aware that the waiting room was filled with people. Keeping his mind on Casey's affairs wasn't likely to get any easier between now and Thursday.

♥ Chapter 6 ♥

"I didn't think Thursday was ever going to get here!" Anna said. "Everybody kept asking me what was going on, because I kept zoning out. I almost blew it with Dawn. I don't know why, since I'm closer to Maria than Dawn. Maria still thinks you're having surgery!"

"That will only be one of many rumors that will go around campus," Michael said. He had struggled too, and given Tina plenty of excuses to tease him.

"Did you get any more news about Bruce?" Anna asked, settling into her seat. "Are they going to let him out on bail?"

"I don't think so. Not with three cases against him."

Anna turned her head to stare out the side window. "We should pray for him," she said.

Michael was surprised. "Have you forgiven him?"

"No," she said. "That's why I need to pray." She folded her hands in her lap and the car grew quiet.

Michael squirmed a little. Even if prayer could play some mysterious part in Bruce's rehabilitation, he wasn't ready to be so generous.

"Now that we're on our way, are you going to give me a hint about where we're going on our honeymoon?" Anna asked after a moment. "You have to tell me soon, or I won't know what to pack."

"Paula's going to pack for you," he said.

53

"What!" Anna howled. "I'll end up with bunny pajamas and a string bikini!"

Michael laughed. "I'm okay with the string bikini, so long as you don't wear it out of our room. But bunny pajamas?"

"They have feet," Anna explained. *Aha!* she thought. If he wanted her to take a swim suit, their honeymoon must involve water. *Lake or ocean*, she wondered. *Florida? A cruise?* "And pink bunnies with white pompons for tails, which makes it lumpy to sleep in. She gave it to me for Christmas when she was six."

Michael laughed as he reached across the console for her hand. "I think I might ask her to pack it, just in case it gets chilly."

"When did you talk to Paula? Don't tell me she called you to try to set up a shower. You don't have a shower for a forty-year-old woman getting married a second time. What would anyone give me? We already have two houses filled with plenty of everything."

"Maybe they would give you sexy negligees," he suggested.

"I do *not* want a shower," Anna said firmly. "If you talk to Paula again, tell her I will be very angry if she has one. But you haven't said how you ended up talking to her the first time. Did she call you?"

"I called her. You used my cell phone last Saturday, so I had both kids' numbers in the call log."

"I should've thought to delete them," she grumbled. "Paula doing my packing?"

"You also put their cell phone numbers on your application, as someone to contact in an emergency," he reminded her. "I would've found a way."

"Did you consider this an emergency?"

"I did," he said. "And they were both willing to cooperate."

"Cooperate with what? What is Andy doing? Selling my Volkswagen to help pay for the honeymoon?"

Michael squeezed her hand. "Let's stop at a jewelry store on our way into town. Have you given any thought to the sort of ring you want?"

"I'll pay for yours," she said. "I already transferred the money out of my savings account."

He changed lanes and passed a slow moving tractor trailer. "Will you want to have your own bank account after we're married?"

"Not especially. Do you want me to sign a pre-marital agreement?"

"Of course not!" he said. "When we get back, I'll have your name added to all my accounts. They'll fix you up with a debit card and a checkbook."

Anna wasn't sure why, but this news made her eyes cloud with tears.

"What's the matter?" he asked with concern.

"Nothing," she said. "It's just sweet."

"I believe marriage is a fifty/fifty proposition," he said firmly.

"Me too. I'll add your name to the deed on my house. Or do you want me to sell it?"

"Let's hold off on making those decisions. What time do you think Paula will get in? I don't think we ought to spend too much time alone …"

"You mean you still don't trust me?" she teased.

"I don't trust *me*," he admitted.

♥

"I made a list," Paula announced, as soon as she and her mother were alone in Anna's bedroom.

Anna was feeling peaceful and tolerant. Away from Bruce, and the watchful eyes at Casey's, she had finally started to relax. She sat down on the bed and patted the space beside her.

"You need to go shopping for rings," Paula began.

"We already did!" Anna jumped up and went to her dresser. She pulled two ring boxes from a bag and opened the smaller one, holding it out for Paula to see. The band was made of black gold, with molded leaves of green and coral.

"I'll bet he would've bought you a big, fat diamond, if you had asked him," Paula sighed.

"He suggested an emerald, but … I fell in love with these."

"Won't the colors wear off?"

"No," Anna assured her. "Don't you like it?"

55

Paula shrugged and turned back to her list. "I thought we'd go shopping tomorrow, to find you a dress. Something classy."

Anna winced. "Michael wants to take me, but you're welcome to go along." She hoped Michael wouldn't mind.

"I'm sure he was just being nice, Mom. Men hate to shop, especially for clothes. Maybe he can do something with Andy while we're gone."

"I'm not sure when Andy's coming," Anna said, returning the rings to her dresser. "Michael really does want to take me. I can't imagine why, but ..."

"The groom is not supposed to see the dress until the bride comes down the aisle," Paula said firmly.

"I'm not coming down the aisle," Anna said. "We'll all walk to the altar together."

Paula rolled her eyes. "What about flowers?"

"Flowers? For a ten minute ceremony?"

"Boutonnières and a bouquet?"

Anna didn't want to waste money on flowers, but she couldn't reject *all* of Paula's suggestions. "Maybe you could take care of that? A rose with baby's breath, for Andy and Michael, and two wrist corsages for us?"

"Did you order a cake?"

"We're not having a reception! Michael is planning to take the four of us to dinner someplace nice. Then he and I will need to leave to catch our plane or train or bus. Or boat, I guess."

"Boat?" Paula repeated, giving her a strange look.

Aha! Anna thought. *He's taking me on a cruise!* She sat down and put her arm around Paula's shoulders. "Would you like a new dress to wear to the wedding?"

"I already bought one," Paula informed her. "I put it on your credit card." She got up and paced around the room. "I guess I'll pack your suitcase while you're dress shopping. I hope he doesn't talk you into some Victorian looking thing."

"He won't talk me into anything. He's not like that." She wrung her hands. "I'm starting to feel stressed."

"You should be excited, not stressed. You're not pregnant, are you?"

Anna was so shocked, it took her a moment to react. Then she jumped up and glared at her daughter. "What did you just ask me?"

"It's a logical question, when people start planning a quick wedding," Paula said defensively. "I understand how things like that can happen, Mom. I'm not ten years old."

"I would rather not hear about your experience on the subject," Anna rebuked her. "Michael and I have *not* slept together." She was furious with Paula for suggesting it. "What else is on your list?" she asked coldly.

Paula wisely abandoned the subject. "I made an appointment for you to get your hair done. Why don't you try a perm? You've been wearing your hair in that goofy bun forever."

Anna plucked the list from Paula's hands, crumpled it, and threw it at the trash can. "This is *my* wedding," she said emphatically. "When you get married, you can play Bridezilla, but this is my wedding. I intend to buy a new dress which I will be able to wear on numerous other occasions. I will wear my hair exactly as it is right now. After the ceremony, we will go to dinner, where we will *not* drink champagne. That's the way Michael and I want it."

"Okay, okay," Paula said, getting up and retrieving her list from the floor. "I didn't actually make the appointment anyway. I just asked them to hold a spot, in case you went along with it. I don't get why you're so crabby! I figured you'd be in a great mood."

Anna *had* been in a great mood. She was nervous, admittedly, but she hadn't felt cross. "What else is on your list?" she asked contritely.

"Never mind," Paula said, dismissing it with a wave of her hand. "What size do you wear?"

"What size what?"

"What size everything. I know you've got clothes you haven't worn for twenty years, so I need to be sure I pack stuff that fits."

"Anything I don't wear regularly is in the closet in the basement," Anna said, hoping it was true. "Are you packing summer or winter clothes?"

"Nice try," Paula said with a grin. "Trust me – you'll like where you're going."

"I'm sure I will," Anna said. She was convinced that they were going on a cruise, and she was worried that she would get seasick.

"Are you going to tell me how this came about?" Paula asked. "When I talked to you last week, you never even mentioned Michael. A few days later, you call to say you're getting married."

"It's a long story," Anna said, unwilling to tell her about Bruce Carlisle. "Once we both admitted how we felt, there didn't seem any reason to wait." That wasn't altogether true, she thought guiltily. She rubbed her knuckles against her chin. What if Michael came back later and said she pushed him into the wedding before he was ready?

Paula watched with fascination. "I've never seen you act like this before. You're a nervous wreck!"

"I'm not," Anna protested, but she was. "I need some fresh air. I'm going to ask Michael to go for a walk."

"It's pouring!" Paula hooted. "I think you'd better take a couple tranquilizers and a long nap instead!"

Anna started out of the room, then she paused. "I do appreciate you dropping everything and coming home on short notice. And I'm sorry if I seem crabby. I'm just nervous. I don't know why. It's not like me. I usually get excited, not nervous. I might get nervous for a minute, but … Anyway … I need to go and see what Michael's doing."

"I'll tag along," Paula said with amusement, trailing her down the stairs.

♥

Michael was in the kitchen, seated at the table with a cup of coffee and his laptop. Two board members were spending the next ten days at Casey's, sharing the job of administrator. They had begged him to stay in touch, at least through emails.

"Want a cup of coffee?" he offered, as soon as Anna came into the room.

"Caffeine would be a bad idea," Paula said, shaking her head behind Anna's back.

"What's the matter?" Michael asked Anna, lowering the lid on his pc and pushing it away.

"I want to take a walk, but it's raining."

"We could take a drive. Would that help?"

"A drive?" she repeated, as if he were crazy.

Michael looked to Paula for help.

"That's a good idea," Paula said. "Go to the park and look at the trees … if you can see them through the rain. You always say nature is soothing."

"All right," Anna agreed. "It's better than nothing."

Michael put his coat on, as he headed to the closet to fetch hers.

"What about dinner?" Paula said. "Should I order a pizza?"

"A pizza?" Anna said, as if she'd never heard of such a thing.

"Pizza sounds great," Michael said. He took out his wallet and handed her a fifty dollar bill, then escorted Anna outside.

They ran to the car and she jumped in, leaning across to open his door.

"This is supposed to quit sometime tomorrow," he said. "The forecast for Saturday is sunshine and blue skies."

"Good, that's good," Anna said, clenching her hands in her lap.

Michael didn't say anything else until he had parked the car in the shelter of a large sycamore tree. "That's where we kissed the very first time," he said, pointing his finger into the park, though the rain made it impossible to see anything. "One minute, you were telling me off. The next minute, we were kissing."

"I'm still embarrassed that I spoke to you that way," she admitted. "You hadn't done anything to deserve it."

"You thought I had lured you to my club so I could seduce you," Michael reminded her. "I'd say that's a very good reason."

"You're very understanding," Anna sighed. She leaned across the console to offer him a kiss. "And patient," she added. "I couldn't put up with me for a minute."

"I couldn't survive *without* you for a minute," he said, wrapping her in both arms, though it was awkward in the cramped space. "Do you want to tell me what's bothering you?"

"I'm just second guessing everything. I feel as if I pushed you into this. I'm the one who proposed, and I'm the one who said we should get married right away."

"You think I wanted to wait?" He cupped her chin in his hand and made her look at him. "I didn't even want to wait a week."

She smiled and rested her cheek on his chest. "Paula asked me if I'm pregnant."

"Seriously?" he said with an angry tone.

"She said it was the logical conclusion, given that we're getting married so quickly."

"No wonder you're stressed out!"

"That's probably part of it," Anna allowed. "She wanted me to change my hairstyle and she wanted to order a cake. I don't know what else she planned."

"What did you say? When she accused you of being pregnant?"

"I said we hadn't slept together. Why did she think I wanted her to come home and play chaperone?"

Michael began to rub her shoulders and she sat forward to make it easier.

"I tried to trick her into giving me a hint about the honeymoon, but she didn't fall for it."

"If that's what's making you nervous, I'll tell you right now," Michael offered.

She lowered her chin, as he began to rub the tense muscles in her neck. "I'm excited about the honeymoon. I'm just nervous about the wedding."

"How can we simplify it, so you can relax and enjoy yourself?"

"Maybe it's not the wedding," she said with uncertainty. "I just wish I had waited for you to ask me. And I should've allowed you to choose the date."

Michael sat back, and she did too. "I wasn't likely to ask you anytime soon," Michael said honestly. "I didn't think you were in love with me. I thought you were learning to *like* me, but once you found out about Jeanne … I was certain you could *never* love me."

Anna shook her head. "I started falling in love with you the moment we met. I remember what a shock it was, when you shook my hand. It felt like electricity or something."

"I felt it too," Michael said. "I thought we must have met before, but I couldn't come up with the occasion. I had just handed your folder to Tina, with a note that said you couldn't be hired. I wanted to snatch it back and tear it up." He reached across the console and rested his hand on her shoulder, strumming her cheek with his thumb.

"What if my car had started and I had driven off into the sunset?" Anna asked. "We would never have seen one another again."

"I would've called you the next day. I would've kept inventing positions at Casey's until you accepted one."

"Really?"

"Really," he said.

She leaned against the door. "I kept trying to hide my feelings because I didn't think you were interested in me romantically."

"What a pair we are," he laughed. "It's some kind of miracle that we've finally gotten together."

"I suppose we have Susie to thank, in a way," Anna mused. "And Bruce too."

Michael didn't comment. He didn't want to think they owed Bruce anything. "I planned to tell you about Jeanne, the day I took you to lunch at my club."

"I sensed I wasn't going to like what you were going to say. I was relieved when you had to hurry back to Casey's."

"We might have drifted further and further apart, if events hadn't forced me to confess. I didn't want to tell you, and you didn't want to know."

"I didn't know what I didn't want to know though," she said earnestly.

Michael smiled as he took her hand and held it between both of his. "Are you feeling better? Do you want to walk in the rain?"

"No thank you," she said, staring out the window. "You handle me very well, you know."

He chuckled. "I'm not sure that's a compliment, but I'll accept it as one." He started the engine and drove slowly back to the house.

When they pulled into the driveway, there was a blue SUV parked to one side.

"That must be Andy's ride," Anna said with surprise. "I didn't expect him until the wee hours." She jumped out of the car and ran to the door, without waiting for Michael.

"Mom!" Andy said, wrapping her in his arms and lifting her feet off the ground. "Hey, Mike! Congratulations!" He reached for Michael's hand while he continued to hug Anna. "I couldn't be happier for both of you. And for Paula and me."

Anna noticed a woman with blond hair, standing in the kitchen, watching with a smile on her face. Paula stood beside her, but Paula wasn't smiling.

"I hope you can say the same," Andy said sheepishly, gesturing to the woman. "This is Beth, my, uh, wife."

"What!" Anna said, pressing her hand over her heart.

"I wanted her to be here for your wedding, but we couldn't figure out how to do it without … you know. Ruining her reputation. We were gonna get married anyway, but we didn't want it to seem like we were trying to steal the limelight. Could you please say something!"

"Congratulations!" Anna said, hurrying to give Beth a hug. "I'm so happy to meet you! Andy's been talking about you for months. I had a feeling you were the one."

Beth hugged her back and Anna knew, instinctively, that she and Andy's wife were going to get along fine. "You finally have a sister," she told Paula, drawing her into a three person hug. "Something she's always wanted," she told Beth.

♥ Chapter 7 ♥

Anna started into the sanctuary, then stopped. Half the pews were filled with members of the congregation.

"I didn't do it!" Paula said, holding up both hands when Anna turned to look at her.

"Do you know these people?" Michael asked with confusion. "Did you get the time wrong?"

"I'm the culprit," Pastor Franklin said in a hushed voice, hurrying up the aisle to meet them. "I asked Sandy to put an announcement in the Sunday bulletin and I didn't think to mention that it should remain confidential until *after* the wedding."

Anna couldn't be angry with the secretary, or the members of the congregation who were turning to smile at her. "It's very sweet!" she told him. "I'm touched. Oh! This is Michael Grant. Michael, this is Pastor Franklin."

The pastor gave Michael's hand a hearty shake. "Are you ready?" he asked, turning back to Anna.

"We're ready," Anna said with excitement. She waited until the minister had returned to the altar before she turned to Michael. He held out his arm and she gripped it.

"I feel self-conscious," Beth tittered, as the wedding march sounded and the audience rose to their feet.

"Just wait," Paula warned. "They're all going to give you the third degree, as soon as the ceremony is over."

Paula's prediction was accurate, for Beth *and* Michael. The members of the congregation surrounded them, doling out hugs and handshakes ... and questions. Michael managed to act as if he didn't mind, but Anna knew he wasn't enjoying himself.

Just when she thought they could finally escape, the pastor ushered them to the basement. Crepe paper streamers were draped from the light fixtures, the tables were covered with starched white cloth and vases of cut flowers. There were casseroles and fried chicken and Styrofoam cups filled with iced tea and coffee.

"Poor Mike," Andy said, when he caught his mother alone. "They're grilling him, to be sure he's good enough for you."

"And they're quizzing me about Beth, to make sure she's good enough for you," Anna said with a shake of her head.

"*I'm* not good enough for *her*," Andy said humbly. "She's a super person. I promise you're gonna like her a lot."

"I can already see that," Anna assured him. "I'm just worried we're gonna miss our plane or train or boat."

"Boat?" Andy said with surprise, confirming her suspicions about a cruise. "They've got one more surprise," he warned. "I'll tell them to do it now."

A few moments later, Pastor Franklin brought Michael to Anna's side, then stepped back as two women wheeled a cart from the kitchen. It held a three tiered wedding cake, beautifully decorated with blue and white frosting. Several cameras flashed, then the top layer of the cake was removed and put into a small box, to be stored in the freezer until their first anniversary. The rest of the cake was sliced and coffee was served and the next time Anna looked at her watch, it was well past the time Michael had said he wanted to leave the house.

"We need to go!" she said frantically. "I'm scared we're going to miss our plane or train or boat."

"Boat?" Michael said with surprise. "Don't worry," he said, squeezing her arm. "I allowed plenty of time."

When they finally got into the car, he leaned over and kissed her. "How do you do, Mrs. Grant. In spite of the chaos and confusion, I'm pretty sure we managed to get married."

"I had no idea they were going to do that," she apologized

again.

"It was fine, Anna. It showed me how well loved you are."

"Start the car!" she urged. "Before they run out to ask us one more thing!"

He started the engine and drove across the parking lot. "I don't hear anything, do you? I guess they didn't string tin cans to the bumper."

"I hope not!" Anna said with alarm.

Michael reached for her hand. "I wish I knew how to help you relax."

"You said you wanted to leave the house at 4:30 and it's nearly 5:00 already."

"I was erring on the side of caution," Michael assured her. "They recommend you arrive at the airport two hours early, and we'll still make that."

"The airport?"

"Yes, but that's all I'll say for now," Michael said with a wink.

♥

"Mom!" Paula fussed. "What's wrong with you? You've flown to Grandma's a dozen times!"

"I get nervous then too."

"Not *this* nervous."

Anna pulled a carry-on bag from her closet shelf. "I think it's because I don't know where we're going. Michael said I should fix a carry-on." She tossed in underwear and socks, then added the T-shirt and cut-off jeans she had worn that morning. "What else?" she asked Paula.

"How about jeans and a few blouses?"

"Blue jeans? On my honeymoon?"

Paula laughed. "I'll take care of this, you go get changed. And wear comfortable shoes. They say your feet swell on a long flight."

A long flight … Anna tried to decide what that meant. "I'd like to wear this," she said, studying her reflection in the mirror. Her wedding dress was pale blue, with a lace inset and tucks below the bodice. "Should I pack it? I might need something dressy."

"I already packed you something dressy."

"Be sure and pack a sweater or jacket, in case it's cold on the plane," Anna instructed.

"I will," Paula said. "Now go get dressed! Before he leaves without you!"

"He wouldn't …" Anna stopped herself, as she realized Paula was only teasing.

♥

As soon as Anna disappeared into the bathroom, Paula took the overnight bag and ran downstairs. "I want to get one thing out of Mom's suitcase," she told Michael. "It will only take a second."

He fished his key ring from his pocket and handed it over. He had removed all but a few keys before leaving Casey's. He wasn't looking forward to sorting them out when he got home.

"This is a little something from me," Paula said, removing a wrapped package from the big suitcase and transferring it to the carry-on. She zipped it up, locked it, and added it to the stack.

"Thank you," Michael told her. "You've already done more than enough. You *and* Andy."

"I didn't do anything, except show up," Andy disagreed.

"Sorry we didn't get here early enough to help," Beth said.

"There wasn't much to do," Michael said. "We wanted to keep it simple and small."

"So much for that," Andy laughed.

"It was nice of your church friends to go to all that trouble," Michael said graciously. "Is your mother nearly ready?" he asked Paula. "Traffic might be heavy."

"I'll run up and annoy her," Paula said.

♥

Finally they were on their way to the airport. Finally they were alone.

"Did you sleep last night?" Anna asked. "I didn't. I was too excited."

66

"Excited or nervous?"

"Both. What about you?"

"Both," he admitted. "More excited than nervous though."

"Me too." She slid down in the seat and put her head back. "We made this as simple as we could, but it was still stressful. I'm sorry about the church. It was totally unexpected."

"Stop apologizing," he said, reaching over to pat her knee. "It was sweet."

"It was also stressful. Anyway, it's over now. We're married. Officially husband and wife. When are you going to tell me where we're going?"

"When do you want me to tell you?"

"Once we get to the airport, I'll be able to figure it out, won't I?"

Michael didn't want her to think L.A. was their final destination. "Hawaii," he said, turning his head, to catch her reaction.

"Hawaii?" Anna said with shock. "Are you kidding? Hawaii?"

"The kids said it's always been your dream, to go to Hawaii someday."

"It has! They were right! Hawaii!" she said again, covering her mouth with both hands. "I'm going to Hawaii!"

"Me too," Michael laughed.

"Have you ever been before?"

"No. I wanted to go somewhere neither of us have ever been. I booked a hotel in Honolulu, but we can switch to one of the other islands, if you have a preference."

"I don't know one from another," Anna said. "How long does it take to get there?" She bounced on the seat.

Michael laughed, but he couldn't turn his head – traffic was heavy. "From St. Louis to Honolulu, somewhere between eight and ten hours."

"That's a long time on an airplane," she said with a nervous giggle.

"We'll have a layover in Los Angeles."

"How long?"

"I went ahead and made reservations at a hotel. We'll fly out from there in the morning. I don't know about you, but I didn't

67

want to spend my wedding night on an airplane." He took a chance and glanced at her – she was smiling.

♥

"First class?" Anna said, following him to the front of the plane. "Don't tell the kids I flew first class. Every time we visit my folks, we criticize people who travel first class."

"Do you want to switch with someone in coach?" he offered.

"No! I want to sit with you," she said, squeezing his arm.

"I meant we'd both switch," he laughed.

"Does it cost a lot more?" she whispered.

"Don't worry about it," Michael said. "I'll look for a second job when we get home."

Anna looked horrified, until he assured her that he was joking.

He handed their boarding passes to a stewardess, and rested his hand on Anna's back as they moved up the aisle. "Do you want the window?"

"It's colder next to the window," she said with a shiver.

"Don't you like to fly?" Michael asked with concern.

"I don't mind it," Anna said. "Wait! Is this an oyster? Should I be honest or polite?"

"I wasn't fooled anyway," he said. He removed his coat and handed it to the stewardess, then sat down and stowed his overnight bag beneath his seat. It contained his laptop, and all the documents for their stay in Hawaii, as well as a change of clothing. If Anna fell asleep during the flight, he would probably log on and help with issues at Casey's.

He ordered a Perrier for himself, but couldn't talk Anna into anything. She played with her chair, putting it up and down a few times, then discovered a magazine in the pocket of the seat in front of her. "Maybe it will have pictures of things to do in Hawaii," she said with renewed excitement. "This must be costing a fortune," she worried. "I appreciate that you wanted it to be special but …"

"Stop worrying about money," Michael scolded. "If we couldn't afford it, I wouldn't have done it."

"That sounds so weird," she said. "*We?* Just because we had a fifteen minute ceremony, now your money is half mine?"

"Not from a legal standpoint, but as far as I'm concerned, we own everything together."

"Do you own the house at Casey's?"

He shook his head. "It belongs to the school. I thought about buying a house, a few years ago, but now I'm glad I didn't. Who knows where we'll want to retire?"

"We might decide to stay in Hawaii and live on the beach," Anna giggled, the magazine forgotten.

"Sounds like a plan," Michael said readily. "Especially if Paula packed that string bikini."

♥

Michael closed the lid of the laptop and watched as Anna tried to get comfortable on the cement floor. They were stranded in Oklahoma, at a private airport that didn't have a real terminal. Half an hour after they left St. Louis, the pilot announced a mechanical problem which required him to land for repairs. Michael had assumed they would be back in the air within the hour … more than three hours ago.

He should have reserved a hotel in St. Louis for their wedding night, but he had worried that they wouldn't be able to get away from her kids. He had been anxious to have Anna to himself – now he was sharing her with strangers.

Anna didn't seem upset by the delay. At first, they sat on their luggage, leaning against the wall, chatting about the wedding and Andy's surprise. When the hour grew late, Anna stretched out on the floor and made a pillow of her carry-on bag. Giving Michael one last smile, she closed her eyes and went to sleep.

Michael was too restless to sit still, let alone sleep. He was grateful for his laptop – Loretta Boswick was sending emails at a record pace, filled with questions only he could answer. He kept at it until the battery died, then he stood and stretched. Gazing down at Anna, he wished he could provide her with blankets and pillows. When she woke up, she was sure to suffer a stiff neck and a sore back.

He walked a few yards away and called Loretta. Mindful of

the passengers who were sleeping all around him, he spoke quietly, until his phone battery died too. He returned to perch on his suitcase and watch Anna sleep, amazed that she could be such a good sport about this disaster.

Michael was elated when a vendor arrived, pushing a cart filled with drinks and snacks. He was first in line and ordered a large coffee, as well as a muffin, a salad, and a sandwich. He checked his watch and nearly groaned. He would have to find someplace to plug in his phone so he could call the hotel in L.A. and cancel their reservation. He was no longer confident that they would be able to arrive in California before the flight to Hawaii departed. Maybe he ought to make backup reservations with another airline ...

When he returned, Anna was gazing around with a confused expression. "I didn't know what you might want, so I got a variety," he said, placing the food before her. "You can go see what else he has, if none of this appeals to you."

Anna reached for the muffin. "Maybe this will settle my stomach," she said, sitting cross-legged as she broke it into pieces. "Want a bite?"

"No thanks," Michael said, sipping his coffee. He removed the plastic wrap from the sandwich and forced himself to eat half of it.

"What's on the sandwich?" Anna asked, dusting muffin crumbs from her fingers.

"I'm not sure," he said, lifting the bread to give her a look. "One of the casseroles at the church supper was pretty spicy. Do you think that's what upset your stomach?"

"Which one?" Anna asked.

"Something with sausage and beans," he recalled. His mouth was still burning from the jalapeno peppers.

"That was *my* casserole!" Anna said, giving him a hurt look.

"Yours?" he said with confusion. "When did you have time to make a ..." She started grinning and he sighed with relief. "How can you go on being so amiable, when everything is going wrong?"

"Philippians 4:12. 'I have learned the secret of being content in any and every situation.' " She looked pleased with herself.

70

"Anyway, in my opinion, everything is going right! We're married and we're on our way to Hawaii! And even if we never make it to Hawaii, I'll be content because wherever I am, you're here too. Wherever 'here' is."

"Somewhere in Oklahoma," Michael sighed. "I'm going to cancel our hotel in Los Angeles, and try to arrange a new flight to the islands. We'll pretend it's our wedding night when we get there."

"Okay," Anna said. She finally noticed her lopsided bun and removed the hair pins, allowing her long, dark hair to flow over her shoulders. "Just so you don't go without me."

"I'm not planning on going anywhere without you, ever again," he said.

♥

"Anna!" Michael said softly, gently shaking her shoulder. "Anna, wake up!"

"We aren't going until Dad gets back from the post office," she said, pushing him away.

Michael chuckled. "We'll be landing in a few minutes. I thought you might want to wake up before we touch down."

Anna sat up and rubbed her eyes, then leaned across him to look out the window. "Are we really in Hawaii?"

"We really are," he assured her. "Finally."

They had arrived in San Antonio around 2:00 a.m., and spent the rest of their wedding night in that airport. They left Texas at six and arrived in California just before seven. The flight to Hawaii was delayed, there was turbulence during the flight to Nevada, they missed their connecting flight to Bellingham … It was now nine p.m., Sunday night.

Anna pressed her nose against the window. "Did you sleep at all?" she asked as she yawned. "I definitely made up for the sleep I lost last week."

"I'm a napper," he said, pulling his carry-on from under his seat. "You never have to worry about me getting enough sleep."

"Just that, I'm wide awake now, and you're probably ready for bed." She realized what she'd said and quickly turned her face away, in case she was blushing. "What are we going to do first? Have you got an itinerary made out? What do you like to do when you're on vacation? I don't even know what you like to do for fun!"

"I don't either. I haven't taken a vacation in years. What kind of stuff do you and the kids do, when you go to Table Rock?"

Anna pulled her suitcase from under her seat and placed it in her lap. "Where's my purse? I lost my purse!"

"I've got it," Michael said, patting his pocket. "We're going to touch down in a minute. You said you like to be warned."

"Thank you. We like to …" She stopped talking as the plane touched the ground, bounced, then touched down again. "Fish. We never catch anything though. And we usually go to a country western show."

"You like country western music?"

"I like almost every kind of music. Except rap. And hard rock. And I'm not that crazy about classical. I like Pop. I like to sing along. And hymns. I like hymns. What kind of music do you like?"

"Hard rock," he said, then laughed at her expression. "I was teasing. I like to listen to show tunes."

"Show tunes?"

"Musicals. Like Brigadoon?" He reached for her bun and tried to right it. "It'll be awhile before I listen to Oklahoma again though," he said morosely.

Anna laughed. "I like musicals too. Do they have shows like that here? Will we do outdoorsy stuff? Or mostly museums? Do they have museums in Hawaii?"

"Pearl Harbor comes to mind."

"Would you like to see Pearl Harbor?"

Michael raised one shoulder. "I got us here. The rest is up to you."

"The pressure's on," Anna pretended to worry. "Do you play golf?"

"I'd like to spend time outdoors, but not learning to play golf."

"Learning?" she said, raising one eyebrow. "I'll have you know I could've gone on the pro circuit when I was in my 30s. Is that what you call it? The pro circuit?" She was pleased that he

72

was laughing. She reached up and pulled out her hair pins, twisted her bun into place, and pushed the pins back in. "I like to hike. Nothing strenuous or difficult though. And I like to swim. Not swim, just splash around in the water. Do you like the water?"

"I like the ocean, but I'm not crazy about chlorinated swimming pools. Do you burn easily?" he asked, tracing his finger across her cheek.

"I tan," she said. "Do you?"

"Yes. But we still need to pick up some sun screen."

The plane taxied to the terminal and the stewardesses began to circulate, helping the passengers gather their things.

"I'm so excited!" Anna said. "I'm glad you've never been here before. It's more fun that way. I wonder if I'll get to see what lava looks like. I know that's weird, but I've always wondered what it looks like."

"There's a boat that will take you out to watch hot lava dribble into the ocean. They recommend it for the people who enjoy white water rafting."

"White water rafting?" Anna repeated anxiously.

"Me neither," he laughed. "But I'm sure we can find you a souvenir made of lava."

"Souvenir hunting … now there's a sport I'm good at!" she said with enthusiasm. "How far to our hotel? Are we going to rent a car?"

"We'll take a taxi. We can rent a car in the lobby of our hotel, when we need one."

"But not tonight," she said.

"No," he agreed. "How about we stay in and make use of room service?"

"That sounds good," she said. "Maybe our hotel can recommend some fun things to do."

"I'm sure there will be brochures in the lobby. And I bookmarked a lot of sites on my laptop. There are dozens of choices. You can swim with the dolphins or a manta ray or …"

"What's a manta ray?" she interrupted.

"A flat sort of fish?" Michael said vaguely. "They have whale watching tours. Or we can go kayaking or scuba diving."

"Are those things you want to do?" Anna asked, uncertain whether he was still teasing.

"Sure," Michael said, tugging gently on her ear lobe. "But my first choice is parasailing."

"I'm not sure what that is, but I'm pretty sure I'm too chicken to do it," Anna said warily.

"It's where they strap you to some kind of parachute and drag you behind a boat until you lift off. You can choose to soar at 400, 800, or 1200 feet."

Anna swallowed hard. "Please tell me you're kidding," she pleaded.

"I'm kidding," he assured her. "I've never been the sort of person who enjoys an adrenaline rush."

Once off the plane, they followed the signs to baggage retrieval. Michael's suitcase was already revolving around the carousel, but after twenty minutes, Anna's luggage still hadn't appeared. They went to the counter and waited patiently while an airline employee worked at her computer. She finally regretted to inform them that Anna's suitcase had been left in Oklahoma, and was now on its way to Atlanta.

"At least you have your carry-on," Michael tried to console her. "And they'll probably have your suitcase delivered to our hotel before you wake up in the morning."

"I know, but …" She had inspected her carry-on while they were stuck in Oklahoma. It contained the items she had tossed in on impulse, and a gift from Paula. They had confiscated her shampoo and conditioner at the airport, so she would have to wash her hair with soap. She looked at Michael and saw that his morale had sunk to a new low. "I'm sure I have everything I need," she said, forcing cheer into her voice. She watched as his expression changed to one of relief and decided that sometimes, it was forgivable to lie about the oysters.

♥ Chapter 8 ♥

Anna investigated their hotel suite with excitement. There was a vase of fresh flowers on the dresser, and a large fruit basket on a table near the sliding glass doors. The carpeting was thick, the bedspread was crisp and new, and everything was sparkling clean.

"Come look," Michael said, opening the drapes to reveal a balcony that faced the ocean.

Anna followed him out and leaned against his side. Before them, there was nothing but a pristine beach and the ocean, glistening black in the moonlight. She took a deep breath of the sea air, then yawned.

Michael yawned too. "I had a difficult time choosing between the first floor, where you could walk out onto the beach, or this, which affords a little more privacy."

"This," Anna said without hesitation. "How did you arrange for the full moon?"

"I had to pay extra," Michael said.

Anna laughed, then she yawned again.

Michael drew her into the circle of his arms and rested his chin on the top of her head. "I vote we put off our wedding night until we've both had about six hours sleep," he said heroically.

"Put it off?" Anna said, spinning around so she could look up at him. "You're not serious!"

He lifted his shoulders, as if to say he wasn't certain whether he was or not.

"I had no idea you were such a wimp," she teased.

He smiled. "I'll go take a shower then?"

"Leave me some hot water," she advised.

♥

Anna held the nightgown under her chin and cringed. The gossamer fabric and plunging neckline were far more risqué than anything she would have chosen. She would tell Michael that Paula picked it out, in case he thought it was sleazy.

Much to her delight, the hotel provided a selection of soaps, shampoos, and conditioners, as well as lotions and powders and a hair dryer. She showered quickly, slipped on the nightgown, and dried her hair. She gazed at her image and debated whether to at least put the hotel robe over her shoulders. Anna was modest by nature, but this was her wedding night and Michael was now her husband. She decided to be daring.

She took a deep breath and started out of the bathroom, wondering whether she would find Michael in bed, or waiting on the balcony. Then she froze, with her hand on the doorknob.

Birth control! She had called her obstetrician and he had renewed an old prescription. Just before they left the house for the airport, she had asked Michael for the key to her suitcase and under Paula's watchful eye, tucked the small bag into a side pocket. Her birth control device was now on its way to Atlanta.

She shrank back from the door and gazed at herself in the mirror again, noting the worry lines that had appeared on her brow. What would Michael say if she told him they needed to postpone their wedding night after all? Perhaps the hotel could give him directions to an all-night pharmacy, or … maybe he had addressed the issue of birth control himself! If not, he was equally responsible for their current dilemma. She had thought of mentioning the subject more than once, but each time, decided to wait for a better moment. In truth, she had hoped Michael would say he wanted to have a baby together, but she wasn't willing to broach that subject until after their wedding night.

She wasn't going to panic. There was little chance she would get pregnant the first time they made love. They could talk about it afterward, and she would apologize. If she was right about the sort of person he was, Michael would apologize too.

But what if she *wasn't* right about the sort of person he was? What if he turned out to be very much like Paul, or even Bruce Carlisle?

Anna closed her eyes and pressed her hands together as she prayed. " 'Do not be anxious about anything and the peace of God will guard your hearts and minds in Christ Jesus.' " How many times in her life had she recited *that* verse! She stood quietly for another moment, then bravely pushed through the door.

♥

Michael sat on the wooden swing on the balcony, struggling to stay awake. Though he was utterly exhausted, he didn't want Anna to catch him snoozing. He opened his eyes when she touched his cheek. She was dressed in a silky white nightgown, fastened down the front with tiny blue bows. Her hair hung loose over her shoulders – little wisps flirted with the breeze. "Wow," he said, embarrassing himself.

"This is a gift from Paula," Anna told him, pinching the pleats of the nightgown. "Otherwise, I would be modeling a pair of cut-off jeans and a T-shirt." She stepped forward and teased her fingernails through the thick dark hair that covered his chest. "This is your last chance to bail until tomorrow night," she offered in a teasing tone.

Michael rested his hands on her shoulders, then let them glide down her arms. Locking his fingers behind her waist, he drew her closer. He didn't want to appear too anxious, but he didn't want her to wonder whether he found her desirable either. He had always enjoyed complete confidence when it came to women, but found himself floundering with Anna. Should he lock her in a passionate embrace, or would she rather talk for a while? He decided to kiss her, gently and tenderly, then untie the top ribbon of her gown. If she pulled away, he would start a conversation. He framed her face in both hands and began to kiss her … and felt his control slipping away. Then he reached for the bow …

and froze.

Birth control! They had never discussed what sort of birth control they would use! How could he not have thought of this? What was he to do? Ask her to wait while he ran down to the lobby, hoping they could direct him to an open pharmacy within walking distance?

"What's the matter?" Anna whispered. She twined her arms around his neck and perched on his thigh.

"Nothing," he said. It wasn't likely that she would get pregnant the first time they made love, was it? He knew such things *could* happen, but surely they were the exception? He combed his fingers through her silky, long hair and touched his lips to hers. In the morning, he would apologize for his lack of foresight, and they would discuss what to use next time. The issue faded from his mind as he finally kissed her the way he had wanted to kiss her since the moment they met.

♥

"I was confident that I had allowed for everything," Michael said, letting Anna set the pace as they walked along the water's edge. "Even if I had anticipated mechanical problems, I would have assumed that the airline would still get us to our destination on time." He couldn't stop talking about the things that had gone wrong since they departed St. Louis.

"The kids and I once had an unexpected overnight in Toledo," Anna recalled. "They built a tent with the clothes out of their suitcases. It's one of their favorite memories."

"Our time in Oklahoma will *never* be one of my favorite memories," he said drily. He squinted in the bright light, then replaced his sunglasses. "When you're accustomed to being in charge, it isn't easy to find yourself stuck in the middle of nowhere, completely powerless."

"You know what they say," Anna taunted with amusement. "If you want to make God laugh, just tell Him your plans."

"God had nothing to do with that fiasco," Michael said. He turned and looked back, surprised that they had walked so far. "Ready to make a one-eighty?"

"Yes," she said. "Walking in sand is harder than walking on dirt. I have a feeling I'm going to have achy legs tonight."

"Good thing you have a husband who will be more than happy to rub them for you." He slung an arm over her shoulders and pulled her against his side. "I don't think about God the way you do," he said pensively. "I was shocked when you suggested we pray about our wedding date. It seemed odd to consult God about something so … incidental? At least to Him …"

"I think we ought to pray about every decision," Anna said staunchly. "Major, minor, and all the ones in between."

"I always strive to do what's right, but I guess that's not the same thing," Michael said thoughtfully.

"Sometimes it is," Anna said. "But sometimes it seems like God is asking us to do the exact opposite of what we think is right, and that's why it's important to pray. Not that He ever asks us to do anything wrong, but … it could seem that way."

"Such as?" Michael asked curiously.

Anna grew quiet for a moment, then she looked up at him and grinned. "Going to your club on a snowy night when there wasn't much chance we'd be able to make it back to Casey's," she said with satisfaction.

Michael laughed. "That wasn't God's idea! I'm stuck with the blame for that idiocy."

" 'Many are the plans in a man's heart, but it is the Lord's purpose that prevails,' " Anna recited. "Didn't some part of your brain warn you that we shouldn't travel in a blizzard?"

Michael frowned. "If I had taken you to the cafeteria, you would've become the subject of ugly rumors. If I had taken you to Briarton, we were bound to run into someone I knew, with the same result."

"Good thing we went to your club instead!" Anna said, wiping her brow with mock relief. "You were missing all night and my car was still there in the morning. The rumors that *did* go around were much worse!"

It was Michael's turn to grow quiet. "You're suggesting that God put the idea in my head and prevented me from considering the weather?"

She looked up at him. "All I know is, God wanted us to go to your club, so we wouldn't be able to get back to Casey's, so we'd go to St. Louis instead."

"He was playing Cupid?"

"Yes," Anna said. She frowned at him. "You said you thought God put me on the third floor of the dorm so I could stop Susie from committing suicide. Isn't this the same thing?"

"I didn't mean it literally." Michael saw her shocked reaction and wished he had softened the denial.

Anna stared down at her feet. "If you learn to look at things that way, *literally*, you won't get so upset the next time you have to spend the night in an airport."

Michael tried to find the weak link in her argument. "If God sent us to my club that night, and dumped enough snow to make it impractical to return to Casey's, then why did we slide off the road and get stuck on a railroad tie? Or would you blame that detail on the other guy?" he teased. "The one with the horns and forked tail?"

"Satan can only act with God's permission," Anna said without smiling. "He doesn't actually have any power of his own. 'Resist the devil and he will flee.' Either way, God can make it turn out good."

"*Good?*" Michael challenged her. "We had to call a tow truck. We didn't get into St. Louis until two a.m. That's *good*?"

"I'm happy with the end results, aren't you?"

Michael squeezed her shoulder. "I think you know the answer to that." He stopped and gazed out at the ocean for a moment. "If God is orchestrating all the details of our lives, why give us free will?" he challenged her.

Anna sat down and stretched her legs toward the water. "So that we can accept or reject Him."

"If I reject Him, then what? The snow stops?" He sat beside her, then leaned back on his elbows.

"I don't know," Anna said. "I think our lives are supposed to be centered on God. He wants to have a relationship with us and He does whatever He has to do to make that happen. There are people who will only turn to God if their lives fall apart, so He has to let their lives fall apart. Other people manage to keep their priorities straight, even if they're showered with blessings. Each life is custom designed to accomplish His purposes." She took off her sunglasses and studied him. "I thought you said you're a Christian."

"I *am* a Christian," he assured her. "Just that … I haven't thought it out as extensively as you have."

"Well, you should," she said. "It's the most important thing in your life."

"*You're* the most important thing in my life," he said with a smile.

"I don't want to come before God," she said sternly. "That's one of the things I've been wrestling with ever since we met. I know I need to keep God in first place, but it isn't easy when you're in love."

Michael decided he would be wise to drop the subject, at least for now. He stood up and reached for her hand, then pulled her into his arms. "I'm certainly glad I took you to my club that night, whether it was my idea or God's." He leaned down and kissed the tip of her nose.

"Me too," she said happily. She started walking again, keeping a tight hold on his hand.

Michael couldn't help himself. Her beliefs were so simplistic, they begged further debate. "What if I hadn't listened? What if I had bought you those peanut butter crackers from a vending machine and sent you off to the women's dorm?"

"God always has a Plan B," Anna said with confidence.

"So if I work against Him …"

"You *can't* work against Him. 'The Lord's purpose *always* prevails.' You can only work against yourself. Like getting stressed out because we were stranded in Oklahoma."

"I wasn't stressed out," Michael said testily.

Anna removed her sunglasses and studied him without smiling.

"Okay, maybe I was," he said sheepishly. "But not nearly as stressed out as you were on Thursday."

"I get stressed out all the time," she admitted. "But that doesn't mean I don't know Who's in charge."

Michael resumed walking. "I'd made reservations at a really nice hotel. I wanted our first night to be perfect."

"It *was* perfect," Anna said. She squeezed his hand and smiled at him.

"Yes it was," he reluctantly agreed. "I take it your parents were church goers?"

Anna laughed. "You could say that! My father made us memorize Scripture and recite it at the dinner table. I sure could've used your photographic memory in those days."

"Do you still read the Bible?"

"Every day," she said without hesitation.

"I used to," Michael remembered. He didn't add that he'd outgrown the habit along with the belief that God could help him find a good parking place.

"You should start again," Anna said. "And memorize some verses of Scripture. It'll help you get through the hard times."

"We're not going to have any hard times," Michael said. "I forbid it!"

Anna laughed and poked his belly. " 'Many are the plans in a man's heart,' " she reminded him. "Will you go to church with me on Sundays?"

He could hear the worry in her voice. "Of course. Wherever you want to go."

When they reached the beach in front of their hotel, Michael rented two chairs and an umbrella. He retrieved his back pack from a locker and they slathered one another with lotion. Then they played in the surf, hunted for shells, and built a sand castle. All the while, Michael couldn't stop thinking about the things Anna had said. If God interfered in people's lives, why had He allowed Jeanne to commit suicide? Why hadn't He prodded Michael to go home early enough to save her life?

"This might be the most beautiful spot on Earth," Anna said, interrupting his thoughts. "I could sit here for the rest of my life and never complain. Until I get hungry again," she added.

"I would not have believed a person your size could eat that much, if I hadn't seen it with my own eyes," Michael told her.

Anna giggled. "It was so good! I think I'm going to gain weight while we're here, if we eat at very many buffets like that one."

"You're going to need new clothes anyway," Michael said,

82

"since it doesn't look like they're going to find your suitcase. I was just thinking we should head over to the mall."

"Shopping is so *not* what I feel like doing," she groaned.

"This is a real anomaly," he said with amusement. "A woman who hates to shop?"

"We're in Hawaii!" Anna reminded him. "There are so many neat things to see and do – I don't want to waste time at a mall. Anyway, I don't need new clothes. I have plenty of clothes at home."

"Paula said your swimming suit is ancient."

"Oh, Paula," Anna said, waving her hand in the air. "She only wears her clothes one season. The worst part is, everything will probably cost ten times as much as it would in St. Louis."

"You're not paying, I am. So drop that argument right now."

"I thought you said half the money is mine," she reminded him.

"So I did. But the money we spend on your clothes is coming out of my half."

♥ Chapter 9 ♥

"A hundred dollars for a cotton dress," Anna said with disgust. "It doesn't even have sleeves!"

"Are sleeves expensive?" Michael teased.

"It's not funny!" she said. "It's easy for you! You just throw on a suit and off you go."

"Hey!" Michael objected. "I have a fashion consultant who helps me choose those suits. It's not as easy as you might think."

Anna gaped at him with surprise.

"I'm kidding," he said, touching her chin with his knuckles. "I order them from a catalog."

"Are you kidding again?" she asked suspiciously.

"Please, will you try it on?" He took the dress and held it beneath her chin. "Yellow is a good color for you."

Anna snatched the dress from his hand and headed for the dressing room. She came out a moment later, and twirled in a circle.

"Fits perfect," Michael said. "Even the length is perfect."

She eyed herself in a full length mirror, turning left, then right.

"Can we check one item off our list?" Michael said hopefully.

"I hate the price," Anna grumbled.

"We'll get you some cheap flip-flops to wear with it. Will that help?"

"Yes," she said.

He laughed. "Get changed, so we can find you a swim suit.

85

And shorts and shirts."

"Girls wear blouses, not shirts," she corrected him.

After the dress was purchased, they wandered along the mall, though Anna didn't have much enthusiasm.

"Need anything in there?" Michael asked, gesturing to a store that featured scantily clad mannequins.

"Ha ha," Anna said, tugging him away. "Seriously … we need to talk about money, Michael."

"Talk or argue?" he asked.

She made a face. "I've never been in a position to act extravagant and …"

"Until now," he interrupted.

"I don't want to!" she pleaded. "I'm afraid it will change me. What if I turn into Paula? She's so materialistic!"

"That will never happen," Michael said with confidence. "You're not made that way."

"Who can predict what might happen if you spoil me? Haven't you ever read articles about the way people change after they win the lottery?"

Michael took her arm and led her to a bench. "Let's come to an understanding right now, so that we never have to argue about this again."

"That would be good," Anna said agreeably.

"All these years, I've been accumulating money," he said in a serious tone. "If the house needs something, the school covers it. I drive an old car and repair it myself. I don't take vacations and I don't have expensive hobbies. I've been banking the bulk of my salary and I'm well paid, Anna."

"Then let's dig a well in Uganda," she said with excitement.

"Dig a well in Uganda?" he repeated with confusion.

She waved her hand. "Let's do something *good* with that money. Let's help those who can't help themselves."

"I give generously to many charities," Michael said tersely. "Is it wrong if I want to spend some of that money on my wife, buying her things she could never afford?"

"It's not wrong for you, but it *is* wrong for me," Anna tried to explain. "A hundred dollars for a dress? I could buy the pattern and fabric and buttons for less than twenty dollars. It feels sinful!"

"Sinful?" he said, raising his eyebrows.

Anna bit her lip. "I believe everything we have belongs to God. Wise stewardship means I don't throw money away. If I can buy just as good a dress for thirty dollars, why spend a hundred? Cheap flip flops last just as long as pricey ones. My ten year old swimsuit is still in good condition and I still like it."

Michael sighed as he stretched his legs out and stared at his very expensive shoes. "Once upon a time, I believed those things too," he remembered. "My parents disgusted me. I refused to wear the clothes my mother bought. I shopped at Goodwill instead." He smiled ruefully. "My dad told me my high ideals would fade in time and it looks like he was right."

"It happens gradually," Anna said, nodding her head.

Michael put an arm around her shoulders and gave her a hug. "Will we return the dress?"

"I'd like to keep it, but I don't want to hear one word from you if I'm still wearing it twenty years from now."

"Twenty years from now," Michael said with a smile. "I like the sound of that." He pulled his phone from his pocket. "Any particular discount store?"

"I promise I'll give in when something is really important to you," she said earnestly.

"Really?" he said, eyes twinkling. "Then can we go back to that store with the sleazy mannequins and see whether they have a clearance rack?"

♥

Michael sat with his arm around Anna, watching as people climbed to the top of the cliff, then dove into the water far below. Both his father and his brother had bragged about diving from the cliffs while they were in Hawaii. While Michael wasn't normally a risk taker, he thought he'd like to try it, just one time, so he could mention it the next time he saw his family. "Do you want to watch me do a belly flop?" he asked Anna, in case he was no longer proficient at diving.

"Do you want to give me a heart attack?" she countered with

widened eyes.

"I'm serious," he said. "I really want to do this."

Anna gripped his wrist so tightly, her knuckles went white. "I'm serious too! I really don't want you to do this!"

"I'll never have this opportunity again," he argued. "I'm not normally tempted to prove my prowess, but for some reason …"

"Please!" Anna said again, gazing into his eyes.

"Nothing is going to happen," he said, aware that he was using the authoritative tone he employed at Casey's. "You need to learn to trust me, if we're going to have a good marriage."

She let go of his arm and scooted away.

"Anna?" he said, wishing he had tried a different tack. "Look at me."

"No," she said. "I'm not going to look at you again until after it's over."

Michael studied the cliff, squinting in the sunlight. He wondered how high it was, how far to the water. The desire to dive left as suddenly as it had come.

"Okay," Anna said, jumping up and reaching for his hand. "Will we hold hands? I saw another couple hold hands when they jumped. I'll be absolutely terrified, but if something is going to happen to you, it might as well happen to me too."

Michael debated whether to say he'd only been teasing … but that would be a lie. "Would you really do it?" he asked, certain she was bluffing.

"Yes." She stuck out her chin, in a gesture that was already becoming familiar to him. "I don't want to spoil your trip by being afraid of things."

"Thank you," he said, pulling her into his arms. "Thank you for caring enough to want to die with me. I think I was suffering a moment of regressed adolescence, to even consider it."

"Really?" she said, sinking onto his knee.

"I'd never even make it up there," he said with a shudder. "If you hadn't objected, I would've climbed halfway and suffered a panic attack."

"Do you have panic attacks?" she asked with surprise.

"I've never had one before, but I would if I tried to climb that cliff. You would've had to come up there and get me."

"Really?" she said doubtfully.

He kissed her again. "I love you," he said. "And I need you, Anna. As much as it pains me to admit such a thing, I desperately need you in my life." Her smile was a great reward for his honesty.

♥

"Did I mention that you look beautiful in yellow?" Michael said, smiling at her across the table.

"Yellow and orange," Anna complained. She dipped her napkin in her water glass and scrubbed at a spot on the bodice of her dress.

"Will it come out, do you think?"

"If not, I'll wear a pin to cover it," she sighed.

The musicians returned to the stage and began to play a slow song. Anna had chosen the restaurant, because it advertised a band that played oldies from the era of their youth.

"May I have this dance?" Michael asked, rising to his feet, extending his hand.

Anna looked up at him with dismay. "I don't dance," she said.

"This particular number does not include any complicated steps," he assured her. "You can just shuffle your feet back and forth in time to the music."

"It's not that," she said. She folded her napkin and laid it to one side. "We weren't allowed to dance when we were kids. My dad said it was one of the devil's ploys to corrupt us."

Michael sat back down and studied her with a puzzled expression. "Do you agree with him?"

Anna lifted one shoulder and chewed her bottom lip. "It hasn't ever been an issue. Paul never took me where there was dancing."

The honeymoon had exceeded Michael's expectations in every way. He didn't want to have an argument on their last night. "It doesn't matter," he said heroically.

"It doesn't look sinful," Anna decided, watching as the floor filled with couples. "So long as they're all married."

"Why would they have to be married?" Michael wondered.

"When two people stand that close together, with their bodies touching … It's likely to lead to something."

"Ah," Michael said, unable to keep from smiling. "Something like the danger of two people who are attracted to one another being alone in a secluded location?"

"I don't think I said 'location,' " she corrected him. "Is your photographic memory failing you?"

"I wouldn't be surprised," Michael said with amusement. "You've definitely had an effect on the rest of my brain."

She smiled, as if this pleased her.

"If the man was not your husband, you could leave an inch or two of space between your torsos," he suggested.

"I think my dad felt that one thing leads to another. And he was mostly referring to a different kind of dancing, where people are gyrating around."

"Gyrating?" Michael repeated, trying not to laugh.

Anna shrugged and watched the dancers, her hands clasped together on the surface of the table.

Michael suspected she was praying, but he wasn't sure what she was praying for. "Yesterday, you explained your beliefs about being 'saved,' " he mused. "Did I understand correctly that, once saved, you no longer have to worry about sin?"

"Just the opposite!" Anna said, shaking her head vehemently. "Once you're saved, you try harder than ever not to sin."

"I see," Michael said thoughtfully. "But if you do happen to sin …"

"Aren't you saved?" Anna interrupted.

Michael had backed himself into a corner again. "I believe the same things you believe, but I'm not sure those statements equate to the same conditions and consequences."

"Huh?" Anna said, lifting her hands, palms up. "I have no idea what you mean by that."

Michael wished he hadn't started the conversation. He did believe that Jesus was the son of God, that he died on the cross as a sacrificial lamb to save mankind, that he rose again from the dead. But did this belief determine where a person would spend eternity? And should it keep a man from dancing with his wife? Was he supposed to involve God in all the details of his life? "At the mall, you promised that you would give in when something

90

was really important to me," he reminded her.

She stood up at once, and held out her arms.

Michael was immediately weighed down with guilt. "I'm sorry," he said quickly. "I shouldn't have said that."

"No, you're right," she disagreed, coming to stand beside his chair. "We are married, right? So it won't matter if it leads to something."

In spite of her words, Michael felt he had badgered her. "No," he decided. "I don't want you to remember anything about our honeymoon with regret."

"I've never danced before," Anna told him. "I would love to add my first dance to my honeymoon memories."

He hesitated, then glanced at the dance floor. Some of the couples looked as if they might engage in 'something more' before they ever returned to their rooms. He saw her father's point. "Are you sure?" he asked, rising to his feet.

"I can't wait," she said, eyes sparkling.

♥ Chapter 10 ♥

"You were already happily married once," Marianne said with a sour expression. She boosted herself onto the grooming table and crossed her arms in a knot. "Now you're happily married again, to a big-shot VIP who looks like a movie star. You got to go to Hawaii on your honeymoon and you came back with a great tan and a bunch of new clothes."

"I *had* to buy new clothes," Anna reminded her.

"Sally said she saw you guys holding hands the other day, when you were walking home from school."

"Oops!" Anna giggled. Tina had walked in on them Friday morning, when they were kissing in Michael's office. Fortunately, his secretary hadn't been offended.

"If you do stuff like that in front of the wrong person, it will ruin both of your reputations."

"Thanks," Anna said, though she didn't feel it was wrong for a married couple to hold hands as they walked home.

"Another thing," Marianne said sternly. "You get to have a dog."

Anna sighed. She had done her share of suffering too, but it would do no good to mention that to Marianne. "I've been blessed, but so have you. Just in different ways."

"Well, maybe I'd like to be blessed in the *same* ways," Marianne pouted. "Maybe I'd like to have *one* happy marriage."

"And maybe you will!" Anna said. "You're still young."

"I'm thirty-six."

Anna bent over to scratch Charlie's ears. He always pressed against her legs when someone spoke in cross tones. "Are you ready to go?" she asked. Marianne often dropped by the Dog House at the end of the school day, because she liked to play with the dogs.

"The thing is," Marianne said, following her into the hallway. "I know every single guy at Casey's and none of them is ever gonna be interested in me."

"Who says you have to meet someone at Casey's?" Anna asked, carefully setting the alarm. "There are lots of places you could meet Mr. Right."

"Yeah? Well, if you see him advertising where he's gonna be next weekend, let me know."

"All right, I will," Anna said. She had never tried to play Cupid before, but it couldn't hurt to focus some intercessory prayers on Marianne's single state.

♥

Michael sat at his desk, reading over requisition forms before he signed them, occasionally glancing through the picture window. After the wedding, he had rearranged his office so that his desk faced the stone house. Even as he watched, the lights in the living room came on. It wasn't easy to keep working when he knew Anna was waiting for him.

By time he got home, she would have showered and fixed dinner. She would probably do a load of laundry too, and sweep the back patio. She kept the cookie jar filled with his favorite homemade cookies, and often baked a pie or cake. His shirts were ironed and arranged in his closet by color, just as he liked them. The house was always clean, and he wasn't allowed to help clean it. Anna reminded him of the little pink bunny that never ran out of energy. It was no use telling her he didn't want her to act as a maid or a housekeeper – he had already tried.

Forcing his mind to the task at hand, he perused the requisition forms from the clinic. Thirty pregnancy tests …

He and Anna still hadn't discussed birth control. He wondered if she had undergone a surgical procedure after Paula was born. It would explain why she hadn't broached the subject, but he shouldn't assume that was the case. He needed to bring it up so they could discuss it and he could stop worrying about an unwanted pregnancy ... unwanted on her part.

Tina knocked on his door and he called for her to come in. He accepted the sheaf of papers she handed him, signing them without proofreading her work. He wondered how long it would be before his secretary decided to have a baby, and whether she would take maternity leave or quit permanently. He would hate to lose her – though young, she was the best secretary he had ever had. He slid his iPad across the desk, so she would be aware of any changes he had made to the next day's schedule.

"Are you ready to go?" he asked.

She looked surprised. "It's not yet five."

"So you'd rather not leave early?"

"Bye!" she laughed, hurrying away.

As Michael walked home, he rehearsed what he should say to Anna. He would assure her that he was willing to use whatever form of birth control she preferred, but leave the option open to have a baby.

Charlie greeted him with exuberance, and Michael took him out for a short run. When they came back, he noted that the table was set, though Anna was nowhere in sight. He removed his suit coat and hung it over a chair in the dining room. "Anna?" he called.

"Be right up!" she yelled from the basement. She appeared a moment later, with an armload of clean towels. "You're early," she said, heading for the bedroom. "What a nice surprise."

He followed her, determined to get the discussion over with – he had put it off too many times already. Loosening his tie, he settled on the edge of the bed to wait while she put the towels away. When she emerged from the bathroom, she stepped between his knees and wrapped her arms around his neck.

"I missed you," he said, and kissed her in a way that proved it.

"I missed you too. Guess what! We placed two dogs! The two that came from the same house? They're going to the same house! Talk about a happy ending!"

"That's great," Michael said. "Congratulations to you and your staff."

"Thanks. I'll pass that on tomorrow. Michael?"

"Yes?" He met her eyes, sensing that she had something important to say."

"Would you care if I decided to quit the pet therapy?"

"Of course not," he assured her, rubbing her shoulders.

"You're sure?"

"I'm positive."

"I'm just thinking about it for now," she said, settling on his knee. "What did you want to talk about? You've got a serious look on your face."

"I do?" he said with amusement. He locked his fingers together and rested his hands on her hip. "Do you know what today is?"

"Wednesday?" she guessed. "No, wait! Thursday!"

Michael laughed. "It's Friday. It's our anniversary! One month tomorrow!"

"Happy Anniversary," she said. "I wish I had thought of it and baked you a cake."

"I only thought of it an hour ago, when I wrote the date for the hundredth time. But it was too late to order roses and …"

"I don't like the smell of roses anyway," she said, wrinkling her nose.

"Good to know," he said. "Anyway, it was too late to order flowers so I had to get creative." He reached into his shirt pocket and pulled out a folded piece of paper. He handed it to her, watching her face as she opened it.

"I don't get it," she admitted, turning the check over, in case he had written something on the back.

"It's a charity that digs wells in Uganda," he explained.

Immediately, she threw her arms around his neck and kissed him. "Michael Grant, you are the best person I know!" she said, her eyes clouding with tears. "I love you! And I love your photographic memory!"

Michael laughed and held her close. It hadn't been easy to think of a gift, since he knew how much she hated extravagance.

"Thank you!" she said. She sandwiched his face between her

96

palms and kissed first his left cheek, then his right, then his lips.

Michael pulled away with reluctance, mindful of the other subject he must address. "Before I forget, there's something else we need to talk about. We've needed to discuss it for a long time, but somehow, neither of us ever brought it up."

"Something good or something bad?" she asked.

"I don't know which column you would put it in. Birth control."

Much to his surprise, she rose from his knee and backed away.

"I assumed you had your tubes tied, after Paula was born," he said with some alarm.

"I didn't," she said, clasping her hands at her waist.

"I thought maybe you assumed I'd had some sort of procedure."

She shook her head. "It never occurred to me."

"Then we need to choose a means of birth control now," he said. "Before it becomes a moot point."

Anna stared into his eyes, biting her lip. "I'm afraid it's already a moot point," she said.

Michael was stunned. "Are you saying you're pregnant?"

She brushed at her eyes with both hands, then she nodded.

Michael could see that she was miserable. He felt confused, and though it was illogical, he felt hurt. Having a child would be the thrill of a lifetime for him, but not if Anna didn't want the baby. "Are you sure?"

"I'm sure," she said. She went to her dresser and opened a drawer. She rummaged around for a moment, closed the drawer and looked at him in the mirror.

"Have you taken a pregnancy test?"

"I don't need to. I've had two children. I recognize the symptoms."

Michael had never seen her in this particular mood and he wasn't sure how to deal with it. "What do you want to do?" he asked, frightened by what she might say.

"Do? What do I want to *do*?" Her face turned pale. "I don't believe in abortion."

"Neither do I." His relief was palpable.

"I'm sorry," she said, lifting her shoulders.

Michael was only sorry that she was sorry. He could think of nothing to say.

Anna went into the bathroom again, and closed the door.

Michael got up and went to his office. He stood at the window, gazing into the back yard, trying to get control of his emotions. He had been a fool to sidestep the issue of birth control. He should've asked her on their wedding night, even if it meant going in search of a pharmacy before they made love the first time. Anna loved children! He would never have guessed that she would consider a baby such bad news.

After a few moments, her reflection appeared in the glass. He shoved his hands in his pockets and waited for her to speak.

"I got a prescription from my obstetrician," she said. "Remember when I asked you to take me to the drug store the Friday before we got married? I wanted you to wait in the car?"

Michael turned around. He should have guessed she was going after birth control.

"I put it in my suitcase, right before we left the house. Remember? I asked you for the key."

"And then your suitcase got lost," he said with understanding.

"I should have asked what you wanted," she said softly. "On our wedding night."

"What *I* wanted?" Michael repeated.

"Whether you would hate having a baby. It's not a decision for one person to make on their own." She touched her nose with the back of her hand. "How did you know?"

"I didn't. I had no idea."

"Then why did you bring it up?"

"I've been telling myself we needed to discuss it, but I always found an excuse to put it off. Today I had a requisition from the clinic, for pregnancy tests. I decided I couldn't put it off any longer."

"Discussing what form of birth control we should use?"

"Whether to *use* birth control." He watched her closely. "Do you want to ask me now?" he said.

"Ask you what?"

"Whether I would hate having a baby?"

"I already know the answer, don't I? I saw how upset you got

98

when I told you."

Michael shook his head. "I wasn't reacting to what you were telling me. I was reacting to your demeanor. You didn't sound thrilled."

"I couldn't be happy about something that makes you unhappy."

"Other than having you as my wife, there is nothing I want more than a child," Michael told her. "I would never have asked you. I knew you'd be too sweet to say 'no,' even if it's the last thing you'd want. And I was worried too. You won't like to hear me say this, but given how tiny you are … Did you have any problems delivering Andy or Paula?"

"No," she said. She was smiling now. "I'm really good at having babies. It's like making pie dough from scratch – once you get the hang of it …"

Michael crossed the distance between them and swept her into his arms. "I'm sure I'm the happiest man on Earth," he said hoarsely.

♥

"Nowadays, girls are just as likely as boys to want to play sports," Anna lectured. "You won't be disappointed if it's a girl, will you?"

"Of course not," Michael told her. He had positioned a comfortable chair beside his desk, to accommodate Anna when she came into his home office to chat. For the past week, she had come in two or three times a night, to talk about the baby. "I'll be equally happy with a girl or a boy," he said honestly. "And I'll enjoy getting involved in anything that interests her or him, be it sports or academia or the arts."

"Good," Anna said. She captured her hands between her knees. "Anyway, we could have another baby after this one."

Michael smiled. "Let's get through this pregnancy before we start planning the next one."

"Or we could adopt," she suggested. She sat back on the chair and closed her eyes. "I hate being nauseated. Some women don't get nauseated. I guess I'm lucky that it only lasts the first few months. Some women are nauseated the whole time, right up until their delivery date."

"Is there anything I can do?" Michael offered.

"Don't talk about it," she said. "I have to try to get my mind on something else."

"Do you want to watch a movie? Or play a game?"

Anna stood up and waved good-bye, then hurried from the room.

Michael debated whether to follow her. Maybe he could fix her a cup of tea, or dampen a wash cloth for her to press against her forehead. He turned to his laptop and Googled "nausea during pregnancy." Did the health food store carry any natural remedies that would help? Anna didn't like to take drugs. She had been sick to her stomach while they were marooned in Oklahoma, and had mentioned her aversion to ingesting chemicals. She hadn't been pregnant then but …

Or had she …

Michael shook his head, as though the act would remove the suspicion from his mind. He didn't want to entertain the possibility, but it constantly assaulted him. What if the baby wasn't his? What if the pregnancy had resulted from a rape that Anna had either repressed, or consciously concealed?

Two days ago, the Briarton sheriff had called with an update on Bruce Carlisle. *Mrs. Brown was lucky*, he told Michael. *Appears she's the only one of the women he didn't rape*. More women had come forward. In almost every case, Bruce had asked them out, encouraged them to drink, then forced them to have sex. Afterward, he called them vulgar names and roughed them up, leaving them bruised and scarred, both physically and emotionally.

Michael had returned to the guard shack, to watch the video of Anna's attack again. He had pressed forward and reverse innumerable times, timing it on his watch. Anna was physically small. Regardless of the tricks she learned from her brothers, she could not have defended herself against a man Bruce's size. Her description of the event would not occupy eleven minutes, but a five minute rape could explain the lapse. When Charlie heard what was happening, he must have become frenzied and found a

100

way to open the gate of his pen. Though he wasn't a huge dog, Anna said he became vicious. Bruce must have released Anna in order to defend himself. Anna had grasped the opportunity to restore her clothing. By the time Russell arrived ...

Had Anna successfully repressed the event, or willfully lied about it? Had she considered the fact that the child might be Bruce's? He studied her closely, each time she talked about the baby. If she was hiding something, she was a very good actress.

Over the years, Michael had grown accustomed to long periods of solitude. Since he married Anna, such occurrences were rare. When he arrived home, she was waiting at the door. She would give him a kiss, then begin to chatter about things of no consequence. Paula was going to Lake of the Ozarks – did he think the weather would hold? Paper towels were on sale at the discount store. What should they buy Andy and Beth for a belated wedding gift? He liked listening to her talk about the students and dogs and AHTs. He never tired of her company – she was so animated and lively, and affectionate. She loved to tease him, and she loved it when he teased her back. They were so compatible, he could scarcely believe it.

Even so ... marriage had been a huge adjustment and now they were expecting a baby. It felt as if he no longer had any control over his own life. One moment, he was a bachelor, dedicated to his career. The next moment, he had a wife and two adult children who called his cell phone almost nightly, just to chat. Twice, Paula had come for an overnight, and the second time, she brought friends along. Andy and Beth were planning to come for a long weekend. He was enjoying his new life, but he sometimes felt overwhelmed. And if he felt that way now, what would it be like after he welcomed his child into the world?

If it was *his* child.

Michael realized he was gritting his teeth and forced himself to relax. Bruce's other victims were young and blond. They liked to drink and party, and had gone along with his advances until he got rough. There could only be one reason why Bruce had made an exception and attacked Anna, who was neither young nor blond nor a party girl – because he hated Michael Grant. How dare he touch Anna! Anna, who never hurt anyone, even when she had cause. Anna, who was so sweet and innocent, so pure and good.

He remembered how worried he was when he went to the women's dormitory to try to find her that night. There was no question whether she heard him knocking and calling her name, but she refused to answer. When she finally called him, she left her message on the landline, though she must know he rarely used it. Women dealt with rape in many different ways. Some immediately summoned law enforcement and cooperated fully, anxious to see the perpetrator arrested and prosecuted. Others went home and showered, scrubbing their body raw. They might reemerge and pretend nothing had happened, and possibly convince themselves that it was all a bad dream.

Anna had feared he would fire her for going downstairs alone. Had she also feared that he would reject her if he found out she had been raped? Some men considered a woman "damaged goods" after a rape. Could Anna have feared that he would react in such a way?

Surely she had considered the pregnancy that might result! And if she had, she must have explored her options. Banned from Casey's, would she be forced to take a secretarial position? Her neighbor was too old to care for an infant – who would watch her baby? To make matters worse, while her emotional state was so precarious, she had discovered Susie in the restroom, threatening to slit her wrists. Aware that Michael had taken the master key from Gayle, Anna had been forced to call him to the rescue. There hadn't been time to plan what she would say about Bruce.

If Michael had stopped to consider what Anna had been through, he would've withheld the story of his past until another time. Instead, he blurted it out, believing it was his final opportunity to make things right.

Perhaps that was the key. Once Michael confessed that he had withheld the truth about *his* past, she had felt justified to withhold the truth about what happened with Bruce. A quick marriage to the administrator must have sounded like the best possible answer to her problem.

From the day they met, Anna had displayed a degree of propriety that was almost nonexistent in modern women. On their

102

first date, when a spring storm dumped eight inches of snow on the highway, he had suggested they remain at his club. Anna misunderstood and vowed to remain seated at a table in the dining room *all night*.

Once he said "yes" to her marriage proposal though, her Victorian manners disappeared. Suddenly, the responsibility for remaining chaste had shifted to his shoulders. She had even teased him that he was afraid to be alone with her! Now it made sense: When she realized that she might already be pregnant, it would have seemed urgent to consummate their marriage as soon as possible …

None of his suppositions meant that Anna did not love him. It only meant she feared losing him if she told the truth about the baby's father. If he and Anna were to adopt a child who was conceived during a rape, he could easily love that child as his own. But to be deceived into playing father to Bruce Carlisle's child …

Women who were raped did not always become pregnant, which meant there was every chance that the baby was actually his. She could have become pregnant on their wedding night, or sometime during the honeymoon. All the pieces fit together if he wanted to believe the child was Bruce's. But they fit together equally well if he wanted to believe the child was his. Anna might not know herself.

If he knew for sure, one way or the other, he might be able to overcome any negative feelings about the child. He could resolve it quickly, if he demanded a paternity test. But if the child *wasn't* Bruce's, if he was altogether wrong and Anna *hadn't* been raped … Would she ever forgive him for doubting her?

She must never find out that he had entertained these suspicions. He must pretend to have complete confidence that the child was his. Maybe it shouldn't matter. Maybe a person ought to regard all children as their own. Wouldn't the world be a better place if they did?

♥ Chapter 11 ♥

Anna hurried into the bathroom and locked the door. She pressed her palms against her abdomen and fought off a surge of nausea. She hadn't been sick like this with either of her previous pregnancies and she wondered if it was an indication that something was wrong. She had tried to tell her mother that it was the odor of the roasting turkey, ignoring the older woman's knowing look.

Why hadn't she talked about birth control with Michael before they got married? If only she had realized how badly he didn't want a child! Now that it was too late to negotiate, he swore he was delighted … but she could see that he was not. Something clouded his eyes, every time she spoke of the baby.

How could she have anticipated this? Michael *loved* children. She still remembered the day they met, when he referred to Casey's students as "my kids." He was kind to all of them, without exception. She had seen him deliver a stern reprimand, more than once, but he always did it gently, with love.

Yet he didn't want *their* baby. Why? Did he fear it would interfere with his job? Was he afraid her attention would be diverted from him? It was hard to create a reason in her mind because none of her theories fit her image of Michael.

Anna's mother had provided her daughter with ample opportunity to talk about her troubles, but Anna refused to speak badly of Michael to anyone. She could see that her mother was in

awe of him, and so was her sister. For the past four days, Nan had
followed Michael around the house, asking him questions and
hanging on his arm. Michael explained things with unending
patience, and returned her affection with plenty of heartfelt hugs.
Maybe he was afraid their baby would be born with Down's
Syndrome, like Nan. It was the reason Anna balked, every time
he urged her to make a doctor's appointment. What if some test
revealed that she was expecting a child with birth defects? Would
Michael make an exception to his pro-life status?

She gagged, but took deep breaths until the nausea subsided.
Michael's family was due to arrive any minute and she was
nervous about meeting them. At some point during the meal,
Michael would announce the pregnancy, and she was nervous
about that too. Michael's family was sure to conclude that she had
trapped him into marriage. Maybe her parents would think the
same, along with Andy and Paula.

Her modern fairy tale had turned into the ancient kind, where
the heroine suffered some tragic fate. Would there be a happy
ending? She doubted it more every day ...

♥

Anna stood with her arm around Michael's waist, waving
good-bye as the last of her family backed from the driveway in
Andy's new Escalade. He was taking Nan and his grandparents to
the airport and seeing them off, saving Anna and Michael from
making the trip to St. Louis. Michael's family had left hours ago,
and taken a good share of the tension with them.

"How are you feeling?" Michael asked, keeping his arm across
her shoulders as he escorted her into the house. "I'm worried you
overdid it, spending all those hours on your feet." He closed the
door, locked it, and drew the curtain.

"I feel fine," she said. "Being pregnant isn't like being sick."

"I know, but ... shouldn't you go to the doctor?"

Anna averted her eyes. "There's no reason to yet."

"My peace of mind isn't a reason?"

"All right," she gave in. "I'll call for an appointment
tomorrow. What's the name of the doctor Tina recommended?"

106

She picked up a few dishes from the kitchen table and carried them to the sink.

"Hardy. Thomas Hardy. I imagine one of his parents taught literature." He followed her, and pulled a clean dish towel from a drawer.

Anna smiled, but it didn't last long. "I *am* tired," she admitted, quickly washing the dishes and setting them in the drainer. "I'll bet you are too."

"I am," he said, drying the glasses and putting them away. "I wasn't comfortable having everyone together. I wanted to keep my parents from saying anything rude or hurtful to your parents, and especially to Nan."

"My parents don't worry much what anyone thinks," Anna assured him. She didn't think either of them had noticed that they were being snubbed.

"My mother drug me into my office for a lecture before she left," Michael said.

"Oh?" Anna said curiously. She turned and leaned against the counter. "What was she lecturing you about?"

"She's worried that you'll ask your mother and Nan to come and help after the baby is born. She thinks your sister would endanger an infant."

"That's what *she* thinks, or that's what *you* think?"

Michael looked shocked. "Did I say or do anything to indicate I had any reservations about Nan while they were visiting?"

"Nan is great with babies," she informed him. "Ask my sister. She begs Nan to come and play with her kids."

Michael hung the dish towel on the hook and turned to study her. "If you would like your mom and Nan to come, I'll be happy to buy them a plane ticket." He came up behind her and began to massage her shoulders. "I know it's late for caffeine, but I could go for a cup of coffee. How about you?"

"You don't have to give up caffeine on my account," Anna said. She was trying not to nag him about his unhealthy habits. Maybe that's what he was upset about …

"You were right about it," Michael admitted. "If I avoid caffeine in the evenings, I can usually sleep the whole night through." He grasped her shoulders and turned her around. "Will

I start drinking it again though, once the baby's born?"

"There will be no need for you to get up with the baby," she said. "I was thinking I'd sleep in the living room, so you're not disturbed. I'd fix a room upstairs but … stairs might be difficult for me at first."

Michael pulled her into his arms and held her, though she kept her body rigid. "I *want* to be disturbed," he whispered. "I don't want to miss one feeding, one diaper, one burp." He held her close, until it was obvious that she wasn't going to relent. "Will you tell me what's wrong, now that they're gone? I can tell that you're upset with me, but I honestly don't know why."

"I'm not upset," she said. She pulled away and slid onto one of the stools at the counter. "I just don't want the baby to create a hardship for you. I don't work, so I'll be the one to get up in the night and handle any extra chores and responsibilities."

"You're not listening," Michael said gruffly. "I *want* to be involved. Please don't deprive me of an experience I've wished for all my life."

Anna wasn't sure what to say. He sounded so sincere, but there were so many clues that told her he was not looking forward to the arrival of the baby. "We have a long time before we need to argue about it," she finally said.

Michael studied her for a moment, then he left the room.

Anna folded her arms on the counter and put her head down. If only he would talk to her! If only she could understand why he was unhappy. She only knew one thing – it started the minute she told him she was pregnant.

♥

"Would you mind if Marianne rode along to church with us this Sunday?" Anna was crocheting an afghan to stretch over the back of the couch. She held it up and perused it with a critical eye. "She's been down in the dumps for weeks."

"I don't mind at all. Especially if you think it will help pull her out of the doldrums. What's she depressed about? Do you know?"

"Me getting married again when she's never been married. And now I'm having another child. She's thirty-six. Even if she

108

met someone, it would be a year before they'd know one another well enough to get married. And then they wouldn't want to have children right away … like we did," she added, glancing at him, to see his reaction.

"It might not be the right choice for her, but I think it's going to work out fine for us," Michael said. He closed the magazine he had been reading and placed it on the coffee table. "Did you have someone in mind? At church?"

"Do you mean am I trying to play Cupid?" She pulled a few lengths of yarn from the skein, letting them drape over her knees. "I don't even know which of the men are single. I just thought it would be a chance for her to meet new people. I didn't invite her yet. I wasn't sure if you would mind."

"I don't mind at all."

"Thank you," Anna said. She bent over the instructions for the afghan, frowning with concentration. "This pattern might be too hard for me," she grumbled.

Michael enjoyed sitting on the couch with her in the evening. He would watch as she crocheted a few rows, then try to tease her out of being cross if she had to rip them out. "I do like Marianne. She only thinks I don't because I've had to reprimand her a few times."

"I remember. For gossiping. But she's doing much better with that nowadays. Have you thought about names?"

"Names?"

"For the baby? I was wondering if you'd like to name him after you?"

Michael was quiet for a moment. "That gets confusing. At least it did with my dad and brother. Do we have reason to believe it's a boy?"

"No," Anna said. "I thought we'd pick a boy name and a girl name, so we're ready in either case."

"Or we could just wait. You'll find out the sex on your next trip, right?"

"Yes, but it's not 100%, you know."

"I *didn't* know. I'll prowl the Internet later, and see if I can come up with a few suggestions."

"After my doctor's appointment, would it be all right to start shopping for a bed and changing table?"

"A changing table?"

"It's a water proof stand where you can change a diaper without bending over. When you have to change a dozen diapers a day, bending over a bed can really get to your back."

"A dozen a day?" he said with surprise.

"Just for the first few months, until he starts sleeping all night."

"You keep using those male pronouns," he pointed out.

"Only when I'm talking to you. When I'm talking to Paula, I say 'her', because I know she'd love a sister."

"I'd love either one," Michael said, repeating words he had spoken numerous times in recent weeks. "As to the changing table, you can buy anything you want or need, for yourself or the baby. I'll be happy to go along and load it in the van for you." He had purchased the van the week after Anna announced her pregnancy, and had lately begun researching car seats and strollers and high chairs, wanting those with the highest safety rating. He scooted closer and watched over her shoulder as she worked to the end of the row. "It's going to be very pretty," he said.

"The baby or the afghan?"

"Both," he replied diplomatically.

Anna dumped her project onto the coffee table and yawned. "I may have to search for an easier pattern," she said realistically.

Michael pulled her into an embrace. He was relieved when she didn't protest, or push him away. He encouraged her to rest her face on his chest, hoping she would fall asleep in his arms. "How long before you'll be able to feel movement?"

"Soon," she said, snuggling against him. "Would you want to feel it sometime, when she moves?"

"Michael chuckled. "Yes, I would love to feel it, *every* time she or he moves."

"Maybe it's twins," Anna yawned. "Heaven forbid!"

♥

Anna leaned across Michael and watched as a robust man in a

110

grey suit sat down in the pew across the aisle. "It's Dr. Hardy!" she said with excitement. "Did you know he goes to church here?"

"No," Michael said, nodding politely at Anna's obstetrician.

Anna turned to Marianne and whispered in her ear. Marianne leaned forward, peered past Michael, then sat back and whispered in Anna's ear. Michael stared forward and hoped the doctor didn't think he was a party to Anna's matchmaking.

When the service ended, Anna held his coat sleeve until   Dr. Hardy stepped into the aisle, then gave him a gentle shove.

"Good morning, Dr. Hardy," Michael said, shaking the man's hand. "Michael Grant, in case you can't place me. And my wife Anna, who is your patient. And this is our friend, Marianne Faraday."

Dr. Hardy shook hands all around, then somehow, he and Marianne moved up the aisle ahead of Anna and Michael.

"I thought you said …" Michael began, but Anna quickly shushed him.

After they shook the pastor's hand, Anna took Michael's arm. "Can we stay for coffee hour?"

"I don't see why not. Do you want me to tell Marianne?"

"She'll figure it out," Anna said with confidence. "Meanwhile, I need a restroom. That's one thing about being pregnant that I could live without."

Michael rested his hand on her shoulder as they walked down a long hallway to the restrooms.

When Anna came out, she peeked into the Sunday school rooms. "I'm just curious," she said. "I taught Sunday school in St. Louis."

"You're not fooling me!" Michael said. "You're trying to give the two of them plenty of time unchaperoned."

"I'm sure there are dozens of people downstairs," Anna said. She peeked up at him, then she giggled.

Michael gave her a gentle hug, in spite of being in church. She had finally stopped saying she wouldn't allow him to help take care of the baby. He was relieved – each time she had said it, it helped convince him that the baby wasn't his.

It didn't matter. He was going to embrace the baby as if it were his own. He would love it and nurture it and never let Anna know that he had guessed her deception.

♥

"We need to call Dr. Hardy and reschedule your appointment," Michael said one morning, just before he needed to leave. "John texted that he's bringing the senator to tour the school. I said I had an appointment I couldn't change and John said I should change it anyway. He doesn't ordinarily ask me to do that."

"It's okay," Anna told him. "There's no reason why I can't drive myself into Briarton."

"I'd rather you didn't. I know it's silly, but …"

"Okay," Anna agreed. "I'll see if he can fit us in tomorrow."

"That would be perfect," Michael said with relief.

An hour later, when Anna called his cell phone, he warned her that he could talk no more than a minute. "John and the senator are here," he explained. "Is everything okay?"

"Fine! Just that … when I called Dr. Hardy's office? He came to the phone. He told me how nice my friend was and asked if she's single! Is that not exciting?"

"It is, Anna, but this isn't a good time to talk."

"Okay. Just that I was wondering if you'd be upset if I kept the appointment and had Marianne take me?"

Michael moved further away from John and the dignitaries he was entertaining. "You're asking me to have a sub take her classes so she can go along to the doctor?" he whispered.

"Never mind," Anna said quickly. "I'm sorry. Out of line."

"Go on and ask her," Michael gave in, "but do not tell a soul, including Marianne, that I went along with this scheme."

"How am I supposed to not tell Marianne?" Anna giggled.

"I don't know. Just don't."

Anna giggled some more. "Okay! I'll call you as soon as I get back."

"Anna?"

"What?" she asked, and he could hear the hesitation in her voice.

"I love you," he said softly. "Tell Marianne to drive carefully.

Remind her that she's transporting precious cargo."

"I love you too," she said.

Michael ended the call with a shake of his head. He couldn't believe he had agreed to let one of his teachers take the morning off to pursue a possible love match.

♥

Anna texted him, as soon as she got home, but when Michael texted back, asking the baby's gender, she didn't reply. He assumed it meant she wanted to give him the news face-to-face. She was working in the kitchen when he came in, and she didn't stop and come to greet him. He removed his coat and hung it over the back of a dining room chair, growing apprehensive. She must have learned that she was carrying a girl. She was certain he wanted a boy, in spite of his insistence that it didn't matter.

"What's the news?" he asked, coming to lean on the counter, so he could see her face.

"Dr. Hardy called. He wanted Marianne's phone number! I'm pretty sure he's going to ask her out. They both kept saying funny stuff to each other while he did the ultra-sound. He did it himself, I'm sure so he could spend more time with Marianne."

Michael couldn't help smiling, even as he shook his head. "Is it too much to ask whether he had any news about our baby?"

Anna put the knife down and turned to face him. "Add an 's,' " she said.

He cocked his head to one side. "What's that supposed to mean?"

"Babies. Plural."

Michael was stunned. "Twins?"

"They run in my family. I probably should have warned you."

"*Warned* me?"

"You act as if you think it's good news," she said warily.

"It's wonderful news." He couldn't stop smiling.

♥

"Long time, no see," Tina said. "Michael told me," she

whispered, mindful of the people in the waiting room. "Twins! I'm so excited for you!"

"Thanks," Anna said. "How did Michael seem?"

Tina stared at her with confusion. "He's thrilled. He's over the top."

Anna wanted to believe it, but if he had been distraught over having one baby, he could only be twice as miserable now. She forced a smile, then went around Tina's desk to the stacks of letters waiting to be folded and placed in envelopes.

"What's wrong?" Tina asked, keeping her voice low.

Anna felt her eyes fill with tears, but she knew she must not confide in Michael's secretary. "You know what they say about pregnant women," she sloughed it off. "We're all emotion."

Tina touched her arm and when Anna turned, she gave her a hug. "If he seems off, it's only because he's worried. He'd kill me for telling you this, but he spends a lot of time on the Internet, researching the birth process and all the things that could go wrong. I peek over his shoulder at the screen, whenever I take him papers to sign." She gestured at the inner office. "He's scared something will happen to you. I guess he waited all these years to fall in love and now he's afraid of losing you."

Anna stared at Tina with a pensive expression. She remembered the night she told Michael she was pregnant. He had admitted his concern, because she was small. Why had she never considered this? Michael was worried that something would go wrong, that's all it was! He was afraid she might die in childbirth.

"Tina, you can't imagine what a good thing you just did. I'm sure you're right! He doesn't like to let on that he worries about things, but … I'm sure you're right!"

Tina smiled back at her. "He'll tell you afterwards. When you bring the babies home and everything is fine, he'll admit how scared he was. Wait and see. He won't say it now because he'd worry that you'd get scared too. You're not scared, are you?"

"Not a bit. I had two children already. There's absolutely nothing to it." She sank into the spare chair. "Thank you!" she said with emotion. "God bless you!"

♥ Chapter 12 ♥

"If the babies hold off until June, I could come and help,"
Paula offered. " 'Course, I don't know how much help I'd be,
since I've never taken care of a baby before."

"It would be a crash course," Anna said, rubbing her abdomen.
She winced and sat down on the side of the bed.

"What's wrong?" Paula asked with alarm.

"Nothing," Anna said, waving her hand. "Just the normal
aches and pains."

"When did you last see the doctor?"

"Yesterday. Did I tell you that he's dating my closest friend? I
sort of fixed them up and now they're talking about getting
married. She used to want a big wedding, but after listening to me
go on about it, she changed her mind and decided small is better.
Hint, hint."

"Since I'm not even dating anyone, it's a non-issue," Paula said
glumly.

"Will you help me peel potatoes?" Anna asked, leading the
way to the kitchen.

"If I have to. When will Michael get home? I finally got you a
wedding gift and I want him to be here when I give it to you."

"Hello!" Michael called from the back door.

"There you go," Anna said, quickening her step. She gave
Michael a hug, then stepped back so he could hug her daughter.

"It's good to see you," Michael told Paula. "Glad you could

make it down."

"We were about to peel potatoes," Anna told him, going to the cabinet where they were stored in a bin.

"You sit," Michael said with authority. "Paula and I will peel potatoes."

Paula winked at her mother and went to the sink.

"Paula has something to tell us," Anna announced. She pulled herself onto a stool and raised her legs onto another.

"It's not something to tell," Paula corrected her. "It's a gift. A belated wedding gift."

"You didn't need to do that ," Michael said. "We could never have pulled off the wedding without your help, and that was gift enough." He glanced at Anna. She had forbidden him to thank Paula for the beautiful nightgown that had been tucked into Anna's carry-on bag.

"I wanted to," Paula insisted. "I got tickets for you to see Phantom of the Opera!"

Anna clapped her hands with excitement. "How did you manage that! I heard it was a sell out!"

"I bought them from one of my sorority sisters. She got them before she realized she had a conflict with the date."

"Thank you so much, Paula. I would come over and hug you, but ..."

"That's okay. You can hug me later."

"Or Michael can hug you for both of us."

"What's wrong?" Paula asked, noting his scowl. "Don't you like musicals?"

"I do," Michael said. "Just not that one, I'm afraid."

Paula looked shocked. "What's wrong with Phantom? Everyone says it's fantastic!"

"So I've heard. But it's a story about madness and that's not my favorite theme."

Paula turned and looked over her shoulder at her mother. Anna shook her head.

"I appreciate the gesture," Michael said. "Please don't feel hurt. Why don't *you* go with your mother? When is the show?"

"The first weekend in May."

"Perfect," Anna said, though she knew she would be

uncomfortable during the drive.

"So ..." Paula persisted. "That's really why you don't want to go? Because the phantom is kind of crazy?"

"Yes," Michael said. "I have never understood why so many authors and playwrights are fascinated by the insane. I don't find it an entertaining subject."

"It's not really about that," Paula pleaded. "It's a love story."

"I'm sorry, Paula," he said. "I hope you'll forgive me."

Paula glanced at her mother, then dropped the last potato into the pot, splashing Michael with water.

"I don't know what your mother has told you, about my past," Michael said, wiping his tie with a dish towel. "My first wife had serious emotional problems and eventually committed suicide. That's as much madness as I can handle in one lifetime."

"I didn't even know you were married before," Paula said in a hushed voice.

"I don't want to get into a long conversation about it," Michael told her. "If your mother feels up to the drive and her doctor says it's okay for her to leave town overnight, would you be available to see it with her?"

"You've been wanting to see it as long as I have," Anna tried to tempt her.

"Sure, fine," Paula said, obviously still disgruntled. "You might want to tell her doctor that I'm going to be a nurse. I could probably deliver the babies in the ladies' room, if they decide to come early."

"Don't even say that," Anna gasped. "I'm going to deliver these babies at Briarton Hospital on or just after my due date."

"So that no one thinks you were pregnant before the wedding?" Paula guessed. "Everybody knows twins come early."

"Not always," Anna protested. "In fact, they usually come a few days late. Don't they?" she added nervously.

♥

"You know what?" Michael said, coming around the counter. "There's just enough time for you to take a nap before dinner."

"I don't need a nap," Anna argued. She yawned, then giggled.

117

"I want to spend time with Paula. We don't get that many chances to talk."

"You can talk after dinner. I'll go in my office and close the door and you can girl talk all night." He lifted her from the stool, ignoring her protests. "Please," he said, gazing into her eyes.

"All right," she agreed, resting her head on his chest. "Carry me like a princess. That's what I used to tell my dad, when I was a little girl. Or so I've heard from my brothers a million times."

"It will be good for Paula and I to have some time alone," he whispered, carefully placing her on the bed. "Don't you think?"

Anna shoved her feet under the quilt and burrowed her face into the pillow. Michael waited a moment, then realized she was already falling asleep. He went to the window and pulled the drapes, then tiptoed from the room.

"Is she okay?" Paula asked, sounding guilty. "I didn't mean to say that, about twins coming early."

Michael debated how to answer. "I think she was more bothered by the insinuation that we slept together before we got married. When I was your age ..." He paused and grinned at her.

Paula slapped her palm on top of her head. "I hate conversations that begin with those words."

"When I was your age," he said again, "children didn't believe their parents possessed the necessary body parts to produce children."

"In this case, we have evidence to the contrary," Paula pointed out. "And I wasn't raised Catholic, so you won't be able to sell me on immaculate conception."

"The Catholics don't have a corner on immaculate conception," he pointed out.

"Neither do you and my mother."

Michael laughed. "Will you help me clean the corn?"

"Yuck!" she complained. "I hate when that hairy stuff gets all over me. Can't we just open a can?"

"It's not as good for you. Fresh vegetables are healthier, especially organic."

"So now you're gonna try and convince me she swallowed a watermelon seed?"

Michael chuckled as he spread a sheet of newspaper over the

118

table.

"I'm sorry about your wife," Paula said. "Is it hard for you to talk about it?"

"Yes," he admitted. "I've always blamed myself." He waited for her to tell him that it wasn't his fault.

"I'm sure I would too," she said. "You didn't have children?"

"No. We hadn't been married very long."

Suddenly Paula covered her face with both hands and began to sob. Michael dropped the ear of corn, wiped his hands on a towel, and drew her into his arms. He hoped she wasn't going to tell him something that would upset her mother.

"I'm so miserable!" she cried. "Everyone in my sorority drinks and if I get drunk, I get sick and then I can't get up the next morning. I've been late for class so many times, I'm on probation. I hate it, because my mom told me this would happen if I joined that sorority!"

Michael abandoned her long enough to fetch a box of tissues from the counter. He kept an arm across her shoulder while she wiped her eyes and blew her nose. "You want something to drink?" he offered, once she seemed calm.

"You mean booze?" she asked, with obvious surprise.

"No," he said. "We don't have a drop of alcohol in the house. Fruit juice, tea, or coffee."

"Coffee," she decided. "Could you not tell my mom? About me drinking? I'm gonna tell her sometime, but not until after she has the babies."

"All right," Michael promised. Though he hated keeping secrets from Anna, he thought this was an exception. "Is there anything I can do to help?"

"You just did," Paula said, giving him a hug. "Thank you for listening and not lecturing."

"You don't need a lecture," he said solemnly. "You've got good common sense and you know exactly what you need to do to resolve this."

Paula squeezed him once more, then stepped back. "If I ever meet someone and get married, will you give me away?" she asked.

Michael was shocked. "I'd be honored," he said with emotion.

♥

Please don't let my water break, Anna prayed silently, as she watched the Phantom emerge from his hiding place, high above the floor of the theater. Her labor had started after the intermission, but she couldn't see her watch so she didn't know how far apart the pains were coming. She hated to make Paula miss the end of the show, but she really didn't want to have her babies in the restroom of a theater.

"Paula," she whispered. "Get me a wheelchair."

Paula's face bleached white. "Are you sure?"

"Shh!" Anna cautioned. "Yes!"

Paula got up and started to move down the row, then turned back and reached for her mother's hand.

Anna took a deep breath and followed her, praying that the next pain would hold off for a few minutes.

Once in the lobby, she sank gratefully into a wheelchair and dug in her purse for her phone. She jiggled her foot as she waited for it to power up, praying that Michael hadn't gone far after he dropped them off. He answered on the first ring.

"Where are you?" she asked desperately.

"I'll meet you at the front door in two minutes," he said.

"Wheel me to the door," Anna told Paula. "Wait!" she said, as they passed a counter laden with souvenirs. "I want a memento. And I want to get something for you, since I caused you to miss the second half."

"Mom! I could care less about souvenirs right now. Let's just go!"

"They're supposed to have CDs you can't buy anywhere else," Anna insisted. She rummaged in her purse and pulled out some bills, shoving them into Paula's hand. "Get us both a CD."

"I just want to go," Paula said, eying her mother with near hysteria.

Anna glared at her. "I had two children. I know what I'm doing!"

Paula made a face and turned to the souvenir counter. "Hello?" she called. "Could somebody please help me here?"

Anna felt a pain coming on, but tried to keep her expression

120

neutral, so no one would guess.

"Hey!" Paula yelled, waving the money over her head. "See the woman in the wheelchair? She's about to have a baby and she wants a CD before she goes to the hospital. Could somebody please wait on me?"

"I can't believe you did that," Anna hissed, when Paula handed her the CDs. "I'm glad you got them though. Maybe the doctor would like to listen to it during the delivery."

Paula wheeled her to the door, darting around obstacles at high speed. "He's here!" she shouted, when she caught sight of Michael, pulling up at the curb in the van.

Anna started to get up, but Michael waved both hands, telling her to stay seated. She sank back and decided to let him take charge. She must focus on delaying the babies until he could get her to a hospital. Any hospital would do, she decided, though she was sorry Dr. Hardy wouldn't get to deliver the twins. Marianne had warned her that this would happen, and she would be sure to remind her of that a hundred times …

Michael slid one arm under her back and the other under her knees. "Put your arms around my neck," he instructed. "Paula, will you go ahead of me, please, and open doors?"

"Maybe you could ask one of the ushers which hospital is closest?" Anna suggested.

"I already know," Michael assured her. "We're not going far, I promise." He put her in the front passenger seat and worked to fasten the safety belt.

Anna waited until he slammed the door before she doubled over and tried to remember the instructions for breathing during a pain. It was no use! She needed to get to a hospital, where someone could coach her.

Paula climbed into the back seat, as Michael slid behind the wheel. He pulled onto the street, moving so slowly, Anna wanted to yell at him to speed it up. "How long will it take to get there?" she asked anxiously.

"How close together are your pains?" Paula wanted to know, leaning over the seat.

"I don't know. I couldn't see my watch in the theater – it was too dark."

Paula groaned with frustration. "Why didn't you tell me sooner?"

"I didn't want you to miss the end of the show."

"Focus on your breathing," Michael told her. "Breathe in through your nose, slowly, and out through your mouth."

"Don't worry," Anna tried to reassure him. "We have a registered nurse in the back seat."

"I am not a registered nurse yet!" Paula protested. "I was bluffing, about delivering the babies in the ladies room. I don't know how to deliver a baby!"

"Well, I do," Michael said. "I've taken plenty of first aid courses over the years, and several included instructions on delivering a baby."

"I am *not* having my babies on the side of the road," Anna said indignantly. "We have plenty of time."

Suddenly a police car pulled in front of the van, lights flashing.

"What did you do?" Paula asked with alarm.

"I called and asked for a police escort," Michael said.

"Wow! That was smart!" she praised him.

"It wasn't necessary," Anna insisted. "But it was smart," she agreed, as another pain unleashed its fury.

"As it turns out, I wasn't the only one thinking ahead. Marianne convinced Dr. Hardy to bring her to St. Louis for the weekend. He's meeting us at the hospital. He won't be able to run the show, but he has a good friend who's happy to have him assist."

Anna heaved a great sigh of relief. "How much further?"

"I'd say … five minutes?"

"Good," Anna said. "Because the pains are coming very close together."

"How close?" Michael asked, and for the first time, he sounded worried.

"I don't know. Maybe two minutes?"

"I think I'm going to faint," Paula said weakly.

"Hang on," Michael told her. "I'll deliver both of you into medical hands as quickly as I can."

♥ Chapter 13 ♥

"Could you get a wheelchair for Dr. Grant?" Dr. Hardy asked one of the nurses.

"For Michael?" Anna said with alarm. "What's wrong with Michael?"

"He's looking a little green around the gills. I wouldn't want to try to pick up a man his size, once he lands on the floor."

"I'm fine," Michael said, but when the wheelchair arrived, he sat down.

"Why don't you take him out and get him a glass of water," Dr. Hardy went on in a cheery voice. "Anna, would you like me to call your daughter in?"

"Thanks, but you'd just end up needing another wheelchair," Anna said.

"I thought she's studying to be a nurse."

"She is," Anna said. "Here comes another one."

"Another pain or another baby?" the doctor teased.

The minute the nurse wheeled Michael into the waiting room, Paula clutched her throat with both hands. "What happened?" she gasped. "Why are you in a wheelchair?"

"He'll be okay in a minute," the nurse assured her. She parked the chair and sat down at Michael's side. "He just got a little light-headed."

"I'm fine," Michael said. "I told her I'm fine."

"You're white as a ghost!" Paula disagreed.

"I promised your mother I would stay with her. I hate letting her down!"

"She's in good hands," the nurse assured him. "Four good hands, not counting the tech and the nurses. So what kind of nurse are you going to be?" she asked Paula.

"I haven't decided yet," Paula said. "Do you always work in the delivery room?"

Michael leaned over and tilted the foot rests out of the way. "I need to get back in there. I promised I would stay. I don't usually have a problem with things like this."

"It's not usually your wife on the table," the nurse chuckled. "They'll come get you as soon as baby number two arrives. Trust me – I've driven lots of daddies around in wheelchairs during the delivery." She pressed the foot pedals back down and watched until Michael reluctantly lifted his feet into place.

"Did you call Andy and Beth?" he asked Paula.

"They should be here any minute."

"Good," Michael said, drumming his fingers on the arm of the chair.

"Beth is pregnant too," Paula told the nurse. "That's my brother's wife. But she's not due for three months."

"Could you please wheel me to the door of the delivery room?" Michael asked with exasperation. "In case she needs me?"

"Sure," the nurse said. "You come too," she invited Paula. "We'll stop by the nursery on the way, to get a peek at … it was a boy, right? What's his name?"

"Tyler," Michael said. He cleared his throat, hoping they wouldn't realize he was choked up.

"The other one is a girl," Paula said, sensing that Michael didn't want to talk. "They're naming her Francine but they're gonna call her Franny. Isn't that sweet?"

When they reached the nursery, Michael got out of the wheelchair and stared through the window at the baby boy in the crib labeled "Grant – Male." Even though he'd anticipated this moment for months, he couldn't comprehend that the baby in the bed had emerged from Anna's womb.

"You could probably go in and hold him," Paula said

"Not yet," Michael said. "I need to see your mother first. I need to know she's all right."

"She's fine, Michael!"

"You can't know that. They may have sent me out of the room because …"

"Stop!" Paula warned him. "Don't forget she's my mother!"

"I'm sorry," Michael said, looking around, as though he were lost. "Where's the delivery room? I got disoriented."

"Look at him! He's gorgeous!" Paula said, learning her forehead against the glass. "He's got peach fuzz."

"Peach fuzz?"

"That little bit of blond hair. I need to dig out our baby pictures so I can see whether he looks like me and Andy. I know they have a different dad, but half their genes are the same. I'm gonna ask Grandma to send mom's baby pictures too."

Michael studied the baby and thought about what Paula was saying. A dad and a mother who both had dark hair, and yet the baby's hair was a pinkish shade of blond. Bruce Carlisle had sandy colored hair. Michael tried to push the thought away.

"When it's a boy and a girl, they can't be identical twins," Paula informed him. "We had that in a class."

"Identical would have to be two of the same sex," Michael agreed.

"Did you know that a woman could actually have twins and each one would be from a different father?" Paula said. "It's very rare though."

Michael had never come across that information and he found it shocking. What if one of the twins was his and the other was Bruce's? He closed his eyes. If it should happen to be true, he didn't want to know. He wanted to treat both of the twins as if they were his biological children. The most important thing was to give them plenty of love and attention. It didn't matter whether they were related to him by blood.

"Sorry," Paula laughed. "I forget that everybody isn't as fascinated with genetics as I am."

"I do find it fascinating," Michael told her. He closed his eyes and wished he had taken Anna's advice to memorize Scripture verses, though he doubted there were any to fit this situation.

"Let's walk back to the waiting room, in case Andy and Beth are here," Paula said, looping her hand through his arm. "Okay, Dad?" she teased, gazing up at him with affection.

♥

Michael shielded his face with one hand, while his knee jiggled up and down. What was taking so long? Something must have gone wrong. He should be with Anna. Paula had gone to find out what was happening but failed to return.

"Hey!" someone said, and he looked up to find Andy.

"I tried to call you!" Michael said, jumping up to shake his hand. "I was worried you might be driving all the way to Briarton. I wasn't sure if Paula thought to tell you where we were."

"We figured it out," Andy said. "Congratulations! We stopped by the nursery on our way in – you've got two good looking babies."

"Two?" Michael said.

"They've got them side by side, wearing a pink hat and a blue hat."

Michael had been about to ask if Franny's hair was blond, but if she was wearing a hat …

"I saw Mom's doctor in the hallway, talking on his cell. At least, Paula said he's Mom's doctor. I'm curious to hear how he came to be in St. Louis at the right time."

"What's he doing in the hallway?" Michael asked with concern. "Where's your mother?"

Andy shrugged. "Don't worry, Mike. Knowing my mom, she's probably sharing recipes with the nurses."

Michael rubbed his forehead. "It seems like they would've …"

"Michael?" Dr. Hardy called, approaching with a smile. "Congratulations! You've got your readymade family! Both babies appear to be in good health and Anna is doing fine."

Michael felt his body sag with relief. He couldn't talk for a moment, and he wondered why the doctor and Andy were chuckling. "When can I see her?" he asked.

"In a few minutes. She wanted to comb her hair before she

126

starts receiving company."

"I'm sorry," Michael said. "This is Andrew, Anna's son from a previous marriage."

"Good to meet you," Dr. Hardy said. "You just graduated law school, right? And got married to the lovely Beth?"

Andy laughed. "Sounds like you've been talking to my mom!"

"She's tired, but I'll bet that won't last long. Tomorrow she'll be arguing to go home."

"Don't let her win that argument," Michael pleaded. "I want to be sure she's all right."

"She's fine," Dr. Hardy tried to soothe him. "If there was any doubt, I wouldn't be out here with you. Marianne wants to know whether she can come by tomorrow to see the babies. Morning or evening, whichever works best for you."

"Of course," Michael said, albeit reluctantly. "Tell her to come whenever she wants."

"She's very pleased with herself, for sharing her premonition."

"It was extremely fortunate," Michael said. "Anna relaxed, the minute I told her you were in town."

"I'm going to set Marianne up in a booth, telling fortunes," Dr. Hardy laughed. "I'll see you later, Michael. Andy, nice to have met you."

"Wait!" Michael called after him. "When can I see Anna?"

Dr. Hardy smiled. "One of the nurses will come get you in a few minutes."

A moment after the doctor disappeared, Paula bustled into the room with Beth. "Aren't they gorgeous?" she asked Andy. "I'm so excited!"

"Good thing they're not *both* girls," Andy pretended to console Michael.

"He should be so lucky," Paula sniffed.

"I think I'll go down to the nursery for another look," Andy said, taking Beth's hand. "Can you get me there? This place is huge. A person could be lost for days."

"I'll stay with Michael," Paula said, sliding into the chair beside his.

"No, go on with your brother," Michael urged her. "I'm fine. I really am."

127

"I think he's trying to say he'd like a minute alone," Andy advised his sister.

♥

Anna couldn't understand why Michael didn't come. Though Dr. Hardy had assured her he was fine, she couldn't help worrying that he wasn't. She still didn't understand why they put him in a wheelchair and took him out of the delivery room.

Finally he appeared, looking nearly as tired as she felt. "Michael!" she chortled. "Did you see them? They're beautiful! I can't believe we were so lucky as to get one of each. Think of the arguments it saved, having twins."

Michael came to the bed and bent over to kiss her. "Why would it have otherwise caused arguments?"

"I wouldn't have wanted to raise an only child and you wouldn't have wanted me to get pregnant again."

He drug a chair to the side of her bed and sat down. "Thank you for being okay," he whispered.

"Me?" she teased. "You're the one who had to be removed in a wheelchair!"

Michael threaded his wrists through the railing and cradled her hand in both of his. "I don't imagine you'll ever let me forget that, will you."

"Not a chance," she grinned. She let her head fall back on the pillow and heaved a great sigh of exhaustion. "You did see them?"

"I saw Tyler, but I haven't seen Franny yet. I was afraid to leave the waiting room, in case Dr. Hardy came looking for me."

"Were you really scared?" Anna asked.

"I wasn't scared, I was ..." He shook his head. "I was terrified. I was convinced you were dying and I didn't understand why the doctor wasn't doing anything about it."

"Well, now you know that having a baby is no big deal," Anna said with nonchalance.

"That's easy for you to say." He finally smiled. "I barely remember this, but once upon a time, I had my entire life under control."

"You just *thought* you did," Anna said with amusement. "God is in control, not us. We make big messes and He makes 'all things work together for good.' "

Michael bowed his head and grew still. If God had control of this situation, why hadn't Tyler been born with hair as dark as Anna's and his?

"Are you praying?" Anna said softly.

"Yes," he said, without looking up, though he wasn't sure his thoughts qualified as prayers. What would he do if only one of the twins had "peach fuzz"? He only wanted to love them equally, without showing preference for the one most likely to be his.

♥

"If only they had waited until June," Anna said with dismay. She and Beth were each feeding a baby in the living room of Anna's St. Louis house. Though there were two adults and two babies, they both felt as if they were under siege. "I'm so sorry for disrupting your lives. I know you must have a million things to do. And I'm sure it's not the easiest thing to cart a baby around on the outside when you're already carrying one on the inside."

"I'm fine," Beth assured her. "It's good practice."

Anna had plenty of friends in St. Louis, but she didn't want to ask them to help. She knew people were going to think she and Michael *had* to get married, because the babies had come early. Even if it were true that twins always came early, there was no guarantee that everyone else knew that.

"Is that Michael?" she asked, jumping up to look out the front window. "He made good time, especially with the rain." For almost a week, Michael had been driving to Casey's every morning, and back to St. Louis at the end of the school day. He wouldn't be talked out of getting up with the babies during the night either, and he was clearly exhausted. Anna opened the front door and he hurried in, quickly removing his raincoat.

"You must have gotten away early," she said.

"I did." He kissed Anna, then kissed Tyler's forehead. "He's looking very alert," he commented. Michael was the only one who could tell the twins apart at a glance.

Beth groaned. "How do you do that? I can only tell who I've got if I change the diaper first."

Michael rubbed his hands together, in case they were chilled. Then he lifted Tyler from Anna's arms, cradling him carefully in the crook of his elbow as he stared into his face. "He looks like a boy and she looks like a girl," he said, as if it were obvious.

Anna watched as he sat down and picked up the bottle. She no longer felt that he didn't want children – it was obvious that he was enjoying every minute. It only made her more confused, because she knew something was still wrong. "Do you want me to make some coffee?" she offered.

"Yes, please. I promise I'll give up caffeine again, as soon as they start school."

"High school or college?" Anna teased. "Is that Andy?" She went to the window and peered out. "He's home early too."

"He mentioned he might take me to dinner," Beth said. "You don't mind, do you?"

"Of course not," Anna and Michael said in unison.

Anna thought both couples were probably anxious for some time apart, so they could have a conversation and not wonder whether it was being overhead.

♥

"I want to go home," Anna said, as soon as Andy and Beth had gone. "I don't like you doing all that driving. I'm scared you're going to fall asleep at the wheel."

"If I feel sleepy, I pull over and get out of the car and stretch my legs," Michael tried to reassure her. He had one baby on his knees, the other in his arm.

"What if you get sleepy before you realize you're getting sleepy? Regardless, I want to go home."

"Do you think you'll be able to handle the two of them on your own while I'm working?" Michael asked doubtfully. "I can come home for a couple of hours at lunchtime, but I'm not sure that will be enough."

"I wish my mom and Nan could come," Anna said wistfully.

"Dad says the tests are all routine and he doesn't need her to hold his hand, but ... I'd feel the same way about leaving you if you were having any sort of medical test."

"And I, you," Michael agreed. "And we don't want to interfere with Paula, while she's working so hard to bring her grades up."

"Marianne could come over for a couple of hours when school lets out every day."

"She's pretty busy planning her wedding," Michael reminded her.

Anna sighed. "I remember we said we wouldn't ever want a nanny, but ...maybe for a few weeks?"

Michael touched Tyler's chin with his fingertip. "I'll start looking for candidates tomorrow."

Anna felt some of the tension ease from her shoulders. "Beth is worn out and I don't think Andy has slept well since we moved in. When I told them they could stay at the house as long as they wanted, I didn't know we'd be moving in with two babies. And to be honest, I think I'd sleep better if I were home."

Michael looked up with a surprised expression. "Casey's feels more like home than the house you lived in for twenty years?"

"Almost twenty-five years," Anna said, quickly adding them up. "It's because *you're* there. It's because it's *our* home."

"Do you want to go back with me Friday morning?" he suggested. "That would give us the weekend to try to get into some kind of routine."

"Babies automatically defy anything that hints of routine," Anna said knowingly.

♥

"Good morning, Dr. Grant," Terri White said pleasantly, pouring coffee into his favorite mug. "I hope you slept well?"

"I did," Michael said, wondering how she knew which mug was his favorite. "I didn't hear a sound all night."

"Good! That's the way it's supposed to work."

"Did you and Anna get any sleep?"

Terri tucked the fringe of her grey hair behind her ears. She was about fifty years old and plump, but only around the middle.

131

"She's sleeping now," Terri said, crossing her arms over her belly, as though aware of his perusal. "We'll take turns napping during the day, as the opportunity arises. Would you like a couple of eggs and some toast?"

"Fixing my breakfast wasn't part of the bargain," Michael said. "I'll get something at school." He debated whether to wake Anna and tell her that he was leaving. "I'll be back for lunch," he told Terri. "Maybe this is one of those opportunities to grab a nap?"

"Thank you," she said. "I might do that."

Michael grabbed his laptop from the dining room table and went out the door, wondering why the nanny made him so uncomfortable. She was respectful and took directions, didn't flirt with him or patronize Anna. He had called all of her references and run a thorough background check that produced nothing. Maybe he wouldn't trust any stranger with the care of his wife and children, no matter how perfect her credentials. Living in a rural area, there hadn't been a large pool of applicants to choose from. After going it alone for more than a week, he and Anna had been exhausted and desperate.

He put his mind on school business, but kept a close eye on the clock. Just before noon, he headed back to the house, unable to shake his concerns. It was relief when he found Anna seated on the couch, feeding Franny. Tyler was settled happily in the Porta-crib, kicking his legs and making contented baby sounds.

"Where's Terri?" Michael asked, sitting beside Anna and lifting Franny from her arms. He draped a diaper over his shoulder and laid her in an upright position, gently patting her back until she burped.

"She's taking a nap," Anna said. "She must not realize the babies are awake, or she would've come rushing to the rescue."

"Is that a bad thing?" Michael asked, trying to hide his own reservations.

"Not really," Anna said. "She takes her job very seriously."

"So you're okay with her staying on?"

"I think so." Anna shrugged. "What about you?"

"She offered to make me some breakfast this morning."

"Is *that* a bad thing?" Anna said with confusion.

"No, but … I think we should stick to the terms of the

agreement."

"She's good with the babies," Anna said. "She definitely knows what she's doing." She stared at him, as though waiting for him to challenge her statement.

"Then we're settled for the next few weeks?" he said, shrugging off his concerns. "Until Paula can come?"

"I think it's going to work out fine," Anna said, handing him the bottle. "If you want to finish feeding Franny, I'll fix you some lunch. Although, now that I think about it, it wasn't part of our agreement, was it? Fixing your meals?"

"You forgot to read the fine print," Michael teased back.

♥

Michael stood in the doorway of his office the next morning, going over some papers with Tina until something made him look out the window. Anna was headed towards the school with one baby in the umbrella stroller, the other perched on her hip. She stumbled, then lurched forward and nearly fell. She looked behind her and when he followed her gaze, he saw that a car was parked in the freshly mown field, where he had imagined playing catch with the twins someday. A man jumped out and yelled something to the nanny, who was running after Anna.

Michael thrust the papers into Tina's hands and ran through the outer office, then down the stairs. Though he didn't say a word, Russell and Scott fell in behind him.

The man was trying to wrestle Tyler away from Anna. The nanny had already pulled Franny from the stroller.

"Anna!" Michael shouted, just as the nanny raised her hand and brought it down on the back of Anna's head. Michael watched helplessly as his wife crumpled to the ground. "Anna!" he shouted again. He was running full out, but it felt as if he were moving in slow motion.

The man and woman ran for the car, glancing over their shoulders at Michael and the security guards.

"I can't get a clear shot!" Russell gasped, and Michael saw that he had drawn his gun for the first time in all the years he'd worked at Casey's.

A shot rang out as something hit Michael's right shoulder with enough force to spin him around. He lost his balance and fell, then struggled back to his feet. He took a few steps and fell again. Russell and Scott were both standing with their legs spread, firing at the car. It veered to the right, then disappeared down the winding road that led to the state highway.

"No!" Michael tried to shout, but his voice came out as a whisper. He crawled toward Anna on his knees, catching himself with one hand, the other hanging useless at his side. "Anna," he said hoarsely, collapsing beside her, trying to pull her against him.

"Don't move her," Scott cautioned, stooping beside him. "In case she has a spinal injury."

Michael stared at him without comprehension. "Go after them!" he ordered. "Get the babies!"

Scott was ripping off his shirt. He fell to the ground and pressed the fabric over Michael's shoulder. "Lie still," he ordered sternly. "You're not bleeding out on my watch!"

"Take care of Anna," Michael said, trying to sound as if he were still in charge. Then he closed his eyes and everything went dark.

♥ Chapter 14 ♥

When Michael opened his eyes, he was afraid, but he didn't know why. There was a fierce pain in his right shoulder, and he suspected he might be having a heart attack. Where was he? He blinked a few times, then gradually began to remember. He had been transported to the hospital in Briarton, after being shot. Anna was also hurt, or possibly dead. The twins had been taken.

He tried to sit up, but his limbs would not cooperate. He tried to call out, but his throat was raw and dry. He cautioned himself to stay calm, though his natural inclination was to panic. Sooner or later, someone would come to check on him and he would demand that they take him to Anna.

Please God, don't let her be dead, he prayed, frantic with worry. Somewhere deep in his subconscious, he labeled himself a hypocrite. How dare he call on God now, when he had judged him powerless all these years! He pushed the thought away …

Where was Russell? Had he also been injured? Michael struggled to bring back the horrific memories. The police would want details, as many as he could manage. They would want a description of the man who had taken his son, and the woman who had snatched his little girl from her stroller. They would want every bit of information he had gathered about the nanny. He needed to call Tina, and tell her where to find the file. It was locked in the bottom left drawer of his desk. His keys … he needed to find out what they had done with his phone and his keys.

The bullet had lodged in his right shoulder. He flexed his right hand and the pain intensified until he feared he would pass out again. He forced himself to breathe slowly and wished, again, that he had been forced to memorize Scripture as a child. He was desperate now, for the kind of comfort only God could offer. He recited the Lord's Prayer, then stumbled through the 23rd Psalm. Over and over, he said the words: " 'Even though I walk through the valley of the shadow of death, I will fear no evil.' Please," he prayed, feeling the sting of tears in his eyes. "Please don't take Anna away from me."

♥

The next time Michael awoke, he heard voices and tried again to call out. Though he had gained some volume and a little strength, it was obvious that no one could hear him. He made himself relax, determined to stay awake until someone appeared. He listened harder and thought one of the voices might be Paula's. Was she crying? If she had gotten the news that her mother had died, she would be inconsolable.

"Someone needs to go to the house," she said, "in case they call for a ransom."

"I imagine the police thought of that," a man's voice replied. "But whoever did this must know that your mom and dad aren't going to be home to answer the phone."

Michael strained his ears, hoping to hear something conclusive about Anna. Why didn't Paula come into his room? Why didn't she come and tell him whether or not her mother was all right?

"May I please see my mother now?" she asked. "She needs to know I'm here, and that my brother is on the way."

"Thank God," Michael whispered, barely stifling a sob. *Anna was alive!*

"You can see her, but you must not mention the babies."

"Why not?" Paula demanded.

Their voices moved away from the door as the man answered, and Michael couldn't decipher his words.

"You mean she doesn't even know they've been kidnapped?"

Paula cried.

♥

"Am I glad to see you!" Michael said, when Russell came quietly into the room. "I need you to take me to Anna immediately."

"Whoa!" Russell said, holding up both hands. "I don't have any jurisdiction in this building, Doc. They aren't about to let me take you anywhere."

It was the first time one of Michael's employees had refused to obey an order. "Is she all right?" he demanded. "Is she conscious?"

Russell came to the bed and rested his hand on Michael's good arm. "She's in and out. There were a couple feds trying to question her, but she hasn't got a clue about what happened. One of the nurses said that's normal for a concussion."

"I'm just grateful she's alive," Michael said. He turned his head, to hide his expression. It brought on a fresh surge of pain. "Does she have other injuries?"

"She's got a knot on her head, and some bruises. Her daughter's here and her son's on the way."

Michael thought of Beth, eight months pregnant. "Did they hurt Charlie?" he asked. "Please tell me they didn't kill Anna's dog."

"They drugged him up, but he was coming out of it when I left. They think he'll be okay."

"What happened?" Michael asked. "Have you got any idea what happened?"

"You do realize ..."

"That they took the babies." Michael swallowed hard.

"I wanna know about you, Doc. All that privacy nonsense ... I couldn't get anything out of your surgeon and neither could Mrs. Grant's daughter."

"They had to operate, to remove the bullet. That's all I know."

"Did it hit any major organs?"

Michael tried to recall what they'd told him. "The only major organ in that vicinity would be my heart. If she'd been a better shot, I guess I'd be dead."

"Thank God for that then," Russell said gruffly. "Are you in a lot of pain?"

"I can handle it," Michael said, though he was gritting his teeth. "Who's in charge? Did the local police call in the FBI?"

"There's a whole mess of alphabet soup roaming all over the school and the hospital. There's some agency that coordinates the rest of them, when a kid is abducted."

"Well, where are they? Everyone knows the first few hours are crucial. They should've questioned me long before this. They're wasting time!"

"They're here in the building," Russell assured him, "and they're taking statements from everybody on campus. It was that nanny you hired, wasn't it?"

"Yes," Michael said. "Get them to release my personal effects so you can get into my desk. There's a file in the bottom left drawer, where I keep my personal papers. Tell Tina to …"

"Whoa, whoa, whoa," Russell said. "I'm not in charge, Doc. I can't do anything unless I clear it with them."

Michael was beginning to realize that tension increased the pain in his shoulder. He forced himself to relax. "Do whatever you can," he said, gripping Russell's hand. He wanted to get out of the bed and take charge. He wanted to force people to do what needed to be done, so that the twins could be found … "Do what you can," he said again.

"You betcha," Russell promised.

♥

"Oh, Paula," Anna said, opening her eyes and finding her daughter seated on the side of her bed. "Did you remember to get bread crumbs?" There was a man standing beside Paula, with his hand on her shoulder. Anna couldn't imagine why Paula had allowed a strange man into her mother's bedroom. "Where's Michael? He should've been back by now. I'm starting to get worried."

Paula looked up at the man, then squeezed her mother's hand. "He'll be back soon," she promised tearfully.

Anna tried to sit up, but a wave of dizziness forced her to fall back on the pillow. "Who is that man?" she demanded.

"This is Dr. Blake," Paula explained. "He's taking care of you."

"You're a doctor?" Anna said, with skepticism. The man had three day's stubble on his chin. "Why does my head hurt so bad?"

The doctor motioned for Paula to move, then took her place. He beamed a light into Anna's eyes and asked her to follow his finger from left to right. "You have a concussion, Anna. Do you know what that is?"

"Of course I do," she said with annoyance. "I just don't know how I got it."

"Let's get you back to normal before we talk about that."

"Where's my husband? He should be back by now. I can't imagine what's keeping him."

"He'll be here soon."

"Am I in the hospital?" she asked, slowly turning her head to take in her surroundings.

"That's the best place to be, after you sustain a concussion," Dr. Blake assured her.

"Sustain," Anna repeated. She decided he really was a doctor. "Where's my husband?" she asked. "He should've been back by now."

♥

Michael heard someone come into the room, and opened his eyes just enough to see that it was Paula. He struggled to sit up.

"Stay still," Paula cautioned him. "I don't think you ought to be moving around."

"Where's your mother?" Michael demanded anxiously. "Is she all right?"

"She's fine. I mean … she's okay. She has a concussion."

"Does she understand what happened? Does she know the twins were kidnapped? She'll never survive this …"

"Don't say that!" Paula rebuked him. "My mother is tough! She can survive anything!"

Michael's head dropped back on the pillow and the ghost of a

139

smile crossed his lips. "Thanks," he said seriously. "You can't know how desperately I needed to hear that."

Paula pulled a chair to the side of his bed and sat down. "Someone said you were shot in the shoulder?" She gazed at the bandages that were wrapped diagonally around his chest.

"I didn't realize I'd been shot. It all happened so fast ..."

"I don't know if you're supposed to talk about it. Do you have any idea who ..."

"The nanny," he said darkly. "And she had an accomplice. A male with dark hair, about her same age. Does your mother remember anything?"

"I don't think so," Paula said. "The doctor said she might never remember what happened during the hour or so before the concussion."

Michael closed his eyes, aware of how the investigation would be hindered by Anna's lack of memory. "I can't understand why no one has questioned me. They're wasting valuable time!"

"They tried to talk to my mom, but she's not making much sense. You do know who did it though? The nanny?"

"Your mom was trying to get to the school, but the nanny caught up with her. She took Franny out of the stroller and the man ... he tried to take Tyler away from your mom but she wouldn't let him go." He stopped for a moment, to try to regain control of his emotions. "The nanny hit your mom on the back of the head and she fell."

Paula covered her mouth with both hands. "I can't believe ..."

"Tell me about your mother. Did she need stitches? Did they have to shave her hair?"

"No," Paula said. "There were no lacerations on her head. Just a lump."

"Just a lump," Michael repeated, wondering how serious it might be.

"I saw that security guard. Scott? He said they've got someone manning the landline at the house, in case there's a call for a ransom."

Michael sagged with relief. "Then they are doing *something*."

"Did the bullet hit a bone?" Paula asked worriedly.

"It lodged in the muscle. You'd better get back to your mother.

Tell her I'm sorry."

"Why should *you* be sorry!"

It wasn't a question, but Michael felt he should try to answer it. "I'm the one who hired the nanny. I called all her references and ran a background check but I obviously missed something."

"Mom said you weren't planning on leaving her alone with the babies, so it didn't matter that much. She said anyone would do, if they could fix a bottle and change a diaper."

"When did she tell you that?" Michael asked.

"A day or so after she started? Terri, right?"

"Terri," Michael said with venom. "Terri White, but I seriously doubt it was her real name."

"Try not to worry," Paula said, brushing at her reddened eyes. "That's what the FBI is for. They'll figure it out. They'll get the babies back in no time." She pressed her fist to her mouth, but a sob escaped.

Michael reached for her hand, in spite of the pain it caused him. Neither of them spoke again for a long time.

♥

Michael heard someone come into the room, but he didn't immediately open his eyes. As the anesthetic wore off, the pain was excruciating. He had to fight hard to remain conscious.

"You need to put them together," he heard Paula whisper. She had been going back and forth, between his room and her mother's. "They'll both rest better if they can see one another."

"Do they have a good relationship?"

Michael opened his eyes and found a young man with dark hair, wearing green scrubs. He looked scruffy and unkempt.

"They're like Romeo and Juliet," Paula told him.

"I hope not," the doctor said.

Paula let out an exasperated sigh. "I just mean they're really close. Inseparable."

"Must be nice," the doctor said. "A relationship that works?"

"Can you please put them together?" Paula pleaded.

Michael opened his eyes a slit and watched as the young man scratched his chin. "I'd have to check with your dad's surgeon,

141

and I imagine he's already left the building."

"I'll bet he has a cell phone, and a pager," Paula persisted.

"Okay," he said. "I'll see what I can do."

♥

"We'll give the two of you a few minutes," Dr. Blake said, though he didn't look comfortable with the idea. "I'll be right outside the door, in case you need anything."

Michael and Anna didn't answer. Paula had talked the doctor into pushing the beds together, after convincing him that her mother would otherwise climb out of her bed and into Michael's, the minute he left the room.

"What happened?" Anna asked Michael. "No one will tell me. They keep saying I'll find out later. I want to know *now*. Where are the twins? Who's got them?"

"Tell me what you *do* remember," Michael suggested.

"Don't play games, Michael! Just tell me what happened!"

"I don't know," he said brokenly. "I'm still trying to piece it together."

"My head is pounding," Anna complained, as she crawled slowly from her bed into his. "You're hurt," she said with surprise, gingerly touching the bandages on his chest. "Please tell me what happened!"

"I don't know," he said again. "I saw you coming across the field, to the school. Through the window in my office."

Anna looked at him with a confused expression. "With the babies? Are they at school? Does Tina have them?"

"No," Michael said gently. "Do you remember coming over to the school?"

"No," she said. "I can't remember anything. I drank some orange juice."

"Where was Terri?"

She was quiet for a minute. "I went downstairs to eat breakfast. She had poured me a glass of juice."

"So you drank some orange juice and then what did you do?"

"I don't know. I couldn't find my phone."

"Were you going to call me?"

142

"I think so." She gazed at him with a fearful expression. "Where was Terri?"

"She was … upstairs. She went upstairs to lie down."

"Where were the babies?" Michael asked softly.

Anna pressed the heels of her hands to her temples. "In the living room. Tyler was in the Porta-crib. He loves that mobile. The one that plays the song from Phantom."

"Where was Franny?"

"In the swing. She was in the swing."

Michael couldn't think of a way to tell her.

"I felt funny," she said. "Like I was gonna fall asleep standing up."

Michael pulled her closer, though his shoulder felt like it was on fire.

"I wanted to call and ask you to come home, because I didn't feel good. But the phone wouldn't work."

"You found your phone?"

"The other phone. The landline. It was dead." She leaned back, to look into his eyes. "Are the babies dead, Michael? Was there an accident?"

"No," he said, smoothing her hair away from her eyes. "They're not dead, but they're missing."

Anna was horrified. "Did I leave them somewhere?"

"No, Anna. They were taken. The nanny took them."

"Where?" she cried. "Where did she take them?"

Michael tried to soothe her, but she pushed his hand away. "I don't know," he said. "There was a man, in a silver car. They put the babies in the car."

"Why didn't you stop her, Michael! Why did you let her take them?" Anna covered her face as she cried. Michael held her, searching his mind for anything he could say to console her. After a long while, she wiped her eyes with the sheet and gently touched the gauze that was wrapped around his shoulder. "Did she hurt you?"

Michael hesitated, then decided it wasn't going to get any easier. "She hurt both of us. She knocked you out and then she shot me."

"No!" Anna cried. "Are you all right? Michael, are you all

143

right?"

"I'm okay," he said, grateful for her concern, though he didn't feel he deserved it. "There are all sorts of law enforcement here. They need to talk to us, as soon as you're ready."

"Did they find the babies?" she asked eagerly.

Michael hoped her confusion was the result of the concussion. "Not yet. They need our help. They need us to tell them everything we can remember."

"She had a suitcase on her bed," Anna said. She wore a look of determination. "It was filled with diapers."

"She planned this, right from the start," Michael said bitterly. He reached for her hand and held it to his cheek. "I knew there was something wrong, but I let it go! I'm sorry, Anna! I'm so sorry!"

"It'll be all right," Anna said, patting his hand. "We'll find the twins. Don't worry."

♥ Chapter 15 ♥

"This is Steven Breen and ... sorry," Paula said helplessly.

"Milt Rhoades," the other man said. They were both holding up badges. "Feel up to answering a few questions?"

"I've felt up to it for hours," Michael said irritably.

"Let's get Mrs. Grant back in her own bed," Dr. Blake said, reaching to assist Anna.

"Why?" Paula protested. "Just leave them alone!"

"Who are you?" Anna asked, gazing at the doctor with suspicion. "Who is he?" she asked Paula.

"This is Lucas Blake," Paula said, though her mother had already been introduced to the doctor numerous times.

"Leave us alone," Anna told him, huddling close to Michael.

Michael found the controller and raised the back of the bed a few inches, wincing with pain.

"He's been refusing any pain meds, because he wanted to be alert when you guys showed up," Paula explained to the agents. "Why did you wait so long to talk to him?"

"We were told you wouldn't be conscious until right about now," Steven apologized to Michael. "Meanwhile, we've been interviewing those who were present at the scene, and doing some forensics."

"Forensics?" Anna said with alarm. "Is that when someone dies?"

"Nobody died," the agent said patiently. "We're hunting for

fingerprints and hair samples." He turned to Michael. "Your secretary said you were in the middle of a discussion when you suddenly ran out of the office."

"I looked out the window and saw Anna coming across the grounds, to the school."

"Did she have the babies with her?"

"No," Anna said. "I wouldn't do that."

"Yes," Michael said. "She had Franny in an umbrella stroller, and she was carrying Tyler. She was staggering."

"Did you think she might have been drinking?"

"I beg your pardon!" Anna protested.

"She doesn't drink," Michael said, "so I knew something was horribly wrong."

"When you got outside, were the babies gone?" Milt prodded.

"No!" Michael said with frustration. "As I left the building, two security guards went with me. The nanny had taken Franny out of the stroller. There was a car parked on the grass and ..."

"What kind of car? Did you notice?"

"Toyota. Recent model. It was silver."

"Okay, go ahead," Steven said, scribbling on a notepad.

"The man was trying to take Tyler away from Anna, but she wouldn't turn loose of him."

"What man?" Anna interrupted with concern. "I don't remember any of this!"

"That's because she hit you," Michael explained calmly. "The nanny hit you on the back of the head. She probably used the butt of the gun. She had to knock you out to get you to turn loose of Tyler."

"That stupid bun probably saved your life!" Paula cried, burying her face in her hands.

Lucas Blake hurried across the room and put his arm over Paula's shoulders.

"I think she drugged me," Anna said. "I could see pieces of something white floating in my orange juice. I was so stupid! I drank it anyway."

Steven continued to scribble, without looking up.

"Go ahead," said Milt. "What can you tell us about the woman?"

146

"We hired her a little more than a week ago," Michael said. "Terri White. At least, that's the name she gave us. She seemed very capable. I interviewed her, then she spent about an hour with Anna and the babies."

"She give you any references?"

"I called them all," Michael said. "I have an agency that does a thorough background check and they didn't find anything." He looked at Anna – she was shielding her eyes with her hand.

"Do you need me to dim the lights?" Lucas asked Anna.

"Yes, please," she said politely. "Who is he?" she asked Michael in a whisper.

"Dr. Blake," Michael said patiently.

"Would you still have the list of references she gave you?" Milt persisted.

"My secretary can send it to you."

"All right. We'll get to that in a minute. Just keep on with your story."

"I didn't like her," Anna said.

"Neither of us cared for her," Michael said, though he hated to admit it.

"What didn't you like about her?" Milt asked with interest.

"I was afraid I was being picky," Anna said, glancing at Michael. "But she did put something in my orange juice this morning. I'm sure she did."

"Is this the first time you've heard this?" Agent Rhoades asked Michael.

"She had just started to tell me when you came in. We've been separated until now."

The agent nodded. "Go ahead, Mrs. Grant."

Anna drew an unsteady breath and looked at Michael.

"You couldn't find your cell phone," he reminded her.

"Yes," she said, her brow furrowed with concentration. "I wanted to call Michael, but the landline was dead. So I went upstairs to the babies' room, to try to find my cell. I saw that there was a suitcase on one of the beds, filled with diapers."

Michael clenched his jaw. He had been uneasy with the nanny right from the start. *Why hadn't he trusted his instincts!*

"That's when the Holy Spirit told me to get the babies and go

147

to the school," Anna said.

"Mom!" Paula said wearily.

"I don't care if you believe me," Anna said stubbornly. "I don't care if anyone believes me."

"And is that what you did?" Steven pressed.

"It was hard. I wanted to lie down on the floor and go to sleep." Anna stared up at the ceiling.

"But you managed somehow?" he pressed.

"I put Franny in the stroller, because she's heavier. Then I went out the back door, but I couldn't go very fast. My legs felt heavy, like they were filled with concrete."

"And that's when you looked out the window and saw Anna approaching?" the agent asked Michael.

Michael smoothed Anna's hair away from her face. "I just happened to glance up," he said.

"The Holy Spirit was telling you to come and help me," Anna said, glaring at Paula.

Paula sighed and shook her head.

"What happened then, Mrs. Grant?"

"I don't know," Anna said with regret. "I can't remember."

"Which is normal after a concussion," Dr. Blake volunteered.

"Will she eventually recover those memories?" the agent asked.

"Not likely," Lucas said.

"I was afraid the guards would shoot and hit one of the babies," Michael said, closing his eyes for a moment.

"Did the guards discharge their weapons?"

"One of them. Maybe both of them. I believe they shot out the tires of the car."

"Oh, Michael," Anna cried. "Do you think they shot the babies by mistake?"

"No, Anna. You know Russell and Scott. You know they wouldn't take a chance like that."

Anna hid her face against his chest.

"I didn't realize I'd been shot," Michael said. "I … couldn't stay on my feet."

"Why would she do this?" Anna cried. "Why would she steal our babies?"

148

Steven rubbed the back of his neck. "There are a lot of reasons why people snatch babies. Maybe she lost one of her own. That's the worst case scenario, because it means she probably isn't going to ask for a ransom."

"A ransom?" Anna gasped.

"It might be an enemy of your husband, and she was just a player," Milt said.

"A player?" Paula repeated.

"They paid her to set it up," he explained. "You didn't recognize the man?" he asked Michael.

"I didn't get a good look at him, but from a distance, no. I didn't recognize him."

"Bruce!" Anna said suddenly. "Bruce did this!"

"Who's Bruce?" Milt asked.

"I already had Russell check," Michael told Anna. "He hasn't gotten out. He's serving time in Kansas City," he explained to the agents. "Bruce Carlisle. He attacked Anna last fall and she pressed charges."

"Mother!" Paula nearly shrieked. "Someone attacked you?"

"Let's stay on task," Steven chided Paula. "We'll want more information on this Bruce," he told Michael. "If your secretary can provide that?"

"Of course," Michael said.

"Given the business you're in, you've surely made a lot of enemies, Dr. Grant. Could this be revenge? You took their kid, now they took yours?"

"I keep a running list of those who have threatened me," Michael said. "My secretary can forward that to you as well."

"Do you think the babies are still alive?" Anna begged.

"Babies are worth a lot more alive," Milt assured her. "They'd have no reason to harm them."

"Worth more?" Anna repeated with confusion.

"We haven't had a call yet, for a ransom, but that could be because they know you're both in the hospital. Or we could be dealing with a black market adoption. Either way, we need to move as fast as we can."

"What's a black market adoption?" Paula asked.

"Given the number of abortions, there aren't many babies

available for adoption anymore. Couples who can't have one of their own are desperate."

"So they buy a kidnapped baby?" Paula said with horror.

"They don't necessarily know the baby was kidnapped," he explained.

"What about Gayle?" Anna asked Michael. "And Helen! What about Helen?"

"Check them out," Michael told the agents, giving their full names. "They were both upset when Anna and I got married. I don't think either of them are capable of such a thing, but I'm in favor of following every lead."

"That's what we like to hear," Milt said. "I've got somebody coming to take DNA samples."

Michael's heartbeat quickened. "What would you need with DNA samples?"

"If we get a baby, we'll have to verify that it's yours."

Suddenly Michael covered his eyes.

"Michael?" Anna said anxiously. "Are you all right?"

"I'm fine," he said.

"Is that where you stick a Q-tip in our mouth?" Anna asked the agent. "Could you just do that to Michael? I'm nauseated and if you stick something icky in my mouth …"

"I need to give Dr. Grant something for the pain," Lucas told the agents. "Are you about finished?"

"No," Steven said. "We're just getting started."

♥

"I think they're sending you home way too soon," Beth said, walking beside Michael's wheelchair as the nurse pushed him onto the elevator.

"I'm fine," Michael said irritably. "Where's Anna?"

"Paula said they'd wait in the lobby," Beth said, patting his good shoulder.

"Paula and Mom will be down in a minute," Andy said, meeting them as they exited the elevator. "Although a minute in this place might mean an hour."

"I hope not," Michael said. "I've never been so anxious to get

150

home."

"Those agents are waiting at the front door," Andy said. "They're going to escort us to Casey's."

"Good. That's good," Michael said. "I wonder what's taking your mom so long." He didn't like it when Anna was out of his sight. He raised his left hand and rubbed at his temples. The doctor had insisted on giving him a pain reliever, promising that it wouldn't make him groggy. He needed to stay alert …

The elevator doors opened and a nurse wheeled Anna into the lobby. Seeing her in her rumpled clothing, seated in a wheelchair, he realized how bad she looked. She had aged into an old woman overnight.

"Where's Paula?" Andy asked. "She's with that doctor again, I'll bet."

"What doctor?" Beth asked with alarm. "What's wrong with Paula?"

"Nothing," Andy assured her. "Leave it to my sister to start up a romance with my mom's doctor."

"I think she's trying to gather information, in case one of us needs medical attention after we get home," Michael said, in Paula's defense.

"Andy, call your sister and tell her we're leaving without her," Anna ordered. "The kidnapper could be calling the house while we're sitting here waiting for Paula." She blinked her eyes, trying to keep the tears from spilling over.

"They've got people sitting beside the phone, around the clock," Michael assured her. It had been three days, and the agents said the chances of a ransom call grew smaller by the minute. If the kidnappers were watching though, they might call as soon as Michael and Anna arrived home.

"Let's go," Michael said, pointing at the door. "I'd rather wait in the car." He felt vulnerable in the crowded lobby. For the first time in his life, he wanted to purchase a gun, and apply for a concealed carry permit. One moment had changed his life, changed who he was and what he believed in. One moment …

♥

"I'm used to sleeping on your right side," Anna complained. "Not that I'm going to be able to sleep. Why don't they call? I was so sure they would call, once we got home."

Michael wrapped his left arm more tightly around her, ignoring the pain in his right shoulder. "We have to accept the possibility that they didn't take the twins with ransom in mind. Milt says black market adoptions have been on the rise. If that's the case, our best chance is for the video they made to go viral."

Anna sat up and pushed her hair away from her face. Since the concussion, she got a headache every time she tried to fasten her hair into a bun. "How do we make that happen?" she asked anxiously.

"We don't," Michael said. "We're relying on the compassion of strangers, to share the post and tweet the information and forward the email."

"Why didn't they take this tack from the beginning?" Anna said angrily. She knew she must not cry, because it upset Michael. She knew he was barely holding it together too, but pretending to be strong and brave for her sake.

"He said they couldn't do it at first, because that kind of publicity will sometimes cause kidnappers to take drastic measures."

Anna got up and went into the bathroom. She splashed her face with cold water, trying to erase the image "drastic measures" had conjured up. When she came back, Michael was propped against the headboard with a magazine. Anna knew he wasn't reading it, because it was opened to an ad for liquor.

"Have you given up thinking it's someone you know?" she asked, hoping her voice sounded strong. "Maybe a disgruntled parent?"

"I haven't given up any theory," Michael said. "There are plenty of people who hate me, but enough to do *this*?" He reached for her hand. "You don't have any enemies, other than Bruce. You didn't have any enemies at all until you became involved with me."

"Think, Michael. Maybe there's someone you haven't considered. Someone who threatened to get even someday?"

"There was one angry father, who swore he would get revenge

on me. I'm not sure if I put his name on the list."

"You should tell the agents!" Anna said with excitement.

"I will in the morning. Unless you think I should wake them?"

"They take turns sleeping," Anna said. She slid out of bed and pulled on her robe. "I think Steven is first shift tonight. I'll go get him."

♥ Chapter 16 ♥

"Look what I brought you," Milt said. He was carrying a tall stack of photo albums. "All the perps' pictures are supposed to be digitized, but these are old, and nobody has gotten to them yet."

Anna went to the table and sat down. She was eager to do anything the agents suggested, in hopes that it would bring her babies home.

"Remember," Milt said, as he watched her flip the cover on the first book. "She might have been wearing colored Contact lenses. She might have lost or gained weight, bleached or dyed her hair."

"She might have had plastic surgery," Steven said, stifling a yawn.

"Mentioning her weight," Michael said thoughtfully. "I remember thinking she had an odd shape. She was chubby, but only around the middle. I wonder if she was wearing some kind of padding."

"I noticed that too," Anna agreed. She studied each picture carefully, tracing her fingernail over the facial features. "I don't think she wore Contacts. I was pretty close to her more than once and I usually notice when people are wearing Contacts."

"Good," Milt said, drawing out his notebook. "Did you think anymore about whether she had an accent? You know how some folks say 'aboot' when they mean 'about'?"

"She spoke like someone from Missouri," Michael said. "She

referred to the refrigerator as the 'icebox.' She called Anna and I 'you guys.' She 'warshed' her hands."

"You're from Missouri and you don't say those things," Anna pointed out.

"My parents corrected me when I did." Michael sat down next to her and studied the pictures in the album. "Judging from the hairstyles, these pictures are pretty old."

"Didn't you say she was about fifty? It's possible she committed a crime before she got savvy enough to cover her tracks so well."

Michael pressed his hand over his eyes as he remembered calling Terri White's references. They had all been fakes, using toss-away phones. He wondered how often he had been duped over the years ... Terri White had not only taken his children, she had robbed him of the confidence to do his job.

"This woman looks familiar," Anna said. "She doesn't look like the nanny, but ... I've seen her before."

Michael leaned over and studied the picture. "Can we take it out of the album?"

When Steven nodded, Anna slipped the photo from its sleeve and placed it on the table between her and Michael.

"It *could* be her," Michael said. He could hear his voice waver. "I might just want it to be," he admitted.

Milt looked enthused. "It's nice to have a lead to chase." He picked up the picture and turned it over. "You never know ..."

"If the picture is that old, how does it even help?" Anna wondered, sagging a little.

"You'd be surprised," Milt said. "They can use age enhancement, change the eye and hair color ... I'm gonna see how fast they can get somebody here with the software program."

Anna jumped up and went to the kitchen. "Anybody want more coffee or something to eat?" She had no appetite, but she continually baked and cooked for the agents.

"What'cha gonna make?" Steven asked, patting his belly.

♥

"You've got company," Milt said, knocking on the open door

156

of the nursery. "Pastor Franklin? From St. Louis, he says."

Anna hurried down the stairs. "What are you doing in our neighborhood?" she asked, giving her minister a hug of welcome.

"I came to see you and Michael. To find out whether there's any way I, or the congregation, can help."

"How did you find out?" Anna asked curiously. "Did you see it on the Internet?"

"Andy called me yesterday."

Anna turned to look at the FBI agent, who was listening in on the conversation. "Sounds like the blitz isn't doing so well," she said sadly.

"Our YouTube video had over a million hits," Milt said defensively.

"I know," Anna said, waving both hands. "I'm sorry."

"No need," Milt said. "You want me to make myself scarce?"

"We can go in Michael's office," Anna said. She suspected Michael would be upset if the agent left because she had company. She knew he was worried that they would soon give up altogether.

"The question is," Pastor Franklin said, following her across the living room, "why didn't *you* call me? You know there are dozens of people who would've been praying for you and offering to help."

Anna shrugged. She closed the door behind them and gestured at Michael's chair.

"How are you holding up?" he asked, continuing to stand.

"I'm doing okay," she said, forcing a smile.

"Hey, Anna. This is me! We've always been honest with one another, haven't we?"

"I'm doing awful!" she cried, hiding her face in her hands. "I have to be so strong for Michael and it's not fair!"

Pastor Franklin put his arms around her and Anna allowed her tears to flow freely for the first time in days. She cried until she was exhausted, then wiped at the wet spot on his shirt. "I'm sorry," she said, sinking into the chair Michael kept beside his desk. "I don't want to burden you with this."

"Burden me, Anna. I'm strong. I can carry it for a while, if it will help." He turned Michael's chair so that he would be facing her when he sat down. "Will we pray before we talk?"

"Yes," she said eagerly. "Please ..."

"Almighty God, you know where Anna and Michael's children are, and You are keeping them safe from harm. You know that we're all looking forward to the moment when you return them into their parents' arms, just as You looked forward to the moment when Your son returned to You. Show us what to do, tell us what to say, in order that we might bring about Your will on earth as it is in heaven. Amen."

Anna opened her eyes and sniffed. She got up and pulled a few tissues from a box on Michael's desk, then sat back down and blotted her eyes. "He insists on blaming himself," she said. "He's convinced that it's his fault and he's so negative ..." She raised her chin and bit her lip. "He says he had a bad feeling about the nanny, but so did I! There was something artificial about her. She was too perfect. It was like she was acting."

"She *was* acting, and she's apparently had plenty of practice. I imagine there aren't many folks who wouldn't have been fooled."

"That's just it," Anna said. "We *weren't* fooled. Either of us. We saw that something was wrong but we ignored it."

"Something like what? Maybe she didn't love children as much as she said she did?"

"She went through the motions, but she wasn't sincere."

"And you could see that?"

"Michael could too, but neither of us admitted it to the other. I didn't want him to keep going without sleep and dragging off to work the next day."

"So even though you saw that she wasn't perfect, you figured she would work okay until you could figure out something else?"

"We were only going to have her for a few weeks," Anna explained. "Until Paula got out of school."

"Then neither of you realized that the nanny was dangerous?"

"Of course not!" Anna said, feeling her temper flare. "Do you think either of us would've tolerated her for one day if we had realized what she was going to do?"

"No, I don't," he said firmly, gazing into her eyes.

She stared at him for a moment, then she tried to smile. "Could you please repeat that with Michael?"

"Men are like that, Anna. He holds himself responsible for your happiness and wellbeing, whether or not it falls under his area of control."

"He's been acting strange the whole time. Ever since he found out I was pregnant." Anna felt guilty to talk behind Michael's back, but she could no longer hold her feelings in. "It wasn't because I trapped him into getting married, if that's what you think. I didn't get pregnant until the honeymoon."

"The thought never crossed my mind," Pastor Franklin assured her. "I've seen you rebuff enough men in the congregation."

"I should've asked him whether he would want to have a baby. I just assumed he would. He loves kids! But as soon as I told him … I don't know. He closed me out. He said he was happy, but he didn't act happy. Well, he did, but … I can't explain it! Things just weren't the same and he wouldn't say why. I was dreading it!"

"Dreading … the birth of the babies?"

"Yes! Especially when I found out there were two. Not because I didn't want them. Because I thought *he* didn't want them. But he's been wonderful. He wants to hold them all the time. He carries them around the house and talks to them about everything. I even heard him teaching Tyler how to change the oil in the car."

"Then why do you feel …"

"I don't know!" she wailed. "Just that something isn't right and he won't say what it is. We're not close anymore. We're like two strangers. We're both acting like that stupid nanny, being polite and saying all the right things but …"

"Do you want me to talk to him?"

Anna pressed her knuckles against her lips. "I don't know. He might be angry with me for getting someone else involved."

Pastor Franklin waited, while Anna mulled it over.

"Yes, please," she finally said. "I know it makes no sense, but I keep thinking if we aren't close, we won't get the babies back. Do you really think we'll get them back?"

"Of course you will. But you're right, Anna. You and Michael need to resolve your differences. You need to be able to put your heads and hands and hearts together when you pray. You need to close your eyes and visualize the twins coming home where they belong. Harboring dark thoughts won't help anyone."

♥

Michael wasn't happy when Anna asked him to come home from school and chat with Pastor Franklin. He appreciated the fact that the minister had driven all the way from St. Louis, but he was buried under a backlog of paperwork and it was the only time he could get his mind off the twins.

Anna handed them each a steaming cup of coffee, then left the room, closing the door behind her.

"I think I'm being set up," Michael said, shifting uncomfortably in his chair.

"Anna hoped we could talk about why you feel responsible."

"Wouldn't you? If your wife was attacked and your children were kidnapped, right before your eyes?"

Pastor Franklin nodded. "My wife had several miscarriages, and I blamed myself for that. But I didn't cause her to miscarry, and you didn't cause a kidnapper to steal your children."

"It's not that simple!" Michael snapped.

Pastor Franklin sat back and rested his hands on the arms of his chair. "I'm not the brightest guy, but I'd probably be able to grasp it, if you could explain."

Michael rolled his eyes at the ceiling. "I know this won't sound very Christian, but … the whole situation feels like karma. It feels like I'm finally getting what I deserve."

"It doesn't sound Christian at all," Pastor Franklin said soberly.

Michael didn't want to do this. He wanted Anna's pastor to go away so he could nurse his wounds – physical and emotional. He wanted to plead "work", so he would have an excuse to disappear, burying his mind in the tasks of the administrator – as he had been doing for more than twenty years.

"Are you one of those men who only attends church to please his wife?" Pastor Franklin asked. "Do you think about other things while Scripture is being read, and doze off during the sermon? Anna tells me your Briarton pastor sticks to the Bible, so I don't think you can blame him for your beliefs. Unless you don't claim to be a Christian?"

"We're all on a journey," Michael said wearily. "Isn't that one of the platitudes you're always trying to sell? Maybe I'm just not far enough along to buy into it."

Pastor Franklin shook his head and sat forward again. "Are you referring to your salvation? Because that's not something you get to 'down the road.' It's the basis of faith. Christ died for your sins. Period."

"It's *my* journey," Michael said firmly. It was not something he wanted to discuss, especially with a minister who would try to back him into a corner.

Pastor Franklin grew quiet. "Let's play with the karma thing for a moment. In your view of things, our sins are weighed against us and we're punished accordingly. Look around you, Michael, and show me the evidence. People do evil things every day and are seemingly rewarded by your secular universe, not punished. Men who murder the innocent have positions of great power. They have more money than they can spend and all the pleasures money can buy. How does that fit your theory of karma?"

Michael rubbed at his temples with his left hand. When he got out of here, he was going to fix himself a large cup of caffeinated coffee, and if Anna objected …

" 'The rain falls on the just and the unjust alike,' does it not?" the pastor persisted. "Don't you know good people who've had nothing but bad luck all their lives?"

"Maybe they're not as good as they appear to be," Michael said lamely.

"Can we apply that to Anna? Is she not as good as she appears to be? I've known her a long time, and I think I know her well. Has she successfully hidden some dark secret from me?"

Michael let his hand drop as he met Pastor Franklin's eyes. "Anna is even better than you think. She puts up with my nonsense and never complains."

"*Almost* never complains," the pastor corrected him.

This came as an unpleasant shock. Michael sat back in his chair and tried to imagine what Anna might have said to the minister. "I'd like to have a transcript of *that* conversation," he said. "It would be helpful if she would voice her complaints to me, rather than a third party."

"Sounds like you're both on the same page then."

Michael stood up and moved behind his chair. It was a tactic that usually intimidated people, because of his physical size.

Pastor Franklin only smiled, as though amused.

"I don't know what you mean by that," Michael said. He pressed his fingertips near the wound on his shoulder, until he realized that he was playing the sympathy card.

"Anna feels certain that something's been bothering you for quite some time, but she's worn out from trying to guess what it might be. You have every right to refuse to speak with me about it, but if you want your marriage to survive, you need to come clean with your wife."

Michael tried to conceal his reaction. "She told you she wants a divorce?" He held his breath as he waited for the answer.

"Don't put words in my mouth," Pastor Franklin said firmly. "The 'D' word was never mentioned and I'm sure it hasn't crossed her mind. Plenty of marriages fail while the couple remains together, especially after a tragedy such as this."

"Did Anna tell you that she was attacked?" Michael asked, giving in to his anger and frustration. "Did she tell you that she was assaulted by a man who intended to rape her?"

The pastor shook his head, wearing a look of concern.

"I didn't think so," Michael said knowingly. "I believe she's in a state of denial about what happened."

"Does this have something to do with what we're discussing? Your failure to own up to whatever's been eating at you? Or is it just another tactic to avoid your own issues ..."

"Maybe if you could convince her to speak openly of *that* incident, to me, I would feel more inclined to share my feelings with her." Michael rested one hand on the back of the chair and stared at the bust of Socrates, who still wore Anna's winter hat. He needed the wisdom of Socrates now.

"I will not carry messages back and forth," Pastor Franklin said. "That would defeat the purpose. If you suspect she hadn't been forthright about this incident, you need to tell her so. You need to explain that when she keeps secrets, you feel the need to

162

do the same."

"She says she's told me everything."

"Then I imagine she has. I've never known her to be deceitful."

Michael wished he could believe what the pastor was saying, but hadn't he just admitted that Anna hadn't even told him about the attack? What was that, if not deceitful?

"If you feel there's more to the story, you must tell her that," Pastor Franklin advised. "You must be upfront and admit that you don't trust her. It may cost you something initially, but it will get the subject into the open, where the light can reveal everything you want and need to know."

Michael didn't shake his head, but he wanted to. Anna would not forgive easily if he shared his suspicions. Especially if he was altogether wrong.

Pastor Franklin sighed. "I'm afraid I haven't done either of you much good. There's an incredible potential here, for a wonderful marriage that will benefit dozens, perhaps hundreds of people. I'd hate to see that fizzle."

"I don't think mending our marriage is a priority right now," Michael said, edging toward the door. "Our children are missing. The only thing that matters is getting them back."

"Point taken, but keep the other in mind. We are engaged in spiritual warfare, Dr. Grant. I'm not sure if that fits into your karma-style scheme of things, but … don't let the devil win this one. Please."

Michael extended his left hand for an awkward shake, then turned and left the room.

♥ Chapter 17 ♥

Michael sat at the kitchen counter, drinking coffee while he scanned his emails. Anna was curled up on the couch, staring listlessly out the window. Michael hadn't shaved and Anna hadn't washed her hair. Though they kept trying to bolster one another, they were sinking deeper into depression every day. Michael blamed himself, and it was somehow tied to his lack of faith in Anna. If he had believed both babies were his, biologically … what then? He would've run faster? He would've dodged the bullet?

Someone knocked on the door and Anna jumped up.

"No!" Michael hollered, before she had taken two steps. "You stay back. Let me answer it."

The two FBI agents had gone somewhere together after breakfast, leaving Michael and Anna alone for the first time since the twins had been taken. They had promised to come back, but Michael felt certain they wouldn't. It had been ten days. Surely it was time for them to label theirs a cold case and move on. He went to the door and carefully pulled the curtain back. Then he unlocked the door and flung it open.

"Tyler!" Michael gasped, as the agent handed him the baby.

"Tyler! Tyler!" Anna shrieked, running across the room. She wrapped her arms around both Michael and the baby, while tears spilled onto her cheeks. "Oh thank you, God. Thank you, Jesus. I knew we would get them back! I knew it!" She gazed expectantly past the agent, then her face fell a little. "Where's Franny?" she asked fearfully.

Milt and Steven exchanged looks. "We've only got the boy for now, but don't you worry, Anna. I promise, we're gonna find your little girl too."

She looked from one to the other, then hurried after Michael, leaving the agents to close the door.

"Why isn't he crying?" Michael asked with concern. "Shouldn't he be crying?"

"He's fine," Anna said. "He's happy to be home, that's all." Together, they unwrapped Tyler from the receiving blankets, examining him closely, to be sure he was unharmed.

Michael stretched his good arm over her shoulders. "I'm so sorry," he said hoarsely. "Anna, I am *so* sorry!"

"We're going to get Franny back too," Anna told him. "You'll see. You've got to believe. You've got to have faith."

"A couple of pediatricians looked him over," Milt said. "They said he looks fine, like he was with good people."

Anna held him up for the agents to see. "He *is* fine," she said, her voice breaking.

"We got lucky," Steven told them, sitting down in Michael's recliner. "The couple who adopted him saw the video on Facebook. It was something you said, Anna. About the way he wiggles his pinky finger while he's drinking a bottle. We showed them the reworked photo of Terri White and they immediately recognized her as the social worker who delivered the baby. They were told he came from a very young unwed mother. They didn't know he was a twin."

"Did you get her?" Michael said. "The nanny?"

"Not yet, but there are multiple agencies working together on this. They're focusing on couples who lost twins, all across the country."

"What'll happen to the people who had Tyler?" Anna asked, hugging him close. "Will they go to prison?"

"I don't know what kind of deal they made," Milt said, rubbing the back of his neck. "But I'm guessing they'll walk away, since they cooperated."

"If the system prosecuted people for adopting black market

babies ..." Michael protested.

"We know," Steven said, with understanding.

♥

They stood side by side at the crib, shoulders touching, watching Tyler sleep.

"I'm afraid to let him out of my sight, even for a minute," Anna said with emotion.

"Me too," Michael agreed. "When I wake up in the morning, if I'm able to sleep, I'll think this was a dream."

"It's a miracle." Anna rested her hand on Tyler's back. "We must not relax our prayers for Franny! I know God will bring her home too, if we don't lose faith."

"Do you feel any better, knowing it wasn't personal?" Michael wondered.

She didn't answer for a long while. "Michael," she finally said. "We need to talk."

Her tone of voice was frightening. *Just because she hadn't mentioned divorce to her pastor, didn't mean it wasn't on her mind.* "Do you want a cup of coffee?" he offered.

"I think I'd better wean myself off of caffeine," Anna said. "Now that we have one of our babies back, we need to start eating healthy again, and getting plenty of sleep."

Michael nodded, though he doubted whether he would ever again get a good night's sleep. "A cup of herbal tea?"

"That sounds perfect." She took a few steps toward the door, then turned back. "Is the monitor turned on?"

He handed her the receiver, then followed her down the stairs. She went to the living room and curled up on a corner of the couch. The agents had gone, this time for good. Now that they knew who had taken the babies, and why, there was no need for them to remain.

"Chamomile," he said, as he handed her a steaming cup.

She took a tiny sip. "It's hot!"

"That's the way most people like it," he teased, replaying a conversation they'd had months before.

"Our first major argument," she remembered, leaning forward, to set the mug on the coffee table. She turned to face him, tipping her head to one side. "What's wrong, Michael? And please don't say 'nothing.' I know there's something and now that we have Tyler back … I need to know what it is! I can't keep on this way, lying awake at night, trying to figure it out. You've got to talk to me, Michael! Is it because you didn't want children?"

Michael leaned against the arm of the couch. "I've told you how badly I wanted children. It's no use saying it again."

She inhaled deeply, as though fighting back tears. "Then why did you react that way, when I told you I was pregnant? As though it was the worst news you could ever get."

"Because of the way *you* acted. You sounded miserable and I blamed myself. I should've asked you about birth control before we ever got married. At the very least, I should've had something on hand, on our wedding night."

"Why didn't you then? You're always so efficient … You never forget anything!"

Michael considered that. "Maybe because I *did* want a child. But it seemed too much to ask, after you'd already raised two children."

"Didn't you imagine that I would've brought the subject up, if I *didn't* want to have a baby? Do you think I'm such a moron that I don't know the facts of life?"

"Of course not," he said, offended by the rebuke. He sat back and pressed his fingers near the wound on his shoulder. "I was afraid. I explained that. I was afraid you'd have trouble delivering the baby, because you're so small. I was scared of losing you."

"And that's all?" she said, watching him closely.

He thought about it. His suspicions about the baby's parentage hadn't come until later, so it wouldn't be a lie to deny them. "That's all," he said.

She uncrossed her arms and retrieved her mug, molding her hands around it, as if she were cold. "The whole time I was pregnant, you slipped further and further away. I thought it might be Paula. That you didn't like having her here so often."

"On the contrary," he said honestly. "Paula is welcome anytime."

"Michael," she said, sounding weary beyond measure.

"Something is wrong between us. It didn't go away after I had the twins, so it can't still be that you were afraid I was going to die. Was it because I was the one to propose? Because I pushed you to get married faster than you wanted?"

"Anna, there's nothing," he said. He couldn't meet her eyes, so he reached for his mug and took a few sips of his coffee. He hadn't specifically asked the agents whether they had tested Tyler's DNA, but he felt certain they had. Tyler was definitely his son ... but was Franny his daughter?

No one else could tell the babies apart. They looked like identical twins, even if it was genetically impossible. Didn't that suggest that the babies could not be from two different fathers?

Suddenly he saw how ridiculous it was. Had there ever been any reason to believe the babies weren't his? The whole scenario had existed in his imagination, and had no basis in fact. He took a deep breath, though it made his shoulder ache. He must never tell Anna about his suspicions! Now that his doubts had been exorcised, she would no longer suffer some vague notion that all was not well. If they eventually got Franny back, everything would be perfect.

"I was afraid you'd been raped," he confessed, ignoring his own counsel. He exhaled with relief, though he knew she was going to be angry. "I thought you were in denial. When people suffer a trauma, they sometimes block it from their memory, as if it never took place." He glanced at her and saw that she was stunned. "I thought you were afraid to tell me the truth," he went on bravely. "Some women think of themselves as damaged goods after they've been raped, and they're sure that's how others will see them – especially a spouse, or boyfriend. I wouldn't have, but you didn't know me well enough to feel confident of that." He stopped talking and watched her closely, unable to guess what she was thinking.

Anna got up and walked across the room. She pulled the drapes back and gazed through the window at the open field that stretched between the house and the school. He wondered if she was envisioning the scene that had been described to her so many times – those horrible moments when the babies were taken.

"You thought I had forgotten I was raped," she said, as if she

169

wanted to be sure she had the facts straight. "Like I can't remember what happened when the babies were kidnapped?"

"You can't remember the kidnapping due to physical causes," he explained. "Blocking the rape from your mind would be a psychological defense."

She continued to stare out the window, but he saw that her fingers were clenched into fists. "So … Bruce raped me and almost killed me. Then he stepped back and allowed me to fix my clothes and let Charlie out of his pen?"

Across the room, Charlie's tail began to thump wildly against the floor, but neither Anna nor Michael smiled.

Michael had reasoned his way through the event many times, but now the explanation eluded him. "I assumed Charlie opened the gate on his own, and that he kept Bruce occupied while you restored your clothing."

"So my first priority was fixing my clothes? After being raped and assaulted?"

Michael thought of how modest she was. He did not think she would've run from the Dog House without covering herself.

"Did Russell say he thought I'd been raped?" She sounded as if she were merely curious.

Michael cleared his throat. "Russell didn't realize you were hurt, so it seemed possible that he didn't realize you'd been raped."

"Maybe Russell lied to you. Maybe Bruce and I were having a good time and he spoiled it."

Michael knew she was trying to hurt him, but the remark still stung. "I never thought you willingly had relations with Bruce."

"Well, that's a comfort," she said sarcastically, finally turning to look at him. "What if I hadn't believed you, when you said Jasmine was your brother's wife? Or what if I accused you of having an affair with her anyway?"

"I never thought you were having an affair with Bruce," he repeated patiently.

"How many times a day do you go in your office with some young sexy teacher who's got a big, fat crush on you?" she demanded. "You close the door and then what? What goes on behind that closed door?"

170

"That's not fair," Michael protested. "Should I have cameras installed, so you can watch to see whether I'm faithful?"

"That's not necessary," Anna said, her eyes glittering. "You know why? Because I *trust* you, Michael! I *trust* you! Not because you're trustworthy. Not because I haven't caught you kissing someone in the cafeteria. I trust you because I *decided* to trust you. For all I know, you cheat on me every single day."

"I have *never* cheated on you," Michael said hopelessly. "I haven't even thought about it. And I don't see how those insinuations are meant to convince me you weren't raped."

"I shouldn't *have* to convince you!" she shouted. "I *told* you I wasn't raped – that should be good enough! Why can't you believe me? I've done nothing to deserve this! I haven't even flirted with anyone!"

"That's not what this is about!" he protested, wondering how he could make her understand. "I didn't think you would lie intentionally. I thought it was involuntary. Like the concussion, but psychological instead of physical."

Anna was shaking her head. "No," she said firmly. "This is about trust. It's about those stupid oysters. You decided right then, that first night, that you would never trust me. And no amount of explaining or apologizing has ever made a difference."

"It has nothing to do with that," Michael said, raking his fingers through his hair.

"You have a double standard, Michael. You lie to me all the time!"

"I do not," Michael said, momentarily as angry as she was. "When have I ever lied to you?"

"You lied about Jeanne. I asked if you were married and you said 'no.' "

"I *wasn't* married. My wife had died."

"So had my husband. What if you asked me whether I was married and I just said 'no'? You would have called that a lie."

"It's not the same thing. You have children."

"What difference does that make?" Anna yelled with exasperation. She paced back and forth in front of the coffee table. "You twist and bend the rules to make them fit your behavior. It's okay for you, but not for me. All those months, torturing me, because you made up some stupid story in your head and once it was there, you refused to believe you were wrong. Michael Grant, wrong?" She laughed, though she was obviously far from amused. "Dr. Michael Grant is *never* wrong. Just ask him, he'll tell you. The only sinless man since Jesus Christ!"

"That's not true," Michael said hotly. "I can think of dozens of times when I've admitted I was wrong. I haven't stopped apologizing since the day the twins were kidnapped, because I failed to uncover the truth about the nanny. I understand why you're angry, but ..."

"No, you don't ," she said through clenched teeth. "You don't even *try* to understand. I'd been trying to find a job for months. If I made a good impression, you would be my new boss. I told you I didn't want oysters, but you ordered them anyway. There were no prices on the stupid menu, but even *I* know that oysters are expensive. What was I supposed to do? Spit it out and say, 'I told you so'?"

Michael squirmed. He wished she would stop bringing up the oysters every time they disagreed.

She returned to the window, holding the drapes out of her way with both hands. She was quiet for a long time, but Michael didn't try to speak. He knew he deserved her anger. He only hoped she would calm down and forgive him without asking for a divorce.

Suddenly she spun around and stared at him. "You thought the baby was Bruce's!" she said, her face white with horror. "That's why you were so upset when I told you I was pregnant!"

He wanted to deny it. He hadn't come to that conclusion immediately, after all ... but he knew the discrepancy would make no difference to Anna. "I didn't think it, but I accepted it as a possibility."

"What's the difference?" she cried.

He tried to remain calm. He had to find a way to explain it, so that she would understand. "Even if it were true, it wasn't as if you were deliberately lying. And I eventually convinced myself that it didn't matter anyway. I decided I would love any child of yours as if it were mine. That seemed even more important when Paula told me that twins could be the result of two different fathers. I didn't want to know if only one of them was mine. I was determined to love them equally, as if they were both mine." He hoped his heroics would make some small difference.

"You told Paula?" she said, incredulous.

"No," he said, raising his left hand. "She was talking about genetics, at the hospital. She's fascinated with the subject. We were standing at the nursery window, looking at Tyler. It was idle conversation."

"So you decided one was yours and one was Bruce's? Again, based on absolutely no evidence?" She turned away and swiped at her eyes. "Which was which? Had you decided that too?"

Michael shifted his weight on the couch, wondering if there was anything he could say or do to fix this. He had been wise to keep his thoughts to himself all those months, and stupid to voice them now. He picked up the monitor and listened until he heard Tyler sigh in his sleep. They should be celebrating, not arguing.

"Were you ever going to tell me?" she asked, without turning around.

"I rarely thought about it, once the twins arrived. It popped into my head from time to time, but I generally dismissed it."

"But why?" Anna pleaded. She turned to look at him and her face was ravaged with defeat. "Why would it pop into your head in the first place?"

He could hear the agony in her voice. If she gave in and cried, perhaps he could comfort her and they could mend fences and start over. "I don't know," he admitted. "I taught myself to listen for facts that seem of no consequence, when I'm dealing with the students. Often some little remark gives it all away. I don't know if it was something you said, or something you didn't say."

"I specifically said I had *not* been raped," she reminded him. "More than once! Do you honestly believe I could wave my magic wand and forget I was raped? That's the craziest thing I've ever heard!"

"It's not unusual, Anna. Many women manage to convince themselves it didn't happen."

"Not me!" she said tearfully. "I'm not made that way! You should know me better than that by now!" She let her hands fall to her sides. "Talk about a liar," she said bitterly. "You've been

173

lying to me every minute of every day, all these months. Don't you ever again say one word to me about honesty, Michael. You're the biggest liar I've ever known."

He wanted desperately to explain it, to himself as well as to her. He wished he knew what she had said, or failed to say, that made him suspect she was hiding something. Surely there was a way to justify his suspicions! "I never understood why you wanted to get married so quickly," he said, relieved that he had found some small defense. "Don't get me wrong – I was all for it. You know I was." He waited for her to agree, but she had sunk into a stony silence. "I expected you to say we should date for a year, or at least six months. And when you called your pastor, it was obvious that you had already discussed the possibility of a quick wedding with him."

Anna gasped. "I explained that! I told him about Casey's and he heard it in my voice – that I had fallen in love with you. He predicted we would get married, but since you hadn't offered me a contract, I told him it couldn't happen. He just smiled and bet me an apple pie I'd be married by Christmas. It was a joke!"

"But can't you see how it seemed to me?" Michael pleaded.

"No," she said, shaking her head. "I only saw that you were unhappy because I was pregnant. I thought you didn't want a child. At least not with me. I thought you were afraid I'd neglect you. I thought … I didn't know *what* to think! And when the twins were taken, by the nanny you recommended …"

"She was the only nanny I could find!" Michael reminded her. "I spent hours online, trying to find a reputable nanny who was willing to relocate for a few weeks. We were desperate and the agency did a background check and found nothing. There wasn't one red flag."

"I thought you set it up!" she said, wiping her eyes with the heels of her hands. "In the hospital, when you told me the babies had been kidnapped … I thought you arranged it. You didn't even want one child, let alone two. How else were you going to get rid of them?"

Michael was so horrified by this accusation, he was speechless.

"I only thought it for a minute," she said in a small voice.

174

"You weren't likely to tell them to actually shoot you, just to keep me from catching on."

Michael clenched his hands tightly together. It made his shoulder throb with pain, but he didn't care.

"I tried so hard to guess what I had done," she said hoarsely, "but I could never have guessed anything like this." She laughed, with a sad and hollow sound. "We were so stupid! Like teenagers, with overactive hormones. We obviously don't love one another. It was infatuation or ... I don't know what to call it, but it wasn't love." She crossed the room, then ran up the stairs.

♥ Chapter 18 ♥

Anna tucked the soft blue blanket around Tyler, trying to believe it wasn't a dream, that one of her babies had come home. At first, she couldn't believe they had been taken. Now she couldn't believe Tyler had come home.

Father, help me! she prayed, folding her hands on the railing of the bed. She *did* love Michael! She loved him more than her own life. How could she suspect him of something so terrible? She had tried to write it off to the concussion, but it wasn't much of an excuse. And what of his doubts about her? People who loved each other did not harbor such ugly thoughts! And to be talking about this now, while Franny was still missing …

She tried to blank her mind, so that God could speak through her pain. She tried to listen, but all she heard was her own voice, crying out at the unfairness of it all.

She backed away from the baby, certain her heart must be breaking. Throughout the whole ordeal, she had forced herself to be stoic, to keep her head up, her thoughts positive. She prided herself on being a strong person, able to bear up under any strain … but now she was falling apart. She couldn't allow it! She had to stay strong until Franny came home!

She searched her memory, trying to come up with a quote from Scripture that could help her through this nightmare. She felt so lost and alone, so helpless and afraid. She grabbed a fluffy white diaper from the changing table and pressed it over her face.

All her life, she had struggled to be good, to obey the ten commandments, to put God first in her life. She didn't claim to be perfect – she knew she was a sinner, but she did not deserve this! No mother deserved this …

Perhaps she was paying for Michael's sins … Maybe that was the underlying reason why she had tried to blame him for the kidnapping. And thinking such evil thoughts, about a man she knew to be so good … maybe she *did* deserve to suffer. She backed into the corner and slid down the wall, giving herself permission to cry until she ran out of tears. Over and over, she had told herself – *you still have Michael*. So long as she had Michael, she could survive anything. Michael was her world, as important as breathing. Sometimes *too* important. Nearly as important as God. Why had she confessed that ridiculous notion – that he arranged to have the twins taken! Could she blame it on the concussion? Could an impact to the brain cause delusions?

I'm falling apart, she realized with terror. All those years with Paul, struggling to please a man who could never be satisfied. Raising two children on her own. Working as a secretary and dodging the unwanted attention of men who were interested in only one thing. Trying to stay out of debt, while providing her children with the things they needed … She had forced herself to press on, no matter the circumstances. And she had succeeded. She had remained standing, fighting, surviving … until now.

She leaned her head against the wall and listened to the silence. What a fool she was! She hadn't succeeded at anything! She bit her lip and closed her eyes and apologized to Jesus. *The battle is not yours, but God's.* How many times in her life had she recited that verse? She had remained strong because she knew Who was fighting her battles. God had brought her through every trauma in her past and God would bring her through this. Left to her own devices, she might as well crawl under the bed and will her heart to stop beating.

Be still and know that I am God. She was exactly where God wanted her to be, even if she didn't know why.

♥

Michael sat frozen on the couch, staring blankly across the room. How could Anna have accused him of something so horrific? He may have insulted her, by suspecting that she had been raped, but that was *nothing* compared to this! Because she sensed that something was bothering him, she concluded that he was a criminal? A monster?

He went to the kitchen and refilled his coffee cup. Maybe he would brew another pot and double the grounds, giving himself the dose of caffeine he craved. He had gotten along fine all these years, drinking caffeinated coffee from early morning until late at night. He didn't need Anna's advice about his diet, or anything else.

How could she believe such a thing! That he would arrange to have his own children kidnapped, because he didn't find fatherhood convenient?

Michael carried his coffee to his office and sat down at his desk. He would do what he always did when he needed to escape his thoughts – focus on his job. His briefcase was stuffed with enough paperwork to keep him busy until the sun came up.

But he didn't reach for his briefcase. He sat back in his chair and replayed the argument instead. He had been a fool to confess! After months of carefully guarding his suspicions, he had blurted them out when they were no longer relevant. He saw now that there had never been any real evidence to support his theory. It was true that some women went into denial, but Anna had, in fact, done her best to recollect every detail. And while it had seemed odd that she could act so near normal the next day, that was just the sort of person Anna was – she kept her problems to herself. Since the kidnapping, whenever they left the house, she greeted familiar faces as if nothing was amiss.

What of the video, and the missing five minutes? That had been nonsense too. How much time had he allowed for her to study the promotional booklet? Had Bruce marked the spot, or had she paged through the book until she found the picture? Once she found it, she would not have been satisfied with a quick glance – she would have studied it until she realized it had been taken years before. Had she read the accompanying text? How long did that take? What sort of dialog went on during her perusal

179

of the book? She had suggested that he and Jeanne might have gotten divorced, then listened as Bruce pointed out the fallacy in such a theory. A conversation like that could take place in thirty seconds, or last ten minutes. They had discussed whether to leave the campus. They had fought over Anna's cell phone. How many moments had it taken Bruce to drag her across the table, to choke her with the collar of her own shirt? Not to mention the time he spent nursing his eye …

Even if there was a five minute lull in the tape, Michael knew that Bruce had not raped Anna. He was too much a coward to attempt it on Casey's campus. There had been no witnesses to his attacks on the other women because he first took them to a secluded location. He knew Michael had a relationship with Anna Brown, and that he had instructed the security guards to keep a close eye on him. Bruce was too clever to take that risk.

Michael didn't understand why he had ever believed that Anna was raped. Why had he fabricated such a ridiculous notion and held onto it all these months, sabotaging what might have been the happiest interlude in his life? Throughout her pregnancy, he had held Anna at arm's length, treating her with polite civility. He had known, on some level of his consciousness, that she was bewildered by his behavior. Why had he punished her? He loved Anna! She was the best thing that had ever happened to him. He couldn't imagine living without her yet … *he had done his best to drive her away.*

On impulse, he got up and went to the bookcase to retrieve his Bible. He carried it to his desk and flipped it open, with no clear idea what he hoped to find within its pages. Since the moment the twins had been taken, Anna had been reciting Scripture. Her logic escaped him. Why pay tribute to the same Being who had allowed the tragedy in the first place?

" 'God is our refuge and strength, an ever-present help in trouble. Therefore, we will not fear, though the earth give way and the mountains fall into the heart of the sea …' " Michael read the words aloud, but they brought him no peace. " 'The Lord is a refuge for the oppressed, a stronghold in times of trouble.' " He snorted with disbelief. *What nonsense! The Lord had yet to serve as a refuge for him!* " 'The Lord is my shepherd, I shall not be in want.' "

He sighed and closed his eyes, suddenly aware of his exhaustion. If only he *did* believe! If only he could turn all his troubles over to the Lord and let Him sort them out. *Find Franny*, he would say. *Explain things to Anna and make her forgive me.*

If you want to make God laugh, tell Him your plans, Anna had recited with amusement, the day they strolled the beach. Michael didn't think it was funny, especially now. At Casey's, he laid his plans carefully and followed them to the letter. He kept a close eye on his schedule and budget. He roamed the school, visiting classrooms without warning, listening to random conversations. He did everything he could possibly do to ensure that the school was run safely and efficiently.

But his best efforts were not enough. Things went wrong on a regular basis. Fights broke out, students were injured, teachers broke the rules, security guards failed to pay attention. He micromanaged when he should let go, and ignored situations that begged his attention. He relied on his sixth sense, but it often failed him. He had *ignored* his sixth sense when he hired Bruce Carlisle, a man who enjoyed brutalizing women. He and Anna had *both* failed to heed their sixth sense when it came to Terri White.

His sixth sense ... where did it come from? He knew how Anna would answer that question: It was the Holy Spirit who had warned her to take the children and flee the nanny. It was the Holy Spirit who had alerted Michael to look out the window towards home.

For the first time, he considered what might have happened if he *hadn't* looked out the window. What if he and the security guards hadn't come running, just as the abduction took place? They wouldn't have known that the nanny was involved, or seen the man in the silver Toyota. What might the nanny and her accomplice have done to Anna if no one had been there to interfere? But if the Holy Spirit had alerted him to look out the window in time to save Anna, why hadn't He given warning sooner, so that Michael could've arrived on time to prevent the kidnapping?

Maybe He had. Maybe it was the Holy Spirit who had been

181

whispering in his ear all along, warning him that the nanny was not to be trusted.

When Anna shared her religious beliefs, during their honeymoon, he had found her childlike faith touching, but somewhat ridiculous. Now he envied her those beliefs. What a relief it would be to stop blaming himself for everything that had gone wrong in his life. The next time they were stranded in an airport, he could simply pull the clothes from his suitcase and build a tent. Such thoughts would surely please Anna, but his intellect wouldn't allow him to accept such a credo.

Tyler had been found ... was it due to a miracle, or to adept federal agents who had followed proper investigative procedure? Anna would point out the fact that she had recognized the nanny's picture in the book of potential suspects. There must be hundreds of photo albums filled with the pictures of thousands of perpetrators. What were the chances that she would pick out that photo, even though it looked nothing like Terri White? How had that album come to be on the top of the stack? Would Anna have noticed the picture if it was in the tenth album she looked at? She would give God the credit for all of it.

Finding the nanny hadn't resulted in the return of Tyler, Michael argued silently. The couple had seen the video on YouTube ... But of course, Anna called *that* a miracle too. Would identifying the nanny help the agents find Franny? Maybe, if they followed every lead and interviewed every known associate. Would Anna ignore the hard work of the agents and give God credit for that?

Anna said it was a miracle that the bullet hadn't struck his heart. He attributed it to the fact that the nanny wasn't a good shot. The doctor said Anna had been saved a cracked skull because she wore her hair in a bun. Did that make her choice of hairstyle some kind of miracle?

It didn't bother Anna that her "miracles" could be explained away. She believed because she wanted to believe. He could offer scientific facts to disprove every one of her miracles and she would only stick out her jaw and keep right on believing.

I trust you because I decided to trust you. That's how simple it was for Anna. It had nothing to do with what she knew or even believed. It was strictly a matter of her will. She made her choice and then she stuck to it, regardless of evidence to the contrary.

If only he had done the same! If only he had decided to trust *her*, against all odds. Why was it so easy for her, and so difficult for him? Because her parents had forced her to memorize Scripture? His parents had taken their sons to church, but it had only been a social event. When Michael became overly devout as a teenager, his father had resorted to ridicule, to snap him out of it. But even back then, when Michael kept God first in his life, he had never believed as Anna did. She prayed all the time, about everything. To her, God was like a friend or a neighbor, or even a close family member.

He remembered the trip home from St. Louis after their disastrous first date. *Why do you call yourself a backslidden Christian?* she had asked. He had started attending church on a more regular basis after that, but the truth was – he had only gone to impress Anna. Pastor Franklin was right – he *was* one of those men who only attends church to please his wife. He *did* think about other things during the sermon.

Are you referring to your salvation? Because that's not something you get to "down the road." Christ died for your sins. Period.

The pastor's words came back to him and he understood, with an inexplicable dose of terror, that he could not dodge the question any longer. He either believed or he did not. Either God was the ruler of the Universe, or He was not. Either Jesus had carried the sins of Michael Grant to the cross, or Michael Grant must go on carrying them himself.

He might never find enough factual evidence to convince the scholarly portion of his brain to fully believe, but wasn't it *just* as impossible to prove that none of it was true? Could it be as simple as Anna made it sound? Could he decide to trust God based on nothing more than the heartfelt desire that it *might* be true?

There are people who will only turn to God if their lives fall apart, so He has to let their lives fall apart. Anna's words came back with the force of a blow. His life *was* falling apart. Was the Holy Spirit whispering in Anna's ear, even now, that she must take Tyler and leave Michael for good? How many people must he lose before he finally got the message?

"All right," he gave in. He pressed his hands together, intentionally flexing his muscles so that he would feel pain in his shoulder. "Here I am, for what it's worth. Forgive me my stubborn heart. Make me worthy of Anna's love. And please … *please*! Give me back my little girl." He choked back a sob, then sat quietly for a long time, just listening.

When he reached to close his Bible, he noticed that he had underlined a verse many years before, in his youth. Curious, he drew the Book closer and read through Psalm 128. " 'May you live to see your children's children,' " he read aloud in a whisper. Just then, Tyler began to cry.

Michael smiled. Maybe there was something to this miracle business after all.

♥

When Tyler began to cry at three a.m., Anna lifted her head and groaned. She had fallen asleep with her back wedged in the corner, her neck cocked sharply to one side.

Michael came into the room and leaned over the bed. "Is it all right if I get him?"

"Yes, please. I have a terrible stiff neck. I guess I fell asleep sitting up and … Yes, please," she said again, rubbing her neck with both hands.

He lifted the baby with his left hand, and carried him to the changing table. Anna watched as he changed Tyler's diaper, and eavesdropped as he told his son how happy he was to have him home.

"Where's Franny?" Michael asked Tyler. "If only you could talk …"

"I'll fix a bottle," Anna said tearfully, and hurried from the room.

"I'm not sure he's hungry," Michael said, bringing him into the kitchen a few minutes later. "It's only been three hours."

Anna bristled. "Are you saying not to feed him?"

"No," he said quickly. "Just that he might not eat it all."

She shook the bottle, then tested the warmth of the formula against her wrist.

"If you sit here, on a stool, I'll rub your neck while you feed him," Michael offered.

Anna hesitated. She hated that things were so awkward between them, but she wasn't ready to forgive. "How's your shoulder?" she asked, boosting herself onto the stool before she took the baby. "You haven't been doing the exercises."

He began to massage the muscles in her neck, with both hands. "This ought to be good therapy for it."

Neither of them spoke for a while, and the only sound was Tyler, sucking the formula from the bottle.

"I'm sorry I hurt you," Michael finally said. He continued to rub her neck, with one hand. "I thought I was being heroic, by keeping it to myself. Now I realize that I was being cowardly."

"Cowardly?"

He sat on the stool next to hers and trained his eyes on the baby. "I was afraid of losing you, if I told you what I was thinking. But in a sense, I lost you anyway." He reached over and tucked the blanket around Tyler. "You ate the oysters to try to impress your new boss. I kept secrets, so keep from offending my *new wife*. I did exactly what I asked you not to do – I lied, to try to spare your feelings."

"I've been reading the Bible a lot since …" She didn't have to finish the sentence. "There are a lot of verses that say not to lie for any reason. Not even for the sake of flattering your new boss." She hated to admit he was right, especially now. "If we had both been honest, about the nanny …" She choked up for a moment, then she went on. "Neither of us liked her. Both of us felt there was something wrong. If we had admitted it, maybe she wouldn't have taken the twins." She swallowed hard, to keep from bursting into tears.

Michael weighed his words before he spoke. "It wouldn't have changed anything, Anna. Once she saw the ad and called for the interview, we were on her list of potential victims. If we hadn't hired her, she wouldn't have aborted the plan – just altered it. She might've come in the middle of the night and … it could've ended a whole lot worse."

185

Anna closed her eyes, unwilling to imagine it.

"I just want you to know how sorry I am that I didn't trust you," Michael said. "I was in the wrong, utterly and completely."

Anna wanted to forgive him, for her own sake. How could she maintain her anger against Michael while trying to deal with so many other powerful emotions! It wasn't as if he had accused her of cheating. He hadn't even accused her of lying deliberately. He had only suggested that she was in denial, that she didn't remember being raped. Yet … he had punished her, all those months, for something she didn't do! "It doesn't make sense, what you said," she told him, hearing the icy edge to her voice. "If I didn't remember being raped, why would I want you to hurry and marry me so I could fool you into thinking the baby was yours? I wouldn't have known there *was* a baby."

"You're absolutely right," he agreed. "It doesn't make sense."

It wasn't the answer she had expected. "Even if I did have some subconscious knowledge that I'd been raped, I couldn't have *known* I was pregnant. It was barely twelve hours after Bruce attacked me."

"You couldn't *know*, but you might have suspected, or just realized it was a possibility."

"How could I be in denial as to being raped, and worried I was pregnant at the same time?"

"You make it sound so obvious, but …"

"It *is* obvious!" she insisted.

Tyler's body stiffened and he started to cry. Michael slid off the stool and went to the kitchen. He put the coffee pot under the spigot and began to fill it with water.

"Did you already drink that whole pot?" Anna said with disapproval. "It's three o'clock in the morning! Maybe you wouldn't suffer such crazy ideas if you allowed your body to get a decent night's sleep." She put Tyler on her shoulder and gently patted his back.

Michael put the pot down, but continued to stand at the sink. "You didn't have any idea what I was thinking, about the rape and the pregnancy. So why would you suspect me of orchestrating the kidnapping of my own children?"

Anna tried to decide if her ugly accusation was any worse than

186

his. "I have an excuse," she said defiantly. "My brain was swollen or bruised or … whatever it was. And I'd been sick with worry for months, trying to figure out what I'd done to make you stop loving me." She slid off the stool and carried Tyler to the living room. Perching on the edge of the couch, she put the baby on her shoulder and did her best to burp him. That had always been Michael's job. She fed one, while he burped the other. She felt tears welling in her eyes and tried to wish them away, then to pray them away. Hadn't they both suffered enough without being alienated from one another now?

But words can never be unsaid.

"Will you try to burp him?" she asked in desperation.

He sat beside her and put Tyler on his good shoulder, struggling to raise his right hand.

"I'm sorry," Anna said softly. "I didn't think about how hard it would be."

"It's fine," Michael insisted, using his left hand instead. "It looks as if he's losing some of his hair."

"That's normal," Anna assured him. "I imagine it will grow in dark." She thought about it for a moment. Bruce's hair was a sandy color. Michael's hair was dark, like hers. Had that contributed to his suspicions? "Paula and Andy both had dark hair when they were born, but it turned white while they were toddlers. I guess it started to turn dark again when they were four or five. I think my hair was the same way." She watched him continue to pat the baby's back. "I wonder if you were born with dark hair. Maybe the babies look like you, when you were an infant."

"Any chance we could postpone this conversation until morning?" Michael asked.

"Are you going to tell me you're too tired to talk, after drinking a whole pot of coffee?"

"That pot holds the equivalent of two mugs," he said wearily.

"If we put it off, we won't talk about it at all," Anna said, choking on her tears. "One of us will pack up and leave and we'll never sort it out."

Michael carefully lowered Tyler from his shoulder and handed him to her. "If anybody's leaving, it will have to be you. I will never leave you, unless you make me. There is nothing you could ever do that would make me stop wanting to be with you."

She bowed her head over the baby and tried to cry without making a sound. "Maybe you won't pack your things and go live somewhere else, but that won't mean you haven't left me."

Michael poked his finger into Tyler's hand, and the baby held on tight. "Would you like me to rub your neck some more?"

Anna knew she would dissolve into a frenzy of tears if he touched her. "He's fallen asleep," she said. "I don't think he was hungry."

"Do you want me to carry him upstairs?" Michael offered.

"I've got him," Anna said, rising and moving slowly across the living room. She glanced back and saw that he had misunderstood. "You could come and help me tuck him in," she suggested.

Michael followed her up the steps, and leaned over the bed as she laid Tyler down. "It's still not real to me," he whispered.

"That we had him, or that we have him back?"

"Both." He backed away, rubbing the muscles in his bad arm. "I'm going to take a shower. Will we ... sleep in the same room?"

Anna gazed across the sleeping baby. In the dim light, she could just see Michael's eyes, filled with fear and sadness and hope. "Of course," she said.

♥ Chapter 19 ♥

Anna sat at the kitchen table, her chin resting on her forearms while she studied a stack of flyers. There was a picture of Tyler, taken the day he turned six months old, with all the information about his missing twin. She heard Michael come into the room, heard him retrieve a mug from the cabinet and pour coffee. She didn't look up until he sat down across from her. "They aren't identical twins," she pointed out. "She may not look like Tyler anymore."

"It's our best guess," Michael said. "Remember how no one could tell them apart when they were born?"

"No one but you." She smiled, remembering how devoted he was to both infants, in spite of his doubts that either of them were actually his. "All newborns look alike."

Michael chuckled. "I'm not sure that statement is politically correct." He stood up and pulled the toaster from a cabinet. "Want some?"

"No thanks. I had cereal."

He retrieved the bread and busied himself making toast. "Don't you think it's better than letting the computer come up with an image?"

"I guess," Anna sighed. "But if these flyers are so effective, why hasn't anyone recognized Tyler and questioned us about whether he's really ours?"

"Almost anywhere we go, people recognize us," Michael said

patiently. "Even if they don't know who we are, they're used to seeing us with Tyler."

"Wouldn't the same thing be true of whoever has Franny? They've been seeing them with her for the past six months, so nobody's going to question them either. The date is right here." She lifted the flyer and indicated the information with the tip of her finger. "If it was effective, someone would stop us and ask us to prove that Tyler is rightfully ours."

"That's a valid point," Michael allowed, "but most people don't pay that much attention."

Most people didn't look at the flyers at all. Anna sometimes stood near the bulletin board at Wal Mart, and watched as people passed by without even giving it a glance.

"Do you think they know that she was a black market baby?" Anna asked. "They must know that we're out there somewhere, wondering if she's still alive. Are there really people who have no conscience? No sense of right and wrong?"

"Yes," Michael said gravely. "Lots of people."

"The kind of people who would want a baby?"

"Evil comes in many guises, Anna. It's probably a couple who appears just as you and I do. Not all sicknesses have visible symptoms. You know that."

"Yes, I do know that," she repeated dismally. "I wanted to do the flyers but ... I thought people would stop us. I've even been carrying a copy of their birth certificates in my purse! I'm sorry," she said with a sigh. "Just because I'm down, that's no reason to drag you down."

Michael buttered his toast, then carried it to the table. "Sometimes I lay awake at night and go over the facts," he confessed. "I'm convinced I missed something that could miraculously lead us straight to Franny. But there isn't anything. Or if there is, I can't find it, and neither can the law enforcement agents who are trained to do just that."

"Why won't Terri White tell who her accomplice was?" Anna wondered, hearing the sound of desperation in her voice. "Why would she sit in prison and let him go free?"

"She's not likely to get out, whether or not she tells," Michael said realistically.

"Steven said they might lighten her sentence. Do you think she's in love with that man? You know, willing to sacrifice herself for him?"

"I don't know." Michael popped the last bite of toast into his mouth and carried his plate to the sink.

Anna knew he didn't like to theorize about what went on in the so-called nanny's head. "I'm going to save a flyer, for Franny's scrap book," she said. "I want her to know how hard we tried to find her. That we didn't give up. I think it will make her feel good, don't you?"

"She'll know how hard we tried to find her without any tangible evidence because once we get her back, we'll tell her, a hundred times a day."

"A *thousand* times a day," Anna corrected him.

"A *million* times day," he corrected her.

Michael wasn't aware that Anna had overheard the hushed conversation between him and the agents, the last time they dropped by with an update. Anna had gone to get Tyler, but paused just outside Michael's office.

"I can't understand why she won't give you the man's name, to save herself," Michael said. A brief silence followed, and then his voice turned hollow. "You think Franny's dead. You figure that's why she won't talk."

"We don't think any such thing," Steven Breen said quickly. "But if Terri White has reason to think it … the charge would change from kidnapping to murder."

Anna had leaned against the wall, clutching Tyler, praying that God would help her forget what she'd just heard. There was another explanation for Terri White's refusal to implicate her partner, and Anna was determined to figure out what it was. Maybe the accomplice had threatened to have her killed? Maybe he was her brother?

"Meanwhile," Michael said, drawing her back to the present. "We do the best we can." He pointed to the stack of flyers. "And we pray."

"Whenever two or more of you," Anna said hopefully.

"There are *hundreds* of people praying that Franny will come home." He returned to the table, but didn't sit down. "I'm

191

surprised you got up so early. Didn't I hear you on the phone with Paula at two a.m.?"

"Paula had never been able to sleep when she's excited. She'd lay awake every Christmas Eve, then fall asleep under the tree the next morning."

"I thought her sorority sisters were spending the night at the house."

"They were. But she wanted to reminisce and she needed either me or Andy for that."

"And she knew better than to wake Andy in the middle of the night," Michael guessed. "Since you're up anyway, should we start getting ready? There's bound to be plenty of last minute details and Paula will need your help."

"She wants to examine your tux, to be sure it matches the others. I don't know what she'll do about it if it doesn't." Anna sighed. "I kept hoping she would change her mind and go with a small wedding."

"Too late now," Michael said, glancing at his watch. "Less than thirty hours to go. Are you suffering Mother of Bridezilla jitters?" he teased, gently massaging her shoulders.

"Maybe that's it," Anna said, tipping her head to gaze up at him. "Whatever I'm suffering, you always have the magic touch."

"Do I?" he asked. Suddenly, he lifted her from the chair and kissed her. "I can't recall whether I ever got around to carrying you over the threshold … Did I?"

"Yes you did," she remembered with a giggle. "When we came back from Hawaii."

"I probably ought to do it again, in case Lucas asks for pointers." He headed slowly toward their bedroom.

"Weren't you the one nagging me to get ready?" Anna teased, twining her arms around his neck.

"If we're late, I'll blame you for being irresistible," he said, silencing her rebuttal with a kiss.

♥

Parents of Abducted Children had called Michael when Franny was missing a year, asking whether he and Anna were

192

interested in visiting parents who had recently lost a child through mysterious circumstances. He had refused, without asking Anna, but a few months later, they agreed to try it. Much to their surprise, the process was a healing one.

"Some good news, some bad news," Michael said, glancing at Anna as he navigated the country roads.

"Three children under the age of three?" Anna said. "I'm not sure that's good news for Beth. It definitely made it much harder for Paula - finding out Beth is pregnant the day she has a second miscarriage." She remembered when Marianne called to say she was expecting a little girl. Anna hoped her friend couldn't tell that her congratulations were less effusive than they should have been.

"She'll get pregnant again," Michael said.

"Having another baby won't make up for the two she lost."

"I'm sure you're right," Michael agreed. He cleared his throat. "Maybe this isn't the best conversation to have when we're on the way to encourage someone whose child has been abducted." They had been visiting couples for several months and knew it was imperative to arrive in a positive frame of mind. Michael reached for Anna's hand. "Guess who called me today."

Anna forced a smile. "Umm ... the president?"

"Susie called. She said to be sure and tell you hello."

"How is she?" Anna asked with interest. She closed her eyes and saw the pretty blond, standing in a shower stall in a beautiful white nightgown, holding a razor blade to her wrist.

"She's teaching fifth grade at a school near her sister's house, and she recently got engaged. She sounded confident and happy."

"I'm glad," Anna said. "Did she ask to come back to Casey's?"

"There was no mention of it. I think the call was for closure."

"I still have her name on my prayer list," Anna said. "I think I'll wait a few more months to cross it off."

"She said she still has Franny on *her* prayer list," Michael said.

Anna turned her head and smiled at her reflection in the window. She loved to hear that people were praying for Franny. "No matter how many times we do this, I feel nervous and uncertain about what to say."

"So do I," Michael admitted.

Michael passed a narrow driveway, then backed up and turned between two large trees. "We're really out in the boondocks," he observed.

Anna sat forward and peered through the windshield. Had someone crept through the woods and snatched the child from their yard? The center hadn't shared details of the abduction.

"How's Paula doing?" Michael asked. "Should we schedule a trip to St. Louis?"

"She's doing terrible, but I'm not sure our presence would help."

"I wonder if they'll consider adoption."

Anna cringed. She had an unnatural dislike for the very word now, because it was the motive for the crime that had stolen her children. "I didn't suggest it. I just listened."

"I think that's where we should start with this couple," Michael said. "Just listen."

"Can we say a prayer before we go in?" Anna asked.

"Good idea," Michael said. He shut off the engine and reached for her hands, folding them inside his own. "Lord, please be with us today and show us how best to offer this couple comfort and hope which can only ever come from one source – Your love."

"Amen," Anna said with emotion. She hopped out of the van and followed Michael to the door, gripping his hand when a young couple answered together.

The man led the way into the kitchen, and offered them tea or coffee. Anna and Michael both declined.

"How long has your little girl been missing?" the woman asked, as soon as they were all seated around the table.

"Eighteen months." Anna felt her throat constrict and paused to take a deep breath. She wasn't going to be of much help if she started crying. "One thing that helps me is to read stories about abducted children who have been recovered."

The woman shifted her gaze to Michael. "You had two children, we only had one. You got your son back. Even if you never get your little girl back, at least you've still got one child."

"It doesn't work that way," Michael said. "If we had a dozen other children, it wouldn't make up for the loss of Franny." He glanced at Anna.

194

"Don't you realize that every day she's missing, there's less chance she'll be found alive?" the woman demanded tearfully.

"We don't choose to believe those statistics," Michael said. "Abducted children are found everyday. Why shouldn't our daughter be one of them?"

"I can't do it!" the woman said bitterly. "I can't keep getting my hopes up."

"Here's my problem," the man said, resting his forearms on the table. "I need to feel like I'm doing something, but there's nothing I can do."

"Men are made that way," Michael said with understanding. "We have to try to fix what's broken, but sometimes it's out of our hands. Even so, every day I do one thing to help bring Franny home. I post an age progression picture on Facebook, or I visit a thread where people report possible sightings of abducted children. There are plenty of little things you can do."

"One thing each day," the man said, reaching to squeeze his wife's shoulder. "I like that idea."

"You go on and do your one thing!" she cried, pushing her chair away from the table. "I can't! I have to face the truth – our baby is dead!" She ran from the room, and a moment later, a door slammed.

"I'm sorry," the man said. "Women take it harder, I guess."

"That's a myth," Michael disagreed. "Men aren't usually willing to show their emotions, but that doesn't mean they don't suffer as much as women do."

The man raised his hand to his face, forming an awning over his eyes.

"Your wife could be right," Michael admitted. "Maybe the next time I see my daughter, she'll be shrouded in the bright lights of Heaven. But I choose not to believe that. I choose to believe that she's alive and she's out there somewhere, waiting for me to find her. I choose to believe that God is watching over Franny and keeping her safe. And one day, He's going to give her back to me. You can choose to believe that too, if you want to."

Anna stared at him with surprise. She had never heard Michael talk that way before.

"People will do their best to discourage you," Michael went

on, "but you don't have to listen to their negative remarks. You can choose to have faith, to believe there's a miracle with your little girl's name on it."

"Thanks," the man said, brushing at his eyes. He stood and shook Michael's hand. "I don't think anyone can help my wife right now, but you've both been a great help to me." He ushered them to the door and closed it softly behind them.

Michael and Anna were both quiet as he backed the van from the driveway and drove slowly along the gravel road.

"I don't want to do this again," Michael said. "It didn't help them and it hurt us."

"Not me," Anna said, digging in her purse for a tissue. "I loved what you said! Especially the part about it being a choice. You're right. I don't have to listen to the people who tell me it's time to move on. I can keep on believing that Franny's alive and that someday, she's going to come back to us." She blew her nose, then turned so that she could see Michael's profile. "You've never said those things to me. About it being a choice."

"You're the one who taught it to me," Michael said. "The night Tyler came home."

Anna made a face. "I don't want to talk about that," she said firmly.

Michael had tried to discuss it with her countless times, and she always reacted the same way. Maybe this was a perfect opportunity, since she was held captive in the van. "I made a wrong choice, Anna, when I failed to trust you. I've admitted that dozens of times. Now the choice is yours – whether or not to forgive me."

"I *have* forgiven you," she said quickly. "I just haven't forgotten."

"I haven't forgotten what you said about me either," he reminded her. "I'm sure I never will."

"I believed that for *one minute*," she protested. "You believed those horrible things about me for almost a year!"

"I'm sorry, Anna. I'm sorry I doubted you. I think I could explain it now, if you'd give me a chance." He glanced at her and saw the set of her jaw, but decided to press on. "Think about how much my life had changed, in such a short time! One minute, I

196

was standing at my window, gazing over at the women's dormitory, wondering whether you'd go out with me. The next minute, you were telling me you loved me and wanted to marry me. A week later, we were on our way to Hawaii! Then, before I had half a chance to adjust to *that*, before *either* of us did ... you were pregnant."

"I did everything wrong!" Anna said tearfully. "I should not have been the one to propose! And then I pushed you to get married in a week!"

"You didn't *push* me," he said. "If I had thought it was possible, I would've wanted to get married that very day."

Anna slumped down in her seat, convincing Michael that she still wasn't ready to let it go.

"I know you felt bad about what you did, when you married Paul to avoid caring for your parents and sister," he said, "but that's not the same thing as blaming yourself for the loss of someone's life. I prided myself on being so smart about human nature, yet I refused to consider what I was asking Jeanne to do. No former prisoner would want to live on the site of their prison! I had been offered my dream job and I wasn't willing to let it slip through my fingers for any reason. I was going to start a new career as the head of a prestigious school! And my father couldn't prevent it, because his firm depended on John Casey's business to survive. Suddenly, overnight, I could implement all those social programs I had dreamt up. I was going to make a difference in the world!" He snorted with disgust. "I made a difference all right! As a result of my unconscionable ambition, Jeanne died! Her life ended! And it was *my* fault!"

"It was *not* your fault," Anna said. "But it's no use telling you that, because you refuse to believe it."

"Maybe you're right," Michael said. "Maybe Jeanne would've killed herself anyway. But she warned me, *that day*, and I ignored her. If I had come home at a reasonable hour, I could have saved her life – that much is a fact. I deserved to suffer for that and I chose my penance – I would never fall in love, never marry, never have children. I had taken her future, so I didn't deserve one of my own."

"That was a stiff penalty even if you *were* responsible," Anna said softly.

Michael saw no point in debating that now. "I eventually grew fond of my martyrdom," he continued. "I began to see myself as nearly saint-like, sacrificing my happiness in some crazy attempt to restore hers. I took pride in my willingness to suffer." He drew a deep breath, unwilling to look over and see her expression. "And then I met you. The only woman who ever managed to slip past my resolve. I fell in love with you, in a heartbeat, and much to my amazement, *you loved me back.* You even wanted to marry me, in spite of what I'd done to Jeanne. And while I was still trying to digest that, you tell me you're expecting my child. It wasn't right, don't you see?" he pleaded earnestly. "I wasn't supposed to have *anything* good in my life. I was meant to suffer, for what I did to Jeanne."

Anna turned to look at him, just as he glanced at her. There was something new in her expression, but he wouldn't allow himself to believe she understood. "I didn't deserve *you*, Anna, let alone a baby. I was delirious with happiness, but I knew it wasn't meant to be mine. And so I found a way to sabotage it."

"By convincing yourself that the babies weren't yours?"

"Yes," he said, with a sag of relief. It was enough to hope that she would understand, even if she couldn't forgive him.

Anna said no more. When they arrived home, she slid out of the van and hurried into the house without a word. Marianne had come to stay with Tyler, and Michael suspected that she and Anna would sit and talk for hours. Marianne and Thomas Hardy had married and were expecting their first child – a girl.

Michael pulled the van into the garage and turned off the engine. He didn't want to go into the house and be polite to Marianne. He didn't know why she disliked him, but she made less and less effort to hide it. Perhaps it was the result of listening to Anna describe his dark heart.

He heard the front door slam and looked in the rear view mirror as Marianne bustled across the driveway. She got into her car and gunned the engine, then backed from the driveway with a squeal of tires. Michael watched until her taillights disappeared down the winding road that led to the state highway.

"Michael?" Anna called, from the door that led into the house.

He pushed the button to close the garage door and followed Anna inside. She went to the kitchen, and began fixing a pot of decaf.

"Marianne said he asked for you the whole time," she relayed cheerfully. "Papa, Papa, Papa. She tried to get him to say Mama, but he wouldn't. I'm afraid I'm going to have to impose a fine."

Michael wasn't in the mood for playful banter. He thought he might close himself in his home office for a few hours. "Have you checked on him?"

"I went right up. He's fast asleep."

"There are a few things I need to get done," he said, heading across the living room.

"Whatever it is, it will have to wait," Anna said. She turned on the coffee pot and approached him with a smile. "At the moment, your wife needs attention and she refuses to be ignored." She slipped her arms around his waist and rested her cheek on his chest.

He hesitated no more than a few seconds before he pulled her close.

"I'm sorry," she said. "I don't normally hold a grudge against anyone, let alone my husband. I just couldn't understand how you could say you loved me, then treat me like … I don't know what. But now I do."

He wasn't sure what she meant.

"It wasn't about me and Bruce," Anna said, leaning back to look up at him. "It was about you and Jeanne. It was about you still not getting what grace is all about. You couldn't allow yourself to be happy. You thought you were supposed to pay penance for your sins forever. It had nothing to do with me."

"No, it didn't," he agreed. "That's what I was trying to say."

"You would've reacted the same way to any kind of good news."

"I'm sure that's true."

"You didn't understand it yourself, did you?"

"No," Michael said. "Not until recently." He bent down and kissed her, and she kissed him back. It felt like the first time they had really kissed in months.

"You can choose to let it go now," Anna said firmly. "If you want to."

"I *do* want to," Michael said. "But it's been part of me for so long …"

"That doesn't mean you can't let it go," she said sternly, tapping her fingertip against his chest.

"I can try."

"Don't say it like that. Say it like you mean it."

"I can try to let it go," Michael said, making his voice strong.

"You're allowed to be happy."

He tried to kiss her, but she held him away. "Say it!" she commanded. "Say, 'I am allowed to be happy now.' "

"I am allowed to be happy now," he said obediently, wearing the ghost of a smile.

"Neither of us can be truly joyful," she sighed. "Not until Franny comes home. But we can find moments of happiness. For Tyler's sake."

"For *all* our sakes," Michael said. "Even Franny's. She won't want to come home to crabby parents, will she?"

"No," Anna agreed. Suddenly she giggled. "Marianne thought I'd lost my mind. She was all ready to sit and talk for two hours."

"How did you get her to leave?" Michael asked curiously.

"I said you and I were in the middle of a big fight and needed to finish it." Anna tipped her head to one side and met his eyes.

Michael wanted to rebuke her, for sharing their personal business, especially with someone who worked at Casey's. Then he understood what that look meant. "You wouldn't do that," he said. "You know that I'm a very private person and you wouldn't ever share our personal business with Marianne. Or with anyone else. Even Paula."

"That's right," Anna said, beaming at him.

Michael understood that he had passed some kind of test. And in a way, Anna had passed some kind of test too.

"You don't really want coffee, do you?" she whispered, tickling her fingers up his back.

"No," he said. "Coffee is the last thing on my mind."

♥ Chapter 20 ♥

"Do you remember when you asked me whether you could visit the students in their dormitories?" Michael asked one morning.

Anna was scrubbing the frying pan, so she didn't turn around. "I asked you that?" she said with confusion. It sounded like something she might have wanted to do, but she didn't remember asking.

"You had just started at Casey's, and I took you on a tour of the campus. I told you I didn't allow anyone to visit the student dorms unless they had specific business there. For some unknown reason, you didn't argue with me about it."

"Ha ha," Anna said in a dry tone, though she was smiling.

"I changed my mind," Michael went on. "I think it's an excellent idea."

Anna glanced over her shoulder. "How come you suddenly changed your mind?" she asked suspiciously.

"There's no conflict, since you no longer work at Casey's. And I've seen how good you are with kids. They might confide in you, about things they wouldn't consider telling anyone else."

Anna opened the dishwasher and began loading the plates and mugs. "Did you check on Tyler?" she asked.

"I did, just as I always do, before I head over to school. He's sound asleep." Michael pointed at the small screen that displayed a video of the three-year-old's bed. "Anna, it's not good for Tyler, or for you. You need to have a life outside the house."

Anna was surprised by this sudden declaration. "You've been talking to Lucas," she accused him. "I *hate* having a psychiatrist in the family!"

"I don't need to hear it from Lucas," Michael persisted. "I know it's true and so do you."

Anna crossed her arms in a sulk. "I am *not* smothering Tyler. I take him to tumbling classes and swim lessons and he has lots of play dates. And while he's there, I visit with other moms and we discuss adult topics."

"Tyler needs to experience life apart from you," Michael said patiently. "Lately, he doesn't even want to go to the restroom with me when we're out. He acts as if he's afraid to leave you."

"Tyler is three," Anna reminded him. "That's normal behavior for a three-year-old."

"Since when do you and I gauge Tyler's progress according to what's normal? Do we want him to be frightened, every time you're out of sight?" He waited a moment, but Anna didn't answer. "Just consider it," he said. "It would be good for him, good for you, and good for me."

"How would it be good for you?" Anna asked doubtfully.

"You could bring him over to the school and he and I could 'hang together', as the kids put it. And it will give me an ear as to how the students are feeling."

Anna laughed. "You really think those kids are going to talk to me, knowing I'm going home to cook dinner for you?"

Michael went to the dining room and put on his suit coat. "It's your decision, of course." He came and kissed her, then went out the door.

Anna finished the dishes, then stood drying her hands on a dish towel, watching the video screen. She leaned over and peered at it more closely. She couldn't tell whether Tyler's chest was rising and falling. *What if he had stopped breathing?*

She raced around the counter and up the stairs, but as she stepped into Tyler's room, he turned his head and mumbled something indiscernible.

Embarrassed, Anna backed into the hallway. "Am I smothering him?" she asked, looking up, as if she could see through the ceiling and the roof. She clenched her hands and tried to view the situation with unbiased eyes. It was true that she was overly protective, but only because Tyler had become more adventurous. When she trusted him to anyone else's care, she felt she had to warn them about his habits. He loved to hide and make her peer behind the couch and recliner, loudly asking Charlie: *Where is Tyler?* When she "found" him, Tyler would shriek with laughter and try to run away. What if Marianne was watching him and he hid from her and she didn't know all his hiding places? What if she assumed he was hiding and he wasn't? What if someone didn't latch the door tight and he slipped outside to find a hiding place? There were so many "what ifs."

No, she decided. Michael was wrong, and so was Lucas and anybody else who said she wasn't a good mother. It was her job to keep Tyler safe and that's what she was doing. Nobody else would ever watch over him as carefully as she did. Not even Michael.

She thought about it all morning. She waited for Michael to mention it again, when he came home for lunch, but he didn't say a word. After Tyler's nap, she changed clothes and put him in his stroller. She called the security guard's shack and asked them to watch for her, then headed for the school.

"Anna!" Tina said with obvious delight, as soon as she entered the office. "And who is this handsome man?"

"Give Tina five," Anna instructed, as she lifted Tyler from the stroller and set him on his feet. To her dismay, he stepped behind her and hid his face. "Sorry," she said. "He's going through a stage."

Tina patted her extended belly. "I am so looking forward to those stages," she said happily. "Did you need to see Dr. Grant?"

"Is he busy?"

"Is he ever *not* busy?" Tina countered. "Should I buzz him, or would you rather surprise him? He's alone and he's not on the landline." She gestured at the dark buttons on her phone.

"Surprise him," Anna decided. She reached behind her and drew Tyler to her side. "You want to surprise Papa?" she tried to entice him.

He hid his face behind one hand, peeking through his fingers at Tina.

Anna went to the door and turned the knob, then ushered Tyler into Michael's office. She closed the door quietly behind her, and tiptoed towards her husband with exaggerated steps. Tyler copied every move.

"Boo!" Michael said, spinning his chair around at the last minute.

Tyler was so startled, his mouth hung open, then his lip began to quiver. By then, Michael had hoisted him onto his shoulder. "Mama's short," he told him.

"Mama short," Tyler agreed, peering down at Anna.

"Rules," Michael said. "Don't promise them anything until you've discussed it with me."

"I didn't say I was going to the dorms," Anna objected.

Michael just smiled.

♥

Before long, Anna was going to the dormitories five days a week. While some of the students ignored her, others seemed to look forward to her visits. Much to her surprise, many of the kids confided in her, asking her not to tell Dr. Grant what they said. Michael proved that he had learned to trust her – he said she should only break their confidence if she felt he needed to know.

When Tristan arrived at Casey's, she immediately began following Anna around the lounge. Sensing that she wanted to speak privately, Anna invited her to a secluded corner for a chat. Tristan hadn't told anyone she was pregnant, for fear her parents would force her to have an abortion. She was fifteen.

School policy did not condone abortion and would not arrange for one. If Tristan wanted to carry the baby full term though, they would help with adoption proceedings.

When Michael contacted Tristan's parents and explained the options, they decided to have her moved to a different facility, where an abortion could be performed.

Tristan begged Anna to intercede. Could she go before a judge and beg for the right to choose her baby's fate?

Michael prepared to contact her parents again, arming himself with statistics about women who spent a lifetime regretting the decision to abort – many eventually committed suicide.

"What if you could tell her parents we already have a couple that wants to adopt the baby?" Anna suggested. She was tucking the last few items into a suitcase, while Michael leaned against the dresser and watched.

"Are you thinking of Paula and Lucas?"

Paula had recently suffered a third miscarriage, and often bemoaned the abortions that were performed in America on a daily basis.

"I could tell her about Tristan and see if she suggests it herself," Anna said.

"Without mentioning names, or making promises," Michael stipulated.

"Should I do it before we go or after we get back?" She clutched her elbows in her hands.

Michael knew she was nervous about leaving Tyler, even though Paula and Lucas were extremely conscientious. He carried her suitcase to the back door, turned on the outside light, then spoke in a quiet voice. "It's only for two nights, and we're not going far. It'll be good for Tyler, and good for us. And it might be good for Paula and Lucas. As to when to tell her … I think it would be best to wait until we get back. Otherwise, she'll be thinking about that all weekend, when we want her focused on Tyler."

Anna went to the living room, where Tyler was building a castle with a massive set of interlocking blocks. "Are you gonna have fun with Paula and Lucas?" she asked him.

"You already asked me that," he said, without turning his head.

"I forgot the answer," Anna prodded.

"Yes," Tyler said. "I'll show Lucas my bug collection and read to Paula."

"*All* your books?" Michael said, perching on the coffee table.

"Most of them," Tyler said. "When are you going?"

"You in a hurry to get rid of us?" Michael teased.

"Not until Paula comes," Tyler said sternly.

"There they are," Anna said, as headlights danced across the ceiling. She hurried to the back door, grabbing Charlie's collar on the way.

"Sorry we're late," Lucas said, carrying two suitcases through the door. "Traffic was terrible on that stretch outside of Columbia." He paused to pet Charlie and was rewarded with a sloppy swipe of his tongue. "Where's the guy?"

"Here he is!" Tyler called from the living room.

Lucas hurried to greet him, while Anna stuck her head out the door, looking for Paula.

"I'm coming!" Paula called, stepping away from the trunk and slamming the lid. "I brought photo albums. Tyler asked me to."

"Photos of what?" Anna said with surprise.

"Me and Andy, when we were little." Paula came in and gave her mother a hug, then shrugged out of her coat and hung it on the back of a dining room chair. "I think he wants to look at pictures of me so he can guess what Franny might look like," she whispered. "Where is he?"

"We're in here, building a fort," Lucas called out.

"It's a castle," Tyler corrected him.

"Are you sure he's only four?" Paula laughed. "Okay, tell me what I need to know so you can leave. Did you make a list? Stupid question."

Anna pointed to the bulletin board. "It's got all the phone numbers and places we're going. We tried to think of everything, but I'm sure there's something we forgot."

"You'll have your cell phones," Paula said without concern.

"If the center calls, ask whether it's about Franny," Anna said. "If it's someone who needs help, explain that we're out of town. But if it's about Franny ..."

"I'll call you right away," Paula promised.

"Did you bring the pictures?" Tyler called.

"Yes I did," Paula laughed. "Go tell him good-bye and scoot," she ordered.

Anna hurried to the living room and stooped beside Tyler. "Can you take a ten second break and give me a hug?"

Tyler sighed with obvious annoyance. He stood up and hugged Anna, then Michael. Then he sat down beside Lucas and resumed his project.

♥

"I'm glad you had fun," Paula said, stretching out on Anna and Michael's bed. "We did too. Tyler is a riot."

"A riot?" Anna repeated.

"He's hilarious! It took us awhile to realize he was trying to be funny. Like when Lucas asked whether ice cream would help him feel better, he said, 'You're a doctor! *You* should know what makes me feel better.'"

"Why did he need something to make him feel better?"

"Mother!" Paula said indignantly.

"Sorry!" Anna said, holding up both hands.

"So? What did you want to talk about?" Paula asked. "Lucas is dying of curiosity."

"I wanted to give you first chance to say 'no,' " Anna said. "If you aren't interested, just say so and the conversation is over."

"Go ahead," Paula said, crossing her arms.

"You know how I said I've been visiting the dorms, to chat with the students? Michael thought they might confide in me."

"The way all our friends used to do," Paula remembered.

Anna liked being reminded of that. "Anyway, one of the students is pregnant and she wants to give the baby up for adoption. She asked if I would help her find a good family."

Paula tipped her head back and stared at the ceiling. "Lucas and I talked all night last night. Spending time with Tyler with no one else around … it was a chance to see how we'd do as parents."

Anna waited, uncertain whether that was meant to be an answer.

"We decided to adopt," Paula said, lowering her chin. "Is this one of those 'God winks' you're always talking about?"

Anna sighed with relief. "Michael said I should warn you that it might not work out, so you don't get your hopes up. Her parents want her to have an abortion."

"When could we meet her? Could we meet her before we go home tomorrow?"

"Are you ready to include Michael and Lucas in the conversation?"

In answer, Paula jumped up and hurried to the living room. "My mom might've found us a baby," she told her husband, flopping down beside him on the couch. "How's that for fast results to prayer?"

Lucas gazed at Anna with appreciative eyes. "Under a cabbage leaf in the back yard?"

"Something like that," Michael said with good humor, making room for Anna in his oversized recliner. "One of the students. I can't give you her name because the young lady is not eighteen. Her parents want her to have an abortion, but she's pro-life. I've been collecting information about the after-effects of abortion on teens, in the hope that her parents can be persuaded to cooperate. They're coming in the morning, because we all know that an abortion needs to be performed as soon as possible, if that's where this will end."

"Are you going to tell them about us?" Lucas asked.

"Providing a solution that's complete with every detail is often a deciding factor," Michael said in answer.

"You mean this has happened before?" Paula said with horror. She slumped back on the couch. "I want a baby so bad and here you are, arranging abortions."

"I don't arrange abortions," Michael protested. "When they opt for abortion, I remove myself from the situation immediately."

"So does this mean we can or can't see the girl tomorrow?" Paula wanted to know.

"It means you'll have to hang around until her parents have come and gone, before I can give you an answer."

"I say we hang around," Lucas said, reaching for Paula's hand. "But you make the final decision, babe."

♥ Chapter 21 ♥

"Paula's here!" Anna called to Andy. She was bent over the oven, basting one of the turkeys.

"Keep an eye on your brother," Andy told Melissa, his oldest daughter. "I'll be right back. I'm gonna help Auntie Paula carry her stuff in."

"Did she bring her babies?" Melissa asked, jumping up and down.

"I'll bet she did," Andy laughed.

"I wonder if we could ask him to wake Beth," Anna whispered to Michael, closing the oven door as Melissa came running into the kitchen. "It's too hard, trying to cook and watch all the kids. Now that Paula's two are walking ..."

"I'll ask Andy as soon as he comes in," Michael promised. "Too bad Nan's not here. She was a tremendous help with the little ones last year."

"I'm sure she's sitting on the floor playing with my sister's grandkids, even as we speak," Anna said wistfully.

"Hey!" Paula said, smiling at her mother. "Happy Turkey Day!"

"Same to you," Anna said, kissing her cheek.

"Oh yeah," Paula said. "I've got an early Christmas gift too." She grabbed the two sides of her coat and pulled it open. "Ta da!" she sang happily. "Twins!"

Anna quickly threw her arms around Paula's shoulders. "That's the best Christmas gift a grandma can get!" she chortled.

"Can you believe it?" said Tristan, the teenager who continued to live with Paula and Lucas, though her baby had been born more than a year ago. "It's like the minute she found out she was gonna adopt my kid, she turned into a baby making machine." Paula had delivered her first baby three months after Tristan gave birth to a little girl.

"Six females," Lucas said, carrying a stack of pie carriers into the kitchen. "I am so outnumbered."

"Seven," Tristan corrected him. "I got a dog! I wanted to bring her, but Paula said Charlie might not appreciate dealing with a puppy."

"Daddy! Daddy!" Melissa called, running to Andy as he returned from waking Beth. "Come and see what Grandma did!"

"Mama didn't do it," Tyler said, following Melissa to the dining room. "It was my idea."

"What was your idea?" Andy asked, stooping to Tyler's level.

"I set a place at the table for Franny," Tyler explained. "In case she comes home for Thanksgiving."

"Good idea," Andy said, though his smile faded.

"I don't believe him," Melissa pouted. "I think he made it up."

"He did not make it up," Andy said firmly. "Remember we told you the story about Franny and Tyler, when they were babies?"

"Like Mommy has a baby in her belly?"

"A little bigger than that," Andy said, picking her up and taking her into the living room. He spoke quietly and everyone else raised their voices, to give them privacy.

Anna pretended she hadn't heard any of it. She kept her back turned, peeling potatoes while she silently communed with her missing child. She told Franny that Tyler had set a place for her, and asked whether she liked pumpkin pie. She held imaginary conversations with Franny more often during the holidays. She thought about asking Lucas if it was unhealthy, but if she gave it up …

"How are you doing?" Michael said, kissing her cheek as he reached for a potato.

"Do you think I was wrong to let him do it?" Anna asked

210

quietly. "Tell me the truth."

"No," Michael said. "I think it was right to let him do it. I'm proud of him for being so thoughtful."

"He takes after his father." Anna said, handing him a paring knife. "It makes the rest of them uncomfortable though. Maybe we should discourage him from talking about Franny when everyone else is here."

"We'll move from that to pretending she never existed. She *does* exist and someday, she will come home and sit at her place on Thanksgiving. When that happens, I want all of our grandkids to know exactly who she is."

Hours later, when everyone had retired to their separate sleeping areas, Anna couldn't shake her feelings of melancholy. "I can't imagine a happier scenario," she whispered to Michael. "A husband I love, who loves me back. Working with troubled kids. A houseful of grandchildren. But without Franny …" She went to the dresser and began to remove her jewelry.

"I know," Michael said, standing behind her, wrapping his arms around her waist. "I feel the same way."

"Paula says it's the same for her." Anna turned in his arms and pressed her ear over his heart. "She says it doesn't matter how you lose a child, it hurts just as much."

"I don't know," Michael said, easing the pins from her hair, allowing it to fall over her shoulders. "It seems to me, the longer you've had a child, the harder it would be to lose them."

"Like John and Erline losing Jeanne?" She had guessed he was thinking of them, but the way his expression darkened made her regret her words. "Paula says we're luckier because we have hope that we'll see Franny again. She says it would be worse if we found out …"

"In either case, we will see Franny again one day." Michael backed up to the bed and sat down, drawing Anna between his knees. "That's why God told us about Heaven ahead of time."

"Then you think …" Anna asked, with some degree of alarm.

"No, I don't," Michael said firmly. "I'm confident that Franny is alive. We have every reason to believe she's a healthy, happy little girl, unaware of what happened to her when she was an infant."

211

"What makes you think she's healthy and happy?" Anna asked, resting her hands on his shoulders, studying his expression.

"The people who had Tyler paid a hundred grand, remember? People don't spend that kind of money on something, then abuse or neglect it."

Anna's smile brightened. "Why haven't you ever said this to me before?"

"Because I hadn't thought of it before. I tried not to think about what sort of life she might have, because I generally thought the worst." He pressed a kiss into the hollow of her throat, and slid his hands from her hips to her waist. Then he glanced over his shoulder, where Tyler slept on a cot in the corner, giving his own bedroom over to company.

"Lucas told Paula we shouldn't let Tyler do stuff like setting a place for Franny at the table," Anna said.

"Tyler was abducted too. Even if he doesn't remember, I'm sure he thinks about it. He probably worries that it could happen again, so when he sees the things we do for Franny, it gives him added security. He knows we would never forget him, never stop doing whatever we could to find him and bring him home. God forbid."

"Amen," Anna said with a shudder.

"When Franny does come home," Michael went on, "he'll tell her about the things we did and it will help her know we didn't go on with our lives and forget about her."

"How do you always manage to say the right thing?" Anna asked, twining her arms around his neck.

"I don't," Michael said. "Ask Paula. She was pretty angry with me today, more than once."

"Oh well," Anna said, making a face. "Letting the babies sit on Charlie? Poor old thing."

Charlie usually slept in Tyler's room, but tonight he had come into their bedroom, to guard Tyler's cot. His tail slapped against Michael's bureau at the mention of his name.

Anna and Michael both smiled, then she kissed him, and teased her fingers through his hair.

"Never promise what you can't deliver," Michael rebuked her

softly. Then he kissed her back. Before long though, he pushed her away and stood up. "Off to the shower," he said, forcing cheer into his voice. "The cold shower."

♥

Anna herded the crowd of six-year-olds into the dining room, and began handing out party favors. She thought Tyler's birthday party had been a success, judging from the smiles on the faces of his school friends. She hoped she had gotten some good video of the special moments for Michael – he had been called to Casey's for some sort of emergency.

One by one, parents arrived to fetch their children, some of them casting an ominous glance across the field that separated the house from the school. One of the women wondered how Anna could bear to live in such close proximity to dangerous juvenile delinquents. Anna only shrugged. None of the crimes committed against her or her family had been perpetrated by Casey's students.

Finally, all the guests were gone, except Marianne's daughters – Aurora and Lorelei. Though they weren't as old as the other children, Anna hadn't minded including them. Taking a trash bag from the pantry, she began to fill it with empty paper cups, crumpled wrapping paper, and half-eaten cake. Tyler and the girls were busy trying out the toys he had received as gifts, and she let her mind roam to plans for an upcoming vacation.

"She will too come back!" Tyler yelled at Aurora, drawing Anna's attention. "Your mom is a liar!"

"Tyler!" Anna gasped. He had learned all sorts of new behavior while attending first grade – most of it bad. "We do not *ever* call anyone a liar." She ordered him to apologize, but he raced up the stairs and slammed his bedroom door.

"A little too much excitement," Anna said, stroking Aurora's hair. She picked up Lorelei, who had shoved her pudgy thumb in her mouth. "Did you girls have a good time?" Marianne had promised to be back before the party was over, but she often ran late. Anna knew Michael had a hard time overlooking this trait in her friend and to be honest, sometimes she did too.

"I did," said the three-year-old, without removing her thumb.

"Well, I didn't," Aurora replied saucily. "My mom is gonna be really mad at Tyler."

Anna wondered what the argument was about, but she decided against showing too much interest. "Would you like to color a picture?" she offered, leading the way to the kitchen. She put Lorelei in a high chair, then went to the dining room for crayons and coloring books. "Here we go," she said, putting it all within reach of both girls. She sat down and paged through a book until she found a picture she liked. "I'm going to use pink, because that's my favorite color."

"Mine too," said Aurora, snatching a book from her sister.

Lorelei looked as if she might cry. Then she sniffed and chose another book.

"Sometimes my cheeks turn pink when I'm excited," Anna said. "Or when I'm mad." She made a face, and both of the girls giggled.

"Tyler's cheeks are pink," Aurora said.

"I wonder why he got so mad," Anna said, without looking at her.

"Because Franny *isn't* coming back," Aurora informed her sternly. "My mom said. And my dad said too."

Anna searched her mind, but there was no reasonable response. She wanted to do what Tyler had done, and call Marianne a liar …

"We're going to Disney World this summer," Aurora informed her.

"Good for you!" Anna said. "I need to run upstairs for a minute. Stay here, please. I'll be right back!" She knew it wasn't wise to leave the girls unattended, but she needed to make sure Tyler was okay.

He was seated on his bed, playing a video game. Michael had asked him to only play with them for one hour after dinner, but he didn't try to hide the game from his mother.

"I came up to see if you were all right," Anna said, ignoring his disobedience. She kissed the top of his head. "I'll come back up as soon as the girls are gone, okay?"

He kept his head bowed over the game and didn't look up.

"I love you," she said, in her sweetest voice. She waited patiently.

"I love you too," he finally snarled.

Anna hurried downstairs and found Marianne looking through the window of the back door, wearing a horrified expression. She let her in, cautioning herself against saying anything she might later regret.

"Where were you?" Marianne demanded. "I've been knocking for ten minutes!"

"Slight exaggeration?" Anna retorted, feeling her temper begin to rise.

"You shouldn't leave Lorelei unattended in a high chair," Marianne lectured, rushing to lift her youngest into her arms. "You didn't even have her strapped in!"

"I was only gone for a second," Anna said. "I had to run up and check on Tyler."

"Tyler says you're a liar, Mommy." Aurora looked pleased with herself.

"What's that about?" Marianne demanded, turning to glare at Anna.

"I think it would be best if we talked about it some other time," Anna said. "When we don't have an audience."

"What's a audience?" Aurora wanted to know.

"Take your sister into the living room," Marianne ordered.

"That's not a good idea," Anna said. "I'll just call you later."

"Are you asking me to leave?" Marianne said indignantly.

Anna bit her lip. "Did you tell Aurora that Franny's never coming home?"

Marianne opened her mouth, but no sound emerged.

"Tyler is understandably upset," Anna said coldly.

Marianne put Lorelei down and gave her a gentle shove towards the living room. "Both of you, go and play," she said. Aurora kicked the table leg as she went by, but neither woman corrected her.

"Listen, Anna," Marianne said, propping her hands on her hips. "Maybe I oughta apologize, but I'm not gonna do it. Somebody needs to say it and since I'm your best friend, I guess the job falls on me. Franny is *not* coming home and you know it.

215

If she's still alive, by some miracle, she doesn't even know you exist."

"And you would know this how?" Anna asked, curling her fingers into fists.

"It's common sense. Everybody knows it. I'll bet Dr. Grant would agree with me, if he thought I wouldn't repeat it to you."

Anna felt her face begin to flush. "That's an insult, to Michael and to me."

"Sorry," Marianne said, but she didn't sound sorry. "You need to move on, Anna. It's like you have a big hole where Franny was, and you need to fill it up with something. Maybe you could adopt a little girl, like Paula did. Thomas and I think it would be good for Tyler, and probably for Dr. Grant too."

Tears stung Anna's eyes, but she was determined not to let them fall. "Marianne, please take your children and leave, before I say something I can't take back."

"I knew you'd get mad," Marianne said, shaking her head with a knowing smile. "But if you think about it, you'll realize I'm right. You can't keep kiddin' yourself and that poor little boy that one day, his sister is gonna pop back into his life. It's crazy!"

"Please leave," Anna said, through clenched teeth.

"Posting all that stuff on the Internet and puttin' up flyers at Wal Mart … you have no idea what she looks like! There's no such thing as identical twins if they're two different sexes. She could have blond hair and blue eyes."

"I'm going upstairs now," Anna said sharply. "Please make sure you lock the door on your way out."

"I'm only sayin' what everybody else is thinkin'," Marianne insisted in a belligerent tone.

"And we all know what an expert you are when it comes to what other people are thinking," Anna lashed out. "Gossip is your best subject, isn't it? Well, here's a great story you can tell: Anna Grant believes her little girl is coming home someday. Some people might say she has an incredible amount of faith, but other people, who are petty and mean and vicious … they'd say she's crazy. Now, will you please take your girls and go home!"

"You bet I will," Marianne said. She ran to the living room and grabbed Lorelei from the coffee table. Yanking on Aurora's hand, she half drug her out the door.

Anna waited until she heard Marianne's car back from the driveway, then she went and closed the door and locked it. She arranged the curtain so no one could see in, then sat down on a kitchen chair and waited for her hands to stop shaking. When she was calm enough, she took her cell phone from her pocket and texted Michael. She asked when he could come home. He answered within seconds, and said he could come immediately, if she needed him. Anna replied with just one word: *please.* Then she got up and went to the living room and watched for him to appear on the sidewalk that stretched between the house and the school.

"What's wrong?" Michael asked with worried eyes, as soon as he came in the door. "Where's Tyler?"

"In his room. He's playing his video game but ... I didn't have the heart to yell at him."

Michael came and put his arms around Anna. "What happened?" he asked.

The minute Anna was wrapped in Michael's embrace, her anger turned to sorrow. "Aurora told Tyler ... that her mom and dad said ... Franny's never coming home."

"And they would know this how?" Michael asked sarcastically.

Anna hammered her forehead into his chest. "That's exactly what I said." She looked up at him. "I used the exact same words."

"You said this to Aurora?"

Anna shook her head. "To Marianne. She was late getting here to pick up the girls."

"What else is new," Michael groused.

"She gave me a big, ugly lecture. She said Franny doesn't ..." Suddenly Anna couldn't talk. She wrenched free and went to the couch and sat down. "She said Franny doesn't even know we exist."

Michael crossed his arms and set his jaw.

"I kept asking her to leave and she wouldn't. She said everybody thinks I'm over the edge."

"She said *what*?" Michael exploded.

217

"Not those words, just … She makes it sound like they all stand around in the hallways, talking about crazy Anna."

"Maybe her and her group, but no one else does," Michael said in a stern tone. "People constantly say supportive things to me. Maybe they saw a little girl on TV who looked like Tyler. Or they ask whether we're aware of some new Internet site, that helps locate kids who were abducted." He paused until Anna looked up at him. "We have no reason to think Franny is not out there somewhere, waiting for us to find her. Don't start doubting yourself, just because Marianne is lacking in faith." Michael's eyes darted across the room. "C'mere, son," he called to Tyler. "You need to hear what Mama and I are saying."

Tyler emerged from the hallway, but drug his feet on the way to the living room. "Some people say Franny is dead," he told his father.

Michael picked him up and held him on one arm. "Franny is *not* dead," he said. "She was adopted by someone, just as you were. The people who adopted you saw the video we made, and gave you back to us. The people who adopted Franny didn't see the video. They don't know Franny was stolen from us, so they're still pretending she's their little girl. But one day, they'll tell Franny she's adopted and she'll start searching for her birth parents. And her brother," he added, tugging Tyler's ear lobe.

"Marianne said we should adopt a different girl," Tyler said earnestly. "Why can't we just do that?"

"Tyler!" Anna said with alarm. "Were you eavesdropping?"

"Because we want Franny," Michael said patiently. "No other little girl will do."

"We could call the other little girl Franny," Tyler suggested.

"Nope," Michael said. He poked a finger into Tyler's ribs. "Tell me this – Is there another Tyler, exactly like you, anywhere in the whole world?"

"No," Tyler said, smiling at his dad. "I just wish she would hurry up and come home. Sometimes I get tired of thinking about it."

"Then take a break," Michael said flippantly. "Think about something else."

"Don't you get tired of thinking about it, Papa?"

Michael put him down and went and sat beside Anna on the couch. "No, son. I never do. I like to imagine where she is and what she looks like. What do you suppose she's wearing right now? Blue jeans or a dress? Does she like bananas? What does she like on her pizza? I think she's very, very smart. I'll bet she's always asking questions. I'll bet her favorite color is … "

"Blue!" Tyler shouted. Blue was his favorite color. He came and sat down between his parents, linking his arms in theirs. "Do you think she's taller than me?" he asked.

"No way," Michael said. "She's probably short, like your mom. Oops!" he pretended to worry, covering his mouth. "Mama hates it when I mention how tiny she is."

"I am *not* tiny," Anna said indignantly, following Michael's lead. "I am huge."

Tyler laughed hysterically.

"I'll bet Franny is funny, like Mama," Michael suggested, winking at Anna.

"Do you think she could beat me on video games?" Tyler asked worriedly.

"*Some* video games," Michael said, after a moment of contemplation.

"Which ones?"

"I don't know," Michael said. "Did you save me a piece of chocolate cake?"

"A big piece," Tyler said. "You didn't eat it, did you Mama?"

Anna looked worried. "I was so hungry!" she pretended to apologize. "And besides, I need to eat a lot so I can get bigger."

"Grrrr," Michael growled. "You know the punishment when you eat Papa Bear's cake?"

"He tickles you!" Tyler warned her with excitement.

Anna pretended to try to get away, but allowed Michael to drag her into his arms. When he started to actually tickle her, she slapped at his hands and begged him to stop.

"Let's go out to dinner," Michael suggested. "In honor of someone's sixth birthday."

"Mine and Franny's!" Tyler said, jumping up and running to the door.

Hours later, Anna came into Michael's home office and sat

down in the spare chair, still clutching her phone.

"How'd it go?" Michael asked, pushing his new reading glasses to the top of his head.

"Okay, I guess. We both said sorry and we both said we forgive each other."

"But you don't think someone was sincere?"

She hesitated. "*She* may have been," she admitted reluctantly.

"You know what they say," Michael admonished her gently. "Holding a grudge is like drinking poison … and hoping the other person will die."

She sighed. "How could she think that adopting a little girl would help us forget about Franny? It was a stupid thing to say."

"Maybe, but did she mean well? Was she honestly wishing she could come up with a solution to your heartbreak?"

"I'm not sure," Anna said. "I think she just wants the old Anna back. For her own sake."

"I liked the old Anna too," Michael said. "But I like the new Anna even better."

"I'm much more serious than I used to be."

"You still like to have fun."

"Do I?"

"Well, you still laugh when I tickle you."

"Please," she said, holding up both hands. "No tickling."

"Anna," he said seriously. "Things will never be right until we have our daughter back. And even then, things will never go back to the way they were."

"What if she's right?" Anna asked softly. "What if we aren't going to get Franny back."

"Do you think she's right?" Michael asked. He pulled his glasses off and tossed them on his desk. Then he switched off the light. "I think she's wrong. I think we will get her back, and all those people who didn't believe will end up being the ones to feel foolish."

His words seemed to carry more weight in the semi-darkness.

"You seem so strong," Anna told him. "So certain. It wasn't all that long ago that I was the one who was trying to convince you not to give up hope."

"It's a choice, Anna. We can choose to give up or we can

choose to go on believing and trusting God. You're the one who taught me that."

"That doesn't mean He always gives us what we want," she said dismally.

"One day, we'll be reunited with Franny," Michael said. He stood up and she did too. They clung together in the darkness.

♥

While Anna met with Tyler's teacher for conferences, he escorted his dad around the school. He showed Michael a picture he had painted, and a book report that was stapled onto a bulletin board. He didn't seem worried about anything his teacher might say to his mother.

Anna emerged from the classroom in tears, though she did her best to blink them away.

"Did Miss Sturgis say I was bad?" Tyler asked with shock.

Anna stooped down to talk to him, though Tyler was almost as tall as she was. "Miss Sturgis says you are always well behaved and that you are smart and talented and creative."

"Yeah, but you're crying," he pointed out.

Michael took Anna's arm and lifted her to her feet, leading her away from the curious stares of other parents. "What's going on?" he asked with concern.

"Miss Sturgis says Tyler can't distinguish between truth and fantasy. She said we should not have decorated Franny's room, as though we're expecting her back any minute. She said we should turn it into a non-descript guest room. *Non-descript*," she repeated bitterly. "She says he's too serious for a seven-year-old because we make him spend too much time reading."

"I *like* to read!" Tyler protested at her elbow.

"Tyler, you want to show Mama the picture you painted?" Michael suggested, patting Anna's shoulder. "I'll meet you at the front door in about ten minutes, okay?"

"Are you gonna yell at Miss Sturgis?" Tyler asked, with more curiosity than concern.

"I will not raise my voice," Michael promised. "I'm just going to explain to her about Franny. Okay?"

"Okay," Tyler said, grabbing his mother's arm and dragging her away.

When Michael approached the front door, about twenty minutes later, he could see that Anna was still upset. "Did Tyler give you the grand tour?" he asked.

"Mom already knows where stuff is," Tyler reminded him. "On account of being a lunch monitor."

"Ahh," Michael said. "Did you show her your picture?"

"He did. And his book report. I'm so proud of him," Anna said, giving Tyler a hug.

"Awk," Tyler complained, pushing her away. "Did you yell at Miss Sturgis, Papa?"

"I did not," Michael assured him. "We just had a chat."

"Did you tell her Franny's not dead?"

"Yes I did," Michael said. "She didn't know the whole story, but now she does."

"Don't worry, Mama," Tyler consoled Anna. "Lots of kids get in trouble with Miss Sturgis, but she's still nice to them the next day."

"Thanks," Anna said seriously.

It was Michael's turn to read Tyler a story that night, and he made it a point to keep reading until Tyler fell asleep. When he came downstairs, Anna was waiting in the living room, with two cups of decaf.

"Let's go in my office and shut the door, just in case," he advised.

"What did you say to her?" Anna asked warily. "I have lunchroom duty tomorrow, so I'd like to be prepared."

"I asked whether she knew that Tyler was also abducted," Michael said, latching the door. "Then I explained how the couple who adopted him saw the YouTube video we made and realized they had adopted a kidnapped baby. I pointed out how many millions of people did *not* see that video, including the couple who adopted Franny."

"Why didn't I think of that?" Anna said with frustration. "Did she seem angry?"

"She was flustered and embarrassed. She asked me to apologize to you on her behalf."

"Do you think she was sincere?"

Michael shrugged. "When I first came into the room, she said I was disrupting her schedule, but Ed and Mary Harrison were next up. Skipper's dad and mom?"

"They seem nice," Anna said, sipping her coffee.

"Ed made a big deal out of introducing me to Miss Sturgis, as the administrator of Casey's. My status may have had something to do with her sudden change in attitude."

"I know how much you hate it when people treat you like a VIP," Anna said with a smile.

"My only concern is how she treats my son and my wife."

Anna made a face. "I shouldn't have let her upset me, but ... Do you think she'll take her resentment out on Tyler?"

"On the contrary. She said they'll add Franny to their prayer list, starting tomorrow."

"I like that," Anna said with satisfaction, but her smile quickly faded. "That doesn't change the things she said about him though. Do you think he's a weird kid?"

"Absolutely," Michael said, without hesitation. "He's exactly like me, when I was his age. Certifiably weird."

Anna hid her grin behind the rim of her mug.

"My brother called me 'Old Weird Mikey,' as a matter of fact. And when my father introduced us to his friends, he would say, 'This is my son, Jerome, and my little old man, Michael.' "

"He did not!" Anna protested with a giggle.

Michael raised one eyebrow. "Do you know the penalty when you accuse Papa Bear of lying?" he asked, wiggling his fingers in tickle mode.

223

♥ Chapter 22 ♥

"Why can't I hear you make the speech?" Tyler demanded. "I'm not a baby so why do I have to go to a babysitter?"

"You're going to a *kid*-sitter, not a *baby*sitter, and all your nephews and nieces are going too," Michael said with nonchalance. "You will be much happier there. It's a long speech and other people will be making even longer speeches. You would get bored."

"I don't get bored when you make a speech at Casey's," Tyler argued.

"I thought we settled this, son. How come you're back on it again?"

"Because Mama said it's an important speech. She said there will be a lot of important people there, like senators. She said you're going to get an award and be on the news."

"That may happen, or it may not," Michael said. "Mama and I think it's important, but we can't be sure if other people will agree."

"Is it to get more schools like Casey's?"

"Something like that."

"I wish I could see you make the speech," Tyler said with a great sigh.

"We'll have a video and when we get home, you can watch it as many times as you want."

"Okay," Tyler gave in. "Who's gonna take the video?"

"Mama."

The eight year old slumped against the counter and held his chin in his hand. "Maybe you could ask Andy to do it. Mama is not very good at taking videos. Remember when she chopped off my head while I was getting my award at school?"

Anna came into the kitchen with a harried look. "I have a feeling there's something I'm forgetting."

"We checked everything off the list as we packed. If it wasn't on the list, we'll buy it there. They do have stores in Washington D.C."

"I lived outside of Washington D.C. for seventeen years," she reminded him.

"Did you remember my travel games?" Tyler asked.

"Yes," Anna said, setting her carry-on at the door. "And your books and your paper and colored pencils."

"Did you remember my pajamas?" Tyler asked. "And my tennis shoes?"

"Yes," Anna said. "I don't think I forgot anything for you, Tyler. It's something for me. Let me think for a minute."

"Anna," Michael warned. "We're running behind schedule."

"We allowed plenty of time on the other end," Anna pointed out. "In case Paula is running late."

"And we'll *need* that time on the other end because Paula *will* be running late."

"Just let me think," Anna insisted. "Let me go in the other room for one minute. Sixty seconds. If it doesn't come to me, I'll give up."

"Go," Michael said, resigned to it. "Tyler, why don't you help me put the luggage in the car."

"Want me to carry the big one?" Tyler asked eagerly. "I brought it up from the basement."

"It was empty then," Michael reminded him. "Go ahead and try."

"Don't let him hurt himself," Anna cautioned.

"The clock is ticking," Michael said, tapping the face of his watch.

♥

226

"Where are Andy and Beth?" Paula demanded. "This isn't my idea of fair, being left with all the kids."

Anna lifted a crying three-year-old with a groan, gazing around the hotel lobby with desperate eyes. It had seemed like a good idea for the three men to register and pick up the keys, while the women sat in the lobby with the children. Then Beth needed a restroom – she was pregnant again – and Anna and Paula told her they would be fine for a few minutes. A few minutes had turned into twenty, and none of the others had returned. The nine children were growing more boisterous by the moment.

"This is ridiculous," Paula complained, scrambling after Andy and Beth's youngest.

"Try to remember what it's like to be pregnant," Anna chided gently. "Maybe she's sick."

"She doesn't *get* sick," Paula retorted.

Anna was happy that her adult kids had opted to come and see Michael receive his award, but she was running low on patience. "Do not stand on the couch!" she scolded Paula's oldest.

"How come you talk nice to their kids and yell at mine?" Paula said with irritation. "I'm perfectly capable of yelling at my own kids, should it be necessary."

"I'm sorry," Anna said. "I don't like trying to watch this many in a public place."

"No one is going to snatch them," Paula rebuked her. "We probably couldn't give one away if we tried."

"Sorry," Michael said, crossing the lobby and taking the three-year-old from Anna.

"Where's Andy and Lucas?" Paula asked, leaning to one side, to look behind him.

"They went to get the suitcases. There was a long line at the desk."

"Do you think they can manage all that luggage by themselves?" Anna asked.

"They took two porters along," Michael assured her.

"Paula? Why don't you go check on Beth," Anna suggested. "Michael and I will stay with the kids until ... here she comes!"

227

"I stopped at the information desk to find out about babysitting services," Beth explained, hurrying over. "I didn't think it would take that long."

"What did you find out?" Michael asked.

"I've got the pamphlet in my purse," Beth told him. "I'll call when we get to our room. Say, Paula," she said with enthusiasm. "Lucas said maybe he and Andy could stay with the kids this afternoon, so you and I can go shopping."

"Oh, yeah?" Paula said, a smile creeping over her face.

♥

"Hi, sweetie," Anna said warmly, stopping to kiss Tyler's forehead as she scurried around the master bedroom of the hotel suite. "Did you have a good time today?"

"Mama?"

"Hmm ... " Anna answered, rummaging in her suitcase.

"Something happened today." Tyler sidled closer.

"Anna?" Michael called, sticking his head out of the bathroom. "Did you pack my cuff links?"

"They're in my jewelry case, on the counter," Anna called back. "I'm going to have to see if Paula or Beth has an extra pair of pantyhose," she thought aloud, going to the hotel phone.

"Mama?" Tyler tried again.

"Just a second, Tyler. Room 823, please," she told the operator. "Did you like the museum, Tyler?"

"It was great," Tyler said, but he didn't smile.

"Beth? By any chance, did you bring an extra pair of panty hose? I managed to poke a hole in mine. Terrific! I'll send Michael as soon as he's dressed."

"Mama?" Tyler said, as she hung up the receiver. "This is somewhat urgent."

Anna smiled. Tyler's vocabulary already rivaled her own. "Can it wait five minutes? Just until I'm dressed?" She was beginning to feel stressed.

"I guess five minutes is okay," he said reluctantly.

"You can time me," Anna promised. "Five minutes, no more."

"Okay," he agreed, starting the timer on his wrist.

"I don't think Tyler had a good time today," Anna told Michael, when she joined him in the enormous bathroom. "You know, I would love to have something like this at home. Two sinks ... you could shave while I brush my teeth."

Michael rinsed his razor and set it aside, then patted his face with a hand towel. "Are my notes in my coat pocket?"

"Unless you took them out."

"I don't remember taking them out, but ... could you check? I certainly hope I'm going to calm down before I get up to the podium. If this keeps up, I'll just stand there and clear my throat for half an hour."

"You'll be fine," Anna assured him. "Remember how nervous you were about doing that thing for channel six last year? You were fine, once it got started."

"That was for a camera. This is live."

"Your subject speaks for itself," she reminded him, a phrase they'd learned to recite whenever either of them were doing something public in support of the school. "Could you zip me up?"

He turned and zipped her zipper, then paused to press his lips to the back of her neck. "I'm going to be looking at you the entire time," he promised. "The source of my courage."

"Just a mirror," she said. "My courage comes from you."

"Mama?" Tyler called, appearing in the doorway. "Five minutes is up."

"What's that about?" Michael asked.

"He wants to tell me something and I asked him to wait five minutes," Anna explained.

"Don't forget to check my pocket for my notes," Michael reminded her.

Anna padded barefoot to the closet, where Michael's suit coat was hanging. "Okay, Tyler," she said patiently, reaching her hand into the left hand pocket and pulling out a small stack of index cards. She looked them over carefully, to be certain none were missing, then turned to her son. "What happened today that made you so unhappy?"

"I'm not unhappy," he said, shoving his hands into his pockets, looking like a miniature version of Michael. "It's just that ..."

"Anna?" Michael called from the bathroom. "Did you find my notes?"

"They're in your pocket," she called back. "Tell you what," she suggested, putting her arm around Tyler's shoulders. "Let's go in your bedroom, where there's not so many distractions."

♥

It's ridiculous, she told herself, staring out the window of the taxi. *A small boy's imagination.* Undoubtedly, it was her fault. Setting a place at the table for Franny, redecorating her bedroom every few years … She had filled his head with nonsense and wild imaginings so that she could hold fast to her own hopes. It had to stop. Now she understood that it had to stop.

"What's the matter?" Michael asked, taking her hand. "Are you nervous for me?"

"Not at all. I have complete confidence in you. You're going to knock 'em dead."

"I hope not," he laughed. "I don't want to go to prison."

What if it wasn't ridiculous though? What if there was any truth to it? After the award celebration, after they returned to the hotel, she would tell Michael. He always remained rational about things. He would gently force her to accept reality, and he would talk to Tyler too. He would be patient and gentle, but firm.

"Anna? What are you thinking about? You're a million miles away."

"Nothing. Silly stuff."

"You're not one to dwell on silly stuff. I can tell something's bothering you. Is it something Tyler said?"

"It's nothing to worry about," Anna assured him. "After the program, I'll tell you the whole story."

"Tell me now. In this traffic, we've probably got half an hour before we get there."

If what Tyler said was true, she might be risking everything by delay. It would be too late to check into it when they got back to the hotel tonight, and by morning ...

"Whatever it is, it would probably be good for me," Michael pressed. "It would get my mind off of the ordeal ahead."

230

"It's nothing! Just little boy stuff."

Michael caught her chin in his hand and turned her head, so he could look into her eyes.

"I don't want to get you worried," Anna said. "I keep thinking you'll say it's too impossible, but if I don't tell you, I'm afraid you'll say, 'if only you'd told me earlier.' "

"Tell me now," he said. "You and Tyler are more important to me than some silly award."

"Some silly award?" she repeated.

"Tell me," he said. "Please?"

♥

"Tell me exactly what happened," Michael said, sitting down on the coffee table, so he and Tyler were eye to eye. "As many details as you can remember."

Tyler drew his knees up under his chin. "Did you already make your speech?"

"Don't worry about it," Michael said with a wave of his hand. "I can always make another speech, son."

"What if I'm wrong?" Tyler whined. "Mama said it's an important speech."

"They moved me to the end of the program. If there's still time, I'll go and make my speech later. This is more important, Tyler. Don't you think so?"

"I don't know," Tyler said, glancing at his mother.

"Well, I think so," Michael said," so tell me about the little girl. When did you first see her?"

Tyler sighed, as though exhausted from dealing with his parents. "When we came back from the Smithsonian, Andy told me and 'Lissa to sit on the couch in the lobby while he talked to some guy. He told us not to get up and not to talk to strangers."

"Good advice," Michael said agreeably. "Was the little girl sitting on the couch too?"

"No," Tyler said, crossing his arms. "She was standing up, with a bunch of other girls."

"Did she talk to you?"

"She curled her finger, you know, like 'c'mere'? But Andy told

231

me not to get off the couch, so I didn't do it. I was trying to study the map of Washington D.C."

"What happened next?" Michael asked, trying to sound nonchalant.

" 'Lissa said she looked like me."

Michael glanced at Anna. "Did you think so?" he asked Tyler.

Tyler shrugged. "I guess."

"Did you talk to her?"

"I couldn't help it," Tyler said, tapping his fingers against his knees. "She came over there. She asked me what I was doing."

"What did you tell her?" Michael's heart had begun to beat faster. He cautioned himself that it was nothing, but … his heart wanted to believe.

"I said 'duh,' because I was looking at the map. Then she said her friends thought we looked like twins."

Michael hoped his expression was neutral. "Was she smiling?"

"She was laughing. Like girls laugh."

"Giggling?" Anna suggested. She came closer and rested one hand on Michael's shoulder.

"I guess," Tyler said, frowning at her.

"Did she say anything else?" Michael's heart was thundering in his ears.

"She thought 'Lissa was my girlfriend," he said, with an unhappy expression. "So I told her she was my niece. That made her laugh too."

"Was her hair long or short?" Anna asked.

"I don't know," Tyler said, beginning to look weary. "Long."

"Did she say anything else?" Michael prodded.

"I asked her if she was Franny."

Anna drew a breath. "What did she say?"

Michael could hear that Anna was beginning to cry, and he suspected it was worrying Tyler.

"She just stared at me," Tyler shrugged. "So I told her my sister got kidnapped a long time ago. I said maybe she was my sister."

Anna went into the kitchenette and began to rattle dishes. Michael knew she was trying to make it easier for Tyler.

"Then some lady came to get her," Tyler said. "She yelled at her for walking away from the group."

"Did you see where the lady took her?"

"I couldn't see."

"You *couldn't* see? You mean they left the hotel?"

"No, they went in the elevator. But they were too far away and I couldn't see what number they pushed."

"Did the lady say anything to you?" Michael asked. He put his hand on Tyler's shoulder, to try to reassure him.

Tyler stared up at the ceiling. "No. She just yelled at the girl. Not mean or anything. She just said she was afraid she would get separated."

"Can you remember anything else?" Michael hoped he wasn't pressing too hard.

Tyler lifted his shoulders and stared glumly at his father. "Do you think it was Franny?" he asked Michael.

Michael wasn't sure how to answer. He *did* think it was Franny, but he knew it was a ridiculous notion that was likely to be disproved. "I don't know, son. What do you think?"

"I think it was Franny," Tyler said, drawing his mouth into a tight line.

♥

"I'm going to call the Center for Missing and Exploited Children," Michael said with barely controlled excitement. He had turned on the TV for Tyler, and left him in the living room. "Hopefully, they can get somebody over here right away."

"It wasn't Franny," Anna said, biting her lip.

"Why do you say that?" Michael asked with surprise. "Are you sure?"

"Michael, be realistic! What are the chances Franny and Tyler are going to recognize each other in a hotel lobby after being separated for eight years?"

"About ten billion to none," Michael admitted. "But that doesn't mean it didn't happen and I'm not going to ignore the possibility."

"What about Tyler? What about putting Tyler through a bunch of nonsense with federal agents and it turns out he was wrong?"

"We'll worry about that if the time comes," Michael said firmly. "Sit with him and help him relax while I go in the bedroom to call. I'm going to try to reach Steven or Milt and ask them to refer us to somebody here."

Anna grabbed a paper towel and blew her nose before she disappeared into the living room.

Michael hesitated. Anna was right. It would be traumatic for all three of them if the little girl wasn't Franny. The likelihood that it *was* Franny was beyond astronomical. Afterwards, they would have to take a lot of flak about their inability to let go of the tragedy and get on with their lives.

Within seconds, he decided he didn't care.

♥

"Dr. Grant? I'm Neal Fossett and this is Ross Carlton. We got a call from a St. Louis agent who worked with you on an abduction case some years ago?" As he spoke, he drew out an identification badge and held it up for Michael's perusal.

"Thank you for coming," Michael said, gesturing to the couch where Anna and Tyler sat waiting. "This may be nothing, but when your agents were actively working with us, they encouraged us to call anytime we thought we might have a lead. This is my wife, Anna, and my son, Tyler."

"They faxed me a copy of your file," Ross said, opening a briefcase and withdrawing a manila folder. "I was looking it over on the way out and apparently, this is the first lead in years?"

"I don't know whether you'll even consider it a lead," Michael said, running his fingers through his hair and leaving it stand on end. "Tyler and his sister are twins. There was a little girl in the lobby today who approached Tyler because her friends noticed that they looked alike. Unfortunately, neither my wife nor I were present."

"Who was with your son?"

"His older brother. Half brother."

"How old is the brother?"

"Andy is an adult," Michael explained. "He had stepped away from Tyler and his daughter for a moment, and that's when the little girl approached. We haven't spoken to Andy yet, so we don't know whether or not he saw the little girl."

"Hi, Tyler," Ross said in a friendly voice. "So, you think maybe you saw your sister today?"

"I don't know if she was my sister, but she looked like me."

"Did you talk to her?"

"Not very much."

Ross sat down on the coffee table and handed Tyler his badge. "Ever thought about being a G-man when you grow up?"

"What's a G-man?" Tyler wondered, examining the badge.

"That's a guy like me," the agent answered with a chuckle. "I work for a special division of the FBI and we look for kids like Franny."

"Like you looked for me when I was missing?"

"Right. And we found you!"

"Thank you," Tyler said politely.

"You're welcome. Your mom and dad gave us a lot of help. Without help, we wouldn't be able to find any of the kids who go missing. So we need you to tell us everything you remember about this little girl, okay?"

"Yeah, but what if it's not Franny?" Tyler asked, chewing on the inside of his mouth.

"So what? No harm, no foul, right? All we're gonna do is ask her parents some questions. But we need to hurry, Tyler. In case they're about to leave the hotel."

"What kind of questions?" Tyler persisted.

"Like when's her birthday. And whether she's adopted."

"If we have the same birthday, then she's probably Franny," Tyler decided.

"Yeah," the agent agreed. "That would be one huge coincidence, wouldn't it?"

Tyler nodded. He turned his head, to look at his parents, then he took a deep breath. "I don't think it's a coincidence," he said. "I'm pretty sure she was my sister."

♥ Chapter 23 ♥

"Are you expecting someone?" Neal asked, when there was a knock on the door.

"We have a grown son and daughter in town, with their families," Anna explained. "My husband was supposed to make a speech tonight, at the Kennedy Center, and I'm afraid we abandoned them there."

"This the son that was in the lobby with Tyler?"

"Yes," Anna said, following him to the door. She stood back and let him open it, then leaned past him to smile at the two couples. "Sorry about the mix-up," she apologized, before they could say anything. "Is it all right if they come in?" she asked the agent.

"Why don't we step out in the hall, so as not to make it any rougher on Tyler," he suggested, holding the door for her.

"What's wrong with Tyler?" Paula demanded, giving the agent a suspicious look.

Anna didn't know whether to speak, or wait for the agent. "This is Agent ... I'm sorry."

"Neal Fossett," he filled in. "Which one of you is Andy, the brother?"

"I am," Andy said. "Why?"

"You left Tyler sitting in the lobby with your daughter this afternoon?"

"I was *right* there," Andy said defensively. "I could see them

237

from where I was standing."

"Nobody is accusing you of anything," Anna soothed him. "We're just trying to find out what happened."

"Nothing happened," Andy insisted. "They were sitting on the couch, for maybe five minutes."

"You didn't see Tyler talking to a little girl?"

Andy looked doubtful. "I may have turned my head for thirty seconds, but ..." His expression grew pained. "I was glancing back and forth and ... well, Tyler's not liar. If he says he talked to some little girl, I guess he did."

"Is your daughter still awake? The one that was sitting with Tyler?"

Beth laughed. "We left nine kids in one room together. I doubt whether any of them fell asleep."

"Mom?" Paula said with concern. "Are you okay?"

"I'm okay," Anna said, throwing her shoulders back. "Just a little stressed."

"*You're* stressed?" Paula accused her. "We thought you guys had an accident!"

"We talked to the head waiter," Anna told her. "He said he would personally see to it that you got the message."

"He did, but not until half an hour into the program. By then, we were frantic."

"Could you bring your daughter down and let us talk with her?" Neal asked Beth. "If the rest of you could go on back to your rooms for now, so there's less confusion ... We'll let you know as soon as there's any news."

"News about what?" Paula demanded. "What's going on?"

Anna looked at the agent, as if asking permission to explain.

"Tyler thinks he saw his sister," Neal said. "We're gonna follow up on it, just in case."

Paula turned to look at Lucas. His lips were drawn into a thin line.

"I'll stay with the other kids and let Andy bring 'Lissa," Beth said. "She behaves better for him."

"Maybe you should let Lucas sit in," Paula suggested. "He's a psychiatrist. He might be able to help, in case it wasn't Franny."

"We'll keep the offer in mind," Neal said politely. "For now, the fewer people, the better."

♥

"Where's Tyler?" Melissa asked, eying Neal with curiosity. "Is he arrested?"

Andy smiled. "Tyler and his papa are in the bedroom, talking to a different guy, while we stay out here and talk to Neal."

"Do you like to shake hands?" Neal asked her.

"I guess so," she said, eying her dad for approval. "Are you gonna arrest Tyler?"

"No way!" he said, settling on the coffee table. "Tyler's a good friend of mine. He told us about something that happened today and I wanted to see if you remember it too."

"About that girl who looked like him?"

Anna saw Andy's eyes widen. She covered her mouth and turned her head.

"Did Mommy or Daddy tell you what we wanted to talk about?" Neal asked with interest.

"We just said you wanted to ask some questions about the little girl she met in the lobby," Andy said. "She was afraid the little girl got kidnapped."

"Where did you go today?" Neal asked Melissa, ignoring Andy and Anna.

"I think it was a museum. They had a really neat gift shop."

"Did you get something good?"

"I got a T-shirt, but my mom went shopping with Auntie Paula yesterday and I got two new outfits for my Barbie."

"Good deal! Now, think real hard, okay. What did you do after you got back from the museum?"

"We played in our room."

"Do you remember something that happened in between?"

"The girl who looks like Tyler?"

"Did you think she looked like Tyler?"

"Kind of."

"Did you hear what she and Tyler talked about?" Neal pressed.

"Umm … She asked him if I was his girlfriend."

"What did Tyler say?"

"Well, first he put his finger in his mouth, like he was gonna throw up. Then he said he was my uncle."

"Do you remember what the little girl looked like?"

"She looked like Tyler."

"Was her hair the same color as Tyler's?"

"Yep. And she was missing her front teeth."

"Was her hair longer than Tyler's?"

"Lots longer, like mine."

"Do you remember what she was wearing?"

"She was wearing a blue skirt and a white shirt and a blue hoody. And she had pierced ears. I want pierced ears but my daddy says not till I'm older. Am I older yet?" she asked Andy.

He just smiled.

"Was it a light blue skirt or a dark blue skirt?" Neal asked.

"It was that kind that has lines, like tic-tac-toe."

"I think she means plaid," Anna suggested.

"They were probably Girl Scouts or something," Melissa elaborated. "All of the girls were wearing the same color skirt."

"How many girls were there?"

"I didn't count them. There were a lot."

"A lot like three? Or a lot like ten?"

"A lot like ten."

Neal sat back and darted a glance at Anna. "So all the girls were wearing blue plaid skirts and white shirts?"

"And blue hoodies," she reminded him.

"Did you see the lady who came and took the little girl away?"

"She wasn't very nice," Melissa informed him with disapproval. "She hollered at her."

"What did she say?"

"That she's supposed to stay with the group, so she doesn't get lost."

"And then what happened."

"Then they left."

"Where did they go?"

"On the elevator."

"What did the lady look like? Did she look like Tyler too?"

"No," Melissa said, shaking her head. "She has yellow hair, like my mom's."

Neal patted Melissa on the shoulder. "You know what? You'd make a good agent, Melissa. You remembered a lot of helpful details."

"What's a detail?" she asked her dad.

"Like a blue plaid skirt," he said. "Are you done with us?"

"Not yet," Neal said. "We'll just take a little break, okay?"

♥

"Michael?" Anna whispered. "Are you asleep?"

"No," Michael laughed. He switched the lamp back on, then turned on his side to look at her. "I was hoping you were. You look exhausted."

"I am, but I know I'm not gonna be able to sleep until they're sure it's not Franny."

"Or until they're sure it *is* Franny?"

"You know it can't be. It's too …"

"Too much like a miracle?" he teased.

"Oh, Michael," she sighed, burrowing against him. "I believe in miracles, you *know* I do. But this is too far-fetched even for me!"

" 'With God, all things are possible.' Isn't that one of your favorite verses?"

"Yes, but …"

"Anna! Stop trying to second guess God! Sometimes He likes to surprise us and maybe this is one of those times. If it's not, we'll have plenty of time to ruminate on how unlikely it was. For now, I choose to believe and I wish you would too."

"I can't!" she protested. "If I let myself believe and …"

"All right," Michael said, smoothing her hair away from her eyes. "I'll believe hard enough for both of us then."

Anna made a choking noise. "We reversed roles," she said. "I was always the believer and you were the doubter."

"Because I did what you're doing. I convinced myself that the good stuff was too unlikely. The bad stuff is far easier to believe, especially when you admit you're a sinner and you know you don't deserve the good stuff. But God has never been about what anyone deserves, Anna. He's about grace. You know that, deep in

241

your heart, because you're the one who taught it to me."

"This goes beyond grace," she said, her voice hoarse with emotion.

"Listen to me," Michael said sternly. "We have been through one of the worst things that could ever happen to any parent. Our children were abducted! But we stayed faithful, just like Job. In fact, our faith grew stronger. Maybe that faith is going to be rewarded and we're going to get our little girl back. But if not, God will see us through the heartbreak and disappointment that follows because *that's what He does*. That's His line of work. He won't desert us and He won't forsake us. And one day, we *will* get Franny back. I *know* we will. This reminds me of the stories people tell when they die and visit Heaven for a few minutes. This is what it's gonna feel like when Franny *does* come home. If not now, someday. There's no reason not to rejoice and enjoy the moment, however long it lasts."

"What if it *is* Franny," Anna said in a small voice. "Think how hard it will be for her! Suddenly someone comes and takes you away from the only parents you've ever known and tells you those people weren't your parents after all and now these people are your parents."

"I thought about that too," Michael admitted. "It will take time for her to adjust. The nightmare would end for us and begin for her."

"What do you think we should do? If it is Franny?"

"We'll take her, of course! She's our child and she belongs with us. She's not theirs, she never was."

"But what if Lucas were to say it would be better for her if …" Anna reached across him to snatch a tissue from a box on the bedside table.

"She's ours," Michael said again. "I've been working with children all my life and they're resilient and adaptable. All they need is to know they're loved. And Franny will know that from the first moment." He reached to turn off the lamp. "Close your eyes. Try to get some sleep. We've got a long day ahead of us, no matter how it turns out."

♥

Anna heard Michael's cell phone ring at 6:30. He hurried off to the kitchen, but she didn't get up. She was daydreaming that the little girl really was Franny and she didn't want to let the dream fade away.

Michael was talking quietly. She suspected it meant he didn't want her to overhear what he was saying. She got up and pulled on her robe and went to the kitchen.

"How can you be certain it's the same little girl Tyler saw in the lobby?" Michael asked.

Anna tried to decide whether that was a positive or negative question.

"Would it be possible for us to see her without her seeing us?"

Anna could hear the hope in his tone. It meant they hadn't eliminated the possibility that the little girl was Franny. She realized she had been holding her breath and exhaled quietly.

"I understand," Michael said, in his best professional voice. "We'll wait here until we hear from you." He shook his head, glancing at Anna, forcing a smile. "Nothing will take our minds off of it," he said adamantly. "We may send Tyler off with the others, but Anna and I will be here all day." He hung up and opened his arms, then buried his face in Anna's hair. "They found the little girl," he said.

♥

"How do they know it's the same little girl?" Paula demanded. "If they don't let you see her ... couldn't they let Tyler see her?"

"They have Tyler's picture," Michael explained patiently. "And they've certainly seen enough of him by now to know whether there's a close resemblance."

"But if it *is* Franny," Paula argued, "you and Mom have every right to see her immediately."

"And if it *isn't* Franny, we don't," Michael replied.

"Wow," Andy said, sinking back on the couch and staring up at the ceiling. "What are the chances of this happening? I was positive it would turn into nothing."

"Are the two of you going to stay in Washington until it's resolved?" Lucas asked.

"Yes, of course," Michael said. "Our biggest concern is Tyler. He's worried about the little girl. He wants to know if this could happen to him, or to one of your kids. What if some other family came along and claimed he was actually their child? We thought it might help if you let him tag along today, wherever you're going. He says he'll think about it no matter where he is, but he'd like to go because time goes quicker when he's with his nieces and nephews."

"Where are we going?" Andy asked his sister. "Do you want to split up or stick together?"

"Stick together," Paula said. "Actually, I feel like we ought to stay here, in case you guys get bad news. But Lucas says you might rest if it's just the two of you."

"Neither of us got any sleep," Michael admitted. "Maybe your mother will drift off, if there's no one here to wait on."

♥

Michael covered the mouthpiece and whispered, "it's the kids."

Anna turned over and stared at a painting of a pastoral scene, trying to determine whether it was meant to be America or some other country. She listened wearily as Michael relayed the most recent news from the FBI agents. The little girl's parents were in Colorado, skiing with friends. She attended a boarding school outside of Chicago and had traveled to the capital with her classmates. The chaperones had, as yet, been unable to reach her parents.

When Michael hung up, Anna turned over again. She put an arm across his waist and closed her eyes and imagined leaving Washington with both of her children. It was a wonderful dream.

♥

"I shouldn't tell you this," Ross said. "We agreed not to tell you anything that would raise your hopes, but ... we convinced the head chaperone that there was no reason not to give us some basic information which might clear up the whole situation

244

immediately. Turns out the little girl was born about a week after Tyler."

Anna's face fell. "Then she couldn't be ..."

"Mrs. Grant," Ross said firmly. "If she was adopted out with fake papers, that's just about right. She was what, a month old? They couldn't fudge her age more than a few days on the document or it would be obvious. I'd say it's a clue in our column."

Anna mulled that over while she pushed her food around her plate. "What's to keep them from checking out and going back to Chicago and we'll never find them again?"

"Well, for one thing, we've got two agents sitting on the group," Ross assured her with a smile. "They go where she goes, every time she leaves the 23rd floor. I kinda thought you might like to get a look at her, see for yourself whether she looks like Tyler's twin. But of course, I can't set that up, or even slip up and mention what floor she's on."

"Ross," Neal said, with a warning in his voice.

Ross grinned. "They tell me I'm too emotional for this line of work," he confided apologetically. "They say I'll be burned out in no time."

"I'm beginning to think you know more than you're telling us," Michael said.

"We really don't," Ross said. "We've got her birthdate and her physical appearance, and that's it. But I'll tell you one thing: if I didn't know it was impossible, I'd swear she and Tyler are identical twins."

"We'd both like to give you some hope," Neal said, "but if it turns out they can prove the little girl is their biological child, it'll be harder to let her go. We're working as hard and fast as we can. We've got agents in Colorado, hunting for the parents, and we've got a judge considering a request for DNA testing. Now, if we could find out whether or not she's adopted, we could really get the ball rolling."

♥

"If they haven't called by now, I guess they're not going to,"

Anna whispered, in case Michael had drifted off to sleep.

"Not necessarily," he said, wide awake. "Her parents might have gone out and the agents will catch them when they return."

"Even so, it will take time to question them and it's two hours earlier there, right?"

"I'm sure you're right," Michael finally agreed. "We should make more of an effort to get some sleep. Otherwise, if we do get to meet her tomorrow, she'll be scared of us."

Anna smiled. "We've got to stop this, Michael. The next call we get will probably be the one that says the little girl is their biological daughter."

"You heard what Ross said. They look like identical twins."

"And we've all heard the theory that everyone has a double, somewhere in the world." Anna shifted her legs restlessly beneath the sheets. "You never asked me what I forgot."

Michael studied her without comprehension.

"Remember when we were leaving home and I said I forgot something and you gave me one minute to remember what it was?"

"What was it?" Michael asked.

"Their birth certificates. I used to carry them all the time, just in case. For some reason, I had a feeling I should bring them along on the trip."

Michael rubbed her shoulder. "Won't it be something if we need them?"

Anna snuggled against him. "If it's not Franny, it will be harder on Tyler than on us. He wants to be a hero. He wants to be the one who saved her."

"Tyler will be fine. We'll *all* be fine, either way."

"Tonight is better than last night," Anna said. "I was so worried that they wouldn't be able to find her again. Then we would always have imagined that we were so close to finding her and missed our chance."

"It's a miracle they did. It's a miracle that the clerk at the front desk knew where to find the little girls wearing blue plaid skirts. Miracles do still happen, every single day."

"We did get Tyler back," Anna said with a smile.

"We found each other," Michael said. "We had two children.

246

We survived the attack by the kidnappers. God showers us with miracles all the time." He gently moved her aside and pushed the covers back. "I'm going to get my Bible."

"Will you read to me?" Anna said. "Read Joseph. The part where he's reunited with his brothers and his dad."

"Good choice," Michael decided, paging through Genesis. He fell asleep a few minutes later, with the book laying open on his chest. He had slept no more than half an hour when the phone rang.

"She's adopted," Neal said with elation.

♥

"I've gone on record saying I don't approve of what Agent Carlton is doing," Neal said in a grave voice. "I think you're inviting lawsuits, at the very least."

"I'm the one taking the risk," Ross said, rolling his eyes. "Her parents have given the school the legal right to make decisions for their daughter if they're unavailable. I'm suggesting we take advantage of that agreement by asking the chaperone to give permission for DNA testing."

Michael knew all about legal aspects of school permission slips. "I believe that would be in case of an emergency only," he said, though he didn't want to take Agent Fossett's side in this argument.

"You don't consider this an emergency?" Ross said with surprise.

Michael regretfully shook his head. "And given my position at Casey's, I couldn't deny knowing that what we were doing was not within the spirit of the law." He had spent a lot of time in prayer during the early morning hours. He was exhausted, but calm. He felt Anna slip her hand into his, but he didn't look at her. He didn't want to be influenced by the anguish in her eyes. "If she isn't our little girl, we don't want to put her or anyone else through that kind of ordeal. And if she *is* our little girl, but we later go before a judge who is sympathetic with the adoptive parents, he could impose a lot of ridiculous conditions that would take months, possibly *years*, to satisfy."

247

Ross sighed. "I just hate seeing the two of you suffer," he said.

"We're doing fine," Anna said bravely.

♥

"I think we should stay," Paula said, glaring at her brother. "You're always there for us in a crisis. And if you need a lawyer, wouldn't it be handy to have Andy here?"

"I'll stay, if you think it will help," Andy said, though he rubbed his forehead in an obvious display of stress.

"Your mother and I appreciate it, but there's nothing you can do," Michael said, looking at Anna, to be sure she was in agreement.

"I was thinking you might want us to take Tyler home for a few days," Lucas offered.

"Thanks, but … I think he needs to be with us," Michael said.

"What *can* we do to help?" Beth asked.

"Pray," Anna said.

"I'll tell you what," Andy said with emotion. "If it turns out to be Franny … you finally made a full-fledged believer out of me, Mom."

"I appreciate that you were willing to come and see me receive that award," Michael said, though he'd already said the same thing countless times.

"They will still give it to you, right?" Paula asked.

"I haven't explained why I was missing," Michael said. "I don't want a news service to pick up the story and turn it into an online drama. Once I explain, I think they'll be understanding."

"Okay, that's it," Andy said, heading for Tyler's bedroom, where nine kids were playing noisily together. "We need to head for the airport, in case we get messed up on the beltway."

Anna wondered whether Michael had made the right decision, keeping Tyler with them. Then she imagined Lucas being the one to tell her son that the little girl wasn't Franny … She put it out of her mind and helped round up jackets and hats and shoes, so the two families could be on their way. She allowed herself, for a few brief seconds, to believe that the next time they all got together, Franny would be there too.

♥

Neal was reading off a clipboard, looking up often to gauge their reaction to his words. "Currently, the little girl's name is Rhiana, and the social worker, who is on her way to officiate, says no one must call her by any other name. Everybody got that?"

"Got it!" Tyler said with enthusiasm.

"Her parents have given permission for DNA testing, though they are certain we will find no issues with the legalities of her adoption. The man who arranged it is a trusted friend whom they have known for many years. Needless to say, there were two agents waiting for him when he arrived at his office this morning."

"Do you think ..." Anna began, then glanced nervously at Tyler and didn't complete her question.

"We'll be keeping you posted," Neal promised. "We're actually going to do the cheek swab on all four of you, if that's okay. The social worker tells us it will give Rhiana peace of mind if she sees everyone undergo the same process."

Tyler stopped bouncing on the couch. "Does it hurt?" he asked stoically.

"Not at all," Ross assured him. "It might tickle a little."

"Then my mom won't like it at all," Tyler warned.

"The social worker didn't object to all three of us being present?" Michael asked.

"Not so far. But if anybody talks out of turn or says the wrong thing, she can evict you."

"You probably shouldn't cry too much," Tyler said sternly, gazing at his mother.

"I'll try not to," Anna promised, as fresh tears welled in her eyes.

"What have they told Rhiana, as to why she's meeting with us?" Michael asked.

Agent Brenner flipped a page on his clipboard. "She knows she was adopted, and she has expressed an interest in meeting her birth parents. Her adoptive parents told her ... correction. They told the school chaperone to tell her that they may have found her

249

birth parents by accident. She immediately expressed enthusiasm in regards to the meeting, even after being warned that you might not be her birth family after all. She knows nothing about the circumstances and we are not allowed to mention any of that. If we do, again, the social worker is permitted to kick us out of the room."

"Can you remember that?" Michael asked Tyler.

"I already told her my sister got kidnapped," he said guiltily.

"That's okay," Ross consoled him. "That was before anybody made up rules so that the meeting would be difficult and uncomfortable for everybody. That's the way bureaucrats like it, right Michael?"

"Ready then?" Neal asked.

"Are you going to remain in the room?" Anna asked them.

"You bet." Neal went into the hallway and waited for them to follow, then headed for the elevator. "It's a conference room and they want the three of you on one side of the table and her on the other. Nothing like making the poor kid feel like an outsider, right off the bat."

"What does that mean?" Tyler asked, walking quickly, to stay in step with the agent. "'Right off the bat?'"

"Right away. Right from the start. I gotta watch myself around you, buddy. You're sharp as a tack. Gonna ask me what that means now?"

"No," Tyler said. "I know how sharp a tack is. Even if we use push pins instead of tacks."

Agent Fossett laughed, pressing the elevator button multiple times as he waited.

"You okay?" Michael asked Anna, putting his arm around her shoulders.

"I'm fine. What about you?" she asked, gazing up into his eyes.

"I'm a nervous wreck," Michael said honestly.

"So am I," Anna admitted.

"I'm not," Tyler said. "She's just a little girl."

♥ Chapter 24 ♥

Anna stepped into the room and stopped. The little girl sat at a conference table, her hands folded neatly on the surface. The moment she spied Anna, she smiled, exposing front teeth that hadn't yet grown all the way in. Her dark hair was fastened into an elaborate French braid, and her eyes were the same shade of smoky green as Anna's.

"Are you my birth family?" she asked.

Anna couldn't answer. The little girl was her child! She knew it with absolute certainty. She ached to run around the table and throw her arms around her. Once she did, she would never turn loose of her again.

Michael gripped her shoulder, a little too hard. She winced and reached to loosen his hand. When she looked up at him, she saw that his face had gone white.

"I'm the boy you talked to in the lobby," Tyler reminded the little girl. "Duh."

The little girl laughed. "What's your sister's name? The one who got kidnapped?"

"Franny," Tyler told her.

A woman in a dark, blue suit sat at the end of the table. She rose and wagged her finger at the children. "The rules were explained to you, before you came into the room," she said. "If you can't follow the rules, we'll have to call an end to this

251

meeting."

"Please," Anna said desperately. "We'll be good." She spoke to the woman without taking her eyes off the little girl. It was Franny. There was no doubt in her mind, but … what if the DNA testing proved that it *wasn't* Franny.

Michael urged Anna to go around the other side of the table, where three chairs were waiting. He cleared his throat and after he sat down, pulled a handkerchief from his pocket and pressed it against his face.

Anna reached under the table and squeezed his knee.

"They're going to stick a Q-tip in your mouth," the little girl said, grinning at Tyler.

"Yours too," Tyler said saucily.

"My friends think you're cute." She covered her mouth with both hands as she giggled.

"Then they must think you're cute too," he said, "cause you look just like me."

"*You* look like *me*," she argued. She turned her eyes on Anna. "Which one of us was born first?"

The social worker held up her hand.

"I'm sorry," the little girl said quickly.

"You're fine," the social worker told her. "We just want to avoid those sorts of questions."

"What grade are you in?" Michael asked her.

"Second. What grade are you in?" she asked Tyler.

"Duh," he said. "Second, of course."

"I thought maybe you're so smart, they moved you up to third."

"Not yet," Tyler said. "Are you smart?"

"Yes, but I don't make good grades. My teachers are always saying I should work harder. Do you play the piano?"

"No," Tyler said, making a face. "Do you?"

"Yes. I'm very talented."

"You shouldn't brag on yourself," Tyler lectured.

"What else do you like to do?" Anna asked. If they said this wasn't her little girl, she would demand that they do the DNA tests over, as many times as it took to prove that it *was* Franny.

"Umm … I like to swim. And someday I want to climb

252

mountains."

"Do you like to read?" Michael asked her. He took Anna's hand under the table.

"Not so much. I like to play video games."

"Me too!" Tyler chortled.

"Do you ride horses?" she asked, turning her eyes on Michael.

"No," Tyler answered. "We don't have a horse."

"We have them at our school, but I don't like to ride them," the little girl said. "They're very sweaty."

"We don't do anything like that at our school," Tyler complained. "Are you gonna get braces?"

"Yes, but not until I'm older. Are you?"

"Yes. But I haven't had any cavities yet."

"I did. I have a big sweet tooth. That's what my housemother says."

"What's a housemother?" Tyler asked.

"A lady who lives in the house with twelve girls and makes sure they do their homework and go to bed on time."

"Have you ever been to Florida?"

Anna looked at Michael. He was smiling. She touched her hand to her lips and realized she was smiling too.

"Twice. Have you?"

"Once," Tyler said. "How old was I when we went to Florida?" he asked Michael.

"Six," Michael told him. "How old were you?" he asked the little girl.

"I went last year with my school," she said. "They had to have one chaperone for every two kids or we couldn't go in the water. I liked the beach but it was dirty. There was black seaweed and it was slimy."

"Don't you ever go anywhere with your adopted parents?" Tyler asked.

She sat back on her chair and crossed her arms. "Not very much," she said. She turned her head to stare at Anna. "Why did you keep him and give me away?" she asked.

"We didn't!" Anna and Michael said together, but the social worker raised a hand to cut them off, before they could say more.

"That question is not within the parameters we agreed on," she said firmly. "It's time we got on with the DNA testing and wrap it up."

"We haven't been here five minutes!" Anna protested.

"If it had been up to me, you wouldn't have had this meeting at all," the social worker said. "It's going to be traumatic for everyone if the DNA tests come out different than you'd like. Who's conducting the test?"

Neal called a lab technician into the room and he and Ross watched as he took samples from all four of them.

"Make sure you get those evidence bags labeled correctly," Ross said.

"Did it tickle?" Tyler asked his mom.

"A little," she said. She smiled at him, then at the little girl. "Did it tickle you?" she asked her.

"A little." She smiled back at Anna, then folded her hands on the table. "Will I get to see you again?" she asked in a small voice.

"We'll see," the social worker said.

"Even if you aren't my birth family, maybe you could adopt me?"

"I thought you're already adopted," Tyler said.

She shrugged. "I don't like it when I have to live at school."

Anna had never understood how parents could send their children away for weeks or months at a time.

"Can I see you tomorrow?" Franny asked.

"We would love to see you tomorrow," Michael told her. "We would love to take you with us right now."

"I wish you hadn't given me away," the little girl sighed. Her happy countenance had turned sober.

"We didn't!" Tyler protested. "Someone stole you from us. From *them*," he corrected himself, pointing at Anna and Michael with both hands.

"Okay, that's enough," the social worker scolded, clapping her hands. "We'll let you know when we have some results. It will probably take ten days or two weeks."

"No way," Ross told her. "We've got a technician lined up, waiting for the samples. We're gonna have results in twenty-four hours, tops."

"You can't go with one tech," she argued.

"Fine. We'll get another one then. We'll get two more. Or three more. How many you want us to get?"

Michael stood up. "Please don't punish us because of hostility between your agencies," he said earnestly. "You must know that all four of us are very anxious to have this resolved."

There was a moment of silence, then the social worker sighed. "We'll see what their tech comes up with," she said, with obvious reluctance.

♥

"Did you hear her say her parents wouldn't care if we adopted her?" Anna whispered. Tyler had finally gone to sleep, but she didn't want to take a chance that he would overhear their conversation.

"Neal said she's been a student at the boarding school since she was six. She goes home for one week at Christmas and nine weeks in the summer."

"I don't understand," Anna said, wiping at her eyes. "Why would someone pay all that money to adopt a child, then send her away?"

"They're holding the family friend who arranged the adoption. He immediately called a lawyer, which always makes a person look guilty."

"I wonder if he'll say he didn't know she had been abducted … Michael? Is there any doubt in your mind?"

"No," Michael said firmly. "None."

"But what if …"

"Don't," he cautioned, placing his fingertips over her lips. "We've been waiting for a miracle for eight long years. Now it's time to rejoice and thank God for delivering our little girl right into our hands. In spite of all the times we doubted, He rewarded what little faith we could muster with this enormous miracle. Every time you start to ask yourself 'what if,' stop and thank Him instead. That was *our little girl*. We all four knew it. If the DNA tests come out wrong, I'll demand they retest in a controlled environment. God will make it come out right, Anna. Trust Him. Believe!"

Anna slid closer and tucked herself under his arm. She thought about the way their relationship had begun. Michael's faith had waned, and she had tried to help him regain it. She hadn't realized that her own faith was wearing thin, as the years went by and Franny wasn't returned. In the end, it was Michael's faith that had carried them through and Michael's faith that was holding them together now.

Suddenly, she felt strong and unafraid. "I believe," she prayed silently. "Help Thou my unbelief!"

Michael sat on the couch, pretending to work at his laptop. It had been thirty minutes since Neal called with the good news, but Michael could not absorb it. He and Anna had prayed for a miracle, and God had answered with a "yes." Sometime today, Franny would be returned to her family. Sometime today, he would hold his little girl in his arms and try not to weep openly with joy.

When someone knocked on the door, Michael slapped his laptop closed and put it on the coffee table. Anna was in the shower and Tyler was still asleep, but he was not about to make Franny wait until he summoned them.

Much to his dismay, it was the social worker.

"May I come in?" she asked politely.

Michael wanted to refuse, but he stepped back and gestured at the living room area.

"I imagine you've heard the news?" she said, making herself comfortable on the couch.

"The DNA testing revealed that Franny is our daughter." He cleared his throat. "I'm not sure why you're here?"

"I came to congratulate you and your wife, and to offer some advice."

"Thank you for your good wishes," Michael said. "As far as advice, though, we're much too excited to undergo any sort of counseling."

"You'll enjoy a much smoother transition if you heed my words. This is an enormous adjustment for everyone, but most of all, for Rhiana. Adopted children fantasize about their birth families and her expectations are going to be far beyond what you can deliver."

Michael took a deep breath. "I appreciate your efforts on Franny's behalf, but we'll seek the help of qualified professionals as soon as we return home."

"Rhiana," she said. "For her sake, you need to continue calling her by the only name she's ever known."

Michael gazed longingly into the hallway. "Perhaps you're unaware of my vocation," he said. "I've been working with children for many years."

"That will be of little help in regards to your own child. Were I to be in this situation, I would seek the advice of a colleague."

Michael forced himself to relax. He must not allow this irritating woman to steal his joy.

"When the agent brings Rhiana upstairs, refrain from any physical display of affection," she went on. "It will make her uncomfortable, at the very least. You need to share these instructions with Mrs. Grant, and your son."

Michael maintained a neutral expression, with great effort.

"I would recommend that you withhold the circumstances of her abduction," she continued. "And you must not quiz her about her adoptive family."

"Thank you," Michael said. He stood up, hoping she would take the hint.

"I'm not finished," she said with authority.

"Oh yes you are," Michael decided. "I'm asking you to go. I'm sure you mean well, but … I'm asking you to go."

The social worker remained seated. "My only interest is the welfare of the child," she said.

Michael's phone vibrated and he quickly pulled it from his pocket. *Bringing FRANNY to you as soon as she's packed*, Ross texted.

Michael's heart kicked into high gear. "Excuse me," he murmured, and hurried into the master bedroom. Once she was dressed, Anna had opened the bathroom door a few inches, to allow the steam to escape. Her wet hair was tangled around her face, but he thought she had never looked more beautiful. He found he could not speak, so he handed her the phone.

She read the message and stared at him with complete astonishment. "I'll be out in a minute," she said, grabbing a comb.

Michael returned to the living room, shocked to find the social worker waiting on the couch. He had already forgotten she was there. "I'm sorry, but I really must ask you to leave," he said.

"I'm going to stay to help with the initial meeting," she said. "For your daughter's sake."

"You have no legal standing here," Michael said, in a rare display of bad temper. "If you don't leave immediately, I will call hotel security and ask them to forcefully remove you."

"Shame on you!" she hissed, as she rose and went to the door.

They stepped into the hallway together, just as the elevator doors slid open, revealing Ross and Franny. With a whoop of delight, Franny dropped her backpack at the agent's feet and sprinted down the hallway. Michael barely had time to stoop down before she leaped into his arms. He clasped her against his chest and held her in a tight embrace as he turned away from their audience. "Franny," he whispered hoarsely.

"I knew you would come get me someday!" Franny sobbed against his shoulder. "I knew you would! I knew you would!"

Michael couldn't speak. He breathed in her little girl scent – strawberries. He would never forget this moment. He would never stop thanking God for His grace and goodness.

After a moment, Franny leaned back in his arms, so she could see his face. "Are you crying?" she asked, pressing her hands to his cheeks.

"Yes," he admitted. "Happy tears."

"Me too!" she giggled. "I'm crying happy tears too. Will I have to go back to school?"

"No," Michael said. "You'll be going home with us. Me and Mama and Tyler."

"Mama? Is that what you call her?"

"No," he laughed. "I call her Anna. But Tyler calls her Mama. You can call her anything you like."

"Does Tyler call you Daddy?"

"Papa. Do you want us to call you Rhiana?"

"My name is Francine," she exclaimed proudly. "Did you call me Francine before you gave me away?"

"We did *not* give you away," Michael said, gazing into her eyes. "You were stolen from us. We have been looking for you every day since you were taken."

"And now you found me."

"And we will never let you go again," he promised.

"Will you keep me until I'm an old lady?" she teased him.

Michael pulled a handkerchief from his pocket and wiped the tears from her face, then his own. "We will keep you until you're ready to go off on your own," Michael said. "If you want to stay until you're an old lady, that will be just fine with us."

Franny laughed and clasped his neck in a tight hug. "Where's Mama?" she asked.

Michael turned to the suite and discovered that Ross and the social worker had gone. "She's fixing her hair. She doesn't know you're here!"

"Let's surprise her," Franny said happily. "Where's Tyler?"

Michael carried her inside and closed and locked the door. "He's a sleepyhead," he whispered, moving quietly to the master bedroom. "You can help me wake him up in a little while."

Anna was bent over, putting on her shoes. When she straightened up and turned around, she gasped and covered her mouth with both hands.

"Mama!" Franny shrieked, sliding to the floor and running into Anna's arms. "I told my friends you were my mother. They said I couldn't know until we had that test, but I *did* know! I knew when you looked at me, when you came in that room."

Anna sat down on the bed and pulled Franny onto her lap. She was laughing and crying all at once, both arms wrapped tightly around her daughter. "Franny, Franny," she cried. "It's a miracle!"

Michael turned away, to try to collect himself before he woke Tyler.

♥

Michael sat down on the end table, where he could see into

259

both bedrooms. Franny would sleep with Anna in the master bedroom tonight, and he would sleep with Tyler. He could see a mound beneath the covers in both beds, from where he sat. Though he was exhausted, he was not ready to let go of this landmark day.

Anna dimmed the lights in the kitchenette and came to stand before him. He pulled her down on one leg and wrapped her in his arms. "What a day," he sighed.

She laid her head on his chest. "What a *wonderful* day," she said happily.

After a moment, he removed the hairpins and untwisted her bun. He tousled her hair over her shoulders, then held her close. "I'm still in shock," he admitted. "I was so sure it was Franny, yet I kept preparing myself for bad news."

"Me too," Anna said. She yawned and snuggled closer. "What did Neal say?"

The agent had called Michael nearly an hour ago. He apologized for interrupting their reunion, but felt they would want to hear his news.

"They got him, Anna. The man who worked with the nanny. The man who wrestled Tyler out of your arms that day. He was a personal friend of the people who adopted Franny. An attorney. He handled dozens of adoptions for people he knew. He's trying to work a deal, if he gives them enough information to return all those children to their rightful families."

Anna was quiet for a long while. "I thought it would give me some relief," she finally said. "I thought I would feel vindicated."

"I'm just glad that he's finally been stopped," Michael said, trying to erase the venom from his voice. "It will take a lot of prayer before I can forgive. The man is a monster."

"The people who adopted Franny … did they know?"

"Neal thinks not. He's going to keep us posted as the investigation proceeds."

"I don't want to fall asleep," Anna told him. "I'm afraid I'll wake up in the morning and it will all have been a wonderful dream."

"Anna … There's something I want to ask you."

She sat up and gazed at him with a wary expression, pushing

her hair away from her eyes.

"I want to retire," he said, watching her closely. "What would you think about that?"

"Retire?" she said with shock. "You're not even fifty!"

"That's the beauty of it," he laughed. "I'm still young enough … *We're* still young enough to do something with our lives."

"Something like what?" Anna wondered.

"I don't know. Home school our kids? Mission work? The four of us together. I want to make every minute count. We came so close to missing Franny's entire childhood; I don't want to miss anything else. I think of all the times Tyler wants to show me something, or do something with me … and I have to say no, because my job is so demanding. What if I had all day, every day, to focus on the three of you?"

"Do we have enough money?" Anna worried.

"We could move into the house in St. Louis, now that Andy and Beth are moving out. You always said it was a great place to raise a family. There might be charity organizations that would pay our basic expenses, if we were willing to work overseas. I browse some of the organizations now and then, when I can't sleep. A Christian organization, so I can freely share what God has done for me. For *us*. It's a lot to hit you with, on a day when your emotions are already in turmoil, but … I was afraid I would talk myself out of it if I didn't say it now."

Suddenly Anna giggled. "You're not asking my permission, are you?" she teased.

"Not your permission, but …"

"Oh, Michael," she sighed. "I never, *ever* have enough time with you. You must know you're describing my favorite dream! The four of us. Four! Not three, four! The four of us going to another country to do mission work? Or … just doing anything! Baking cookies, shoveling snow … It won't matter, so long as we're all doing it together."

Michael didn't speak, but he held her close, breathing in the scent of her shampoo as he teased his fingers through her hair. Gradually, her body went limp, as she drifted to sleep. He shifted her weight to his good arm and continued to sit on the end table, ignoring the lack of comfort. He looked down the hallway to the room where Tyler was sleeping, then to the master bedroom. He could see Franny's dark hair, spread over her pillow and it brought a new lump to his throat.

He had to find a way to share what he had learned, about God and forgiveness and grace. He wanted to help other men who suffered delusions of power, as he had. All the years he ruled Casey's like a little emperor, aware that his subjects cowered when he appeared, and did his bidding without question … until Anna came along. She had turned his world upside down and inside out, refusing to bow to him, ignoring his position and eventually, his size. He had been Goliath, until this tiny woman took on the role of David in his life. He had done much good for many, but he hadn't understood the very principles he was trying to teach.

He no longer doubted whether God had deliberately brought them together. If he hadn't succumbed to God's will and followed his heart, where would he be today? The bigger question was *who* would he be. In time, he would've become irascible, a curmudgeon who couldn't be pleased or satisfied. He had already begun to mete out justice according to his opinions, even if they weren't based on fact. As his loneliness became unbearable, he would have taken his frustration out on those who surrounded him. One day, he would've retired and moved into a condo, surrounded by books and magazines, spending the bulk of every day surfing the Internet for news about Casey's. He would've died alone and there would've been no one to miss him.

"How blessed am I among men," he said softly.

"I promise I'll do it tomorrow," Anna murmured, as he rose with her in his arms.

He tucked her in beside Franny, then circled the bed and stood gazing down at his daughter. She was a beautiful little girl, and she seemed to have a beautiful spirit. She had chattered away all afternoon, in between hugging him, hugging Anna, and teasing Tyler. She reminded him of Anna in so many ways, and he suspected she was going to look more like her mother than Paula did. There would be problems, as they all adjusted, but Michael knew God would bring them through those difficulties too.

Faith. There was no other ingredient so important to

happiness. This was his message and he was determined to find a way to share it with other men. *Let go*, he would tell them. *Stop trying to run the world. Put your life in God's hands and trust Him, because He'll do a far better job than you could ever hope to do yourself.*

The End

Thank you for reading Not by Chance -
I hope you enjoyed it!
You can learn how Anna and Michael met in
Another Chance. - Book #1.
The Grant family's story continues in:
#3 - One More Chance
#4 - Take a Chance
#5 - A Good Chance
#6 - Leave it to Chance

A Series of Chances, a boxed set,
contains the first five books.

Maggie's Mondays
is the first book in another series called
Solomon's Woods, followed by
The 7th Wave.

If you prefer standalone books, I hope you'll try:
Billie's Opportunity
Rescuing Ladybugs
Quicksand!
Miss Eden's Garden
Wrestling Ichabod

And for children - A Hole in the Fence - it's free!

Made in United States
Cleveland, OH
25 February 2025

14689725R00163